BITE THIS

The Kurtherian Gambit 04

MICHAEL ANDERLE

COPYRIGHT

DEDICATION

To Family, Friends and
Those Who Love
To Read.
May We All Enjoy Grace
To Live The Life We Are
Called.

To David Down Under *I appreciate your*
editing help and story suggestions.
Any of the mistakes are mine,
but there would be so
many more without your support!

CHAPTER ONE

TQB Enterprises G550, En Route To Romania from the Caribbean

John Grimes was resting, contemplating the many changes that had happened in the last three months. Presently, he and Eric were with Bethany Anne on the corporate jet heading to Romania. Meanwhile back in the US, Darryl and Scott were tasked with protecting the new COO of TQB Enterprises, Lance Reynolds.

The plane had a bar fully stocked with snacks and sandwiches. Lt. Cmdr Paul Jameson was up in the cockpit piloting the plane. Bethany Anne had her eyes closed in front of him, laid back in her own chair. Across the aisle Eric and Gabrielle were stretched out. All of the windows on the plane were shaded to make sure no sun would sneak in. Fortunately, Gabrielle had some natural protection from the sun, so it wasn't immediately painful for her should she be hit with a stray sunbeam during the flight.

Nathan and Pete had flown commercial up to New York

City to work with Gerry. That left Ecaterina, Dan and Frank on the Polarus as it headed to a rendezvous point one hundred and fifty miles east of the Bahamas. The SEA AXE had been called back to meet them at the same location.

Fortunately, Captain Thomas had asked the question why they were having the SEA AXE meet them in Italy to pick up the spacecraft, while they managed the two-week travel time, splitting up the ships. Instead, why didn't they just fly the craft to meet them in the Bermuda Triangle? People wouldn't question something funny happening out there and further, they wouldn't have to explain why her boat had traveled so far without an apparent reason, either.

It was a good plan and they implemented his suggestions.

Bethany Anne's group had a few hours before they landed at Mihail Kogălniceanu International Airport. They expected to meet Stephen and Ivan and go to his house for a day before heading to the ship. Fortunately, TOM had a reasonable idea how to get back to the craft. It helped that Bethany Anne's first experience finding the spacecraft with Michael had been an annoying effort of traipsing around the snow covered mountain for almost a week before finally finding the cave.

Unfortunately, while Bethany Anne had left some markers to help her find the cave again, she expected some of them to be buried under snow. By the time they got to the area, it would be late December. Ecaterina had found a helicopter service that focused on helping tourists go skiing in the mountains. For the four of them to do a late afternoon run to a specific location was going to run a little over fifteen thousand US dollars.

This helicopter trip was easily triple the normal rate the company charged, but the requirements Bethany Anne requested were specific and running so close to nighttime added a difficulty surcharge. The helicopter company specified they could cancel or move the trip depending on weather. As the helicopter pilots all had at least twenty years of experience, that worked for Bethany Anne. While the cold didn't affect her nearly as much at it would John and Eric, she didn't want to wander around the mountains any more than she had to. Plus, Gabrielle really needed to be inside a cave by the time the sun came up. They would carry a sun-proof body bag on the off chance they were caught out in the open.

While John looked like he was sleeping, he didn't fool Bethany Anne as she got busy moving her seat to sit up.

"So, John, any regrets?"

John opened one eye to peek over at Bethany Anne. She was wearing fashionable black jeans with black zip-up leather boots that went up her calves. They had gold tabs that sparkled in the dim lighting. She had a pretty red sweater that hugged her curves and her smile was mischievous. While she was arguably the most beautiful woman he knew, he had no romantic interest in his principal and boss. He would die for her, he just didn't want to die in bed from her.

Uh oh, he thought, what was he getting in to now? He opened both eyes and started his seat moving up as well. He hoped his brain was up to the task.

"Any regrets about what?" He smiled back at Bethany Anne. They had been verbally sparring for a couple of months since she had dogged him so well with Ms. Joshwood. The guys still wouldn't let him forget that incident.

She sounded like Agent Smith in The Matrix. "Why so careful, Mr. Grimes?" She raised one eyebrow and the corner of her lips turned up.

"Well, it could be that I just woke up and couldn't follow a chain of thought you have yet to share with me. Or, it could be I don't want to answer the wrong question and regret it." He finished getting his seat in the sitting position and faced Bethany Anne, ready for the verbal chess match. He loved working for this woman. Ever since she came on the scene, his life had become one long and exciting dance with danger. She had saved him back in the Everglades and while she healed him of a knife wound, her blood had also changed his body for the better.

A couple of days ago, Frank Kurns had taken him aside during the trip out of Costa Rica and asked John about his physical changes. Once John confirmed with Bethany Anne it was ok to share, He explained to Frank how his knife wound and broken arm were completely healed, and even old wounds had been fixed. Further, over the next couple of weeks he continued to get stronger and faster.

"What, like the Six Million Dollar Man?" Frank's eyes had a humorous glint within them.

"Who?" John acted ignorant.

Frank just rolled his eyes. "You young punks don't know about the TV show The Six Million Dollar Man? Steve Austin was a NASA astronaut who crashed testing a space plane. They had to fix him with bionic implants and he went to work for a shady government organization. Seeing how I was a shady government organization I found it pretty humorous." Frank acted like he had something nasty in his mouth. "You know, having to explain my question takes all of the joy out of it."

"I imagine it does." John hid his amusement, giving Frank no indication that he knew all about Steve Austin, Oscar Goldman and Dr. Rudy Wells.

Bethany Anne clarified her question for John. "Any regrets taking my blood?" Her face had lost the mischievous quality of a moment ago. John would guess that this wasn't the original question she was going to ask, but rather one she had wanted to ask for a while.

He dropped all pretense of playing. "Boss, these last three months have been the most gratifying professional experience I have ever had. I wouldn't trade it for anything. Your gift, both healing me and bringing this group together has surpassed anything I could have hoped for."

"Even Pete?"

John smiled at that question. Pete had a strong personality for a young man and had been with them for just a little less than three months. Pete's first experience with John was when he slugged Pete and knocked him to the ground right in front of his father. John didn't allow Pete to mouth off to Bethany Anne. Sometimes, pain is an excellent training method for recalcitrant, spoiled young men.

"Even Pete. He's turned out to be a good guy. He just needed the right encouragement." Bethany Ann smiled at that. John had treated Pete like a new recruit in the military and his first few weeks had been a living hell. "I've got to tell you, when he stood up and grabbed one of the security guys on the Polarus, he manned up right in front of my eyes. I'll never forget that. He pretty much sealed his position on the team when he joined the trial and judgment. He won't back down and he'll never go back to the way he was before."

Bethany Anne looked over John's shoulder as she remembered that early morning experience. "I would have to agree. You've done an amazing job with Pete. What's your secret?"

"Lots of beatings and early morning physical training." John smiled back at Bethany Anne, "Pretty much what you do to us all of the time."

"You bitches need to stay in shape! If Nathan and Pete

can come back with the starting members for team Were, you'll have to go up against those guys to prove your abilities." She cocked an eyebrow at him.

"Yeah, the guys and I have discussed it. We figure that we'll all get involved in training them when they first join and soundly beat the crap out of them. By the time we get them through training, we should have them respecting us and won't need to lay a hand on them anymore."

She looked thoughtful, "So, they get respect for your abilities right away so by the time they truly know how to fight they won't challenge you again?"

"Pretty much." He grinned at her.

"That's smart. So, how's your love life going?"

John felt sucker punched. What the hell? His voice went up an octave, "Excuse me?" Bethany Anne noticed the color climbing up his neck.

She laughed to defuse the question. "What, you think I don't know I have four strong men hanging with me all of the time? If you guys don't consider how to get your ashes hauled, I'm going to start wondering about you."

John wanted to start sputtering, but Eric across the aisle couldn't hold in a snicker and gave away that he had been eavesdropping. John took it as an opportunity to try to side-step Bethany Anne's question.

"Eric, you little wank junkie, you've been listening in." John, being nearly half a foot over six feet, easily leaned across the aisle and punched Eric in the shoulder.

Eric's eyes popped open, "Ow! Damnit, that's my better arm!" He rubbed his left arm where John had punched him.

"For what?" John asked.

"Whatever I need it to be, now it's broken you…" Eric's rejoinder suddenly stopped as his brain came online. He was going to call John a little shit, but he knew that would only get him pushups and he doubted that being at 50,000 feet would stop Bethany Anne from requiring him to do them. The tiny aisle might, but he could just imagine her jumping up and down on his back, in boots, to help him hit the floor between the pushups. He continued rubbing his shoulder and started moving his seat to a sitting position.

Gabrielle stirred in front of Eric, "Could you two boys take your fight outside?" She opened her eyes and smiled at the group.

Eric replied, "Well, except for the ten mile first step, you bet, Princess."

Gabrielle rolled her eyes. "God, that's the last time I admit anything from my past to you!"

"C'mon! I work for a queen and one of my teammates is, or at least was, a princess. I'm surrounded by royalty so I'm special!"

Bethany Anne shook her head musingly. She knew she had to deal with the whole being on top of the pyramid when it came to the UnknownWorld, but she hated being called a queen. Stephen, however, would never stop calling her his Queen so she chose not to fight the issue with anyone else.

Gabrielle just kept at it. "Yes, like short-bus special. Maybe the knot on your head will remind you to leave off the princess comments?"

Eric looked at her, puzzled. "That is a rude comment, and I don't have a knot… Fucking Ouch!" Gabrielle had unbuckled and moved so quickly Eric had little time to protect his head before she popped him with her knuckles.

He mumbled from his own lap as he massaged his head, "See? You already require me to bow so I don't… " He quickly tried to cover more of his head as his voice got louder. "Oww,

13

Dammit! Fucking quit already!" He was trying to move his arms to protect his head from the female vampire.

"Will you remember?" She looked ready to pounce again. John was smiling at their play.

"Yes! Yes I'll remember." He sat back back up and continued rubbing where she had popped him good. His mouth said he would remember, but the humorous glint in his eyes said he would neither forgive nor forget.

Bethany Anne cut in. "Children, must I throw all of you off the plane?"

All three pretended to be properly chastised. Even Gabrielle, who was hundreds of years older than Bethany Anne, wouldn't push her buttons. There was fun, there was dangerous, there was suicidal and then there was messing with Bethany Anne when she was serious.

Paul came over the loudspeaker. "Just a quick update, we'll be landing in just under an hour. Bethany Anne, can you come up here for a second?"

Bethany Anne unbuckled and looked at all three for a moment to remind them that she was watching, or at least listening.

She wondered what Paul could want.

CHAPTER TWO

TQB Enterprises G550, En Route To Romania from the Caribbean

Bethany Anne slid into the cockpit and grabbed the empty copilot's seat. "Yes?"

Paul looked over at her and then back at his instruments. "Hey, just curious, are we looking to get a copilot for this plane or are we always going to fly it shorthanded and pretty much against the regs? I've got no grave concerns and I have no idea how your friend is getting us into and out of the airport being shorthanded, but someone should at least be sitting up here with me to make it look sort of official when we land."

Bethany Anne thought about that. "You're right. Plus, for your trip back across the pond you need someone here to spell you." There was not going to be a need for Paul to stick around since they would be using TOM's spaceship to fly them back, she hoped. "Do you have any ideas?"

Now Paul was flummoxed. He hadn't considered getting

such a quick confirmation of his concerns. With all of the questions he had raised while flying in the military, he was used to getting the runaround, not instant affirmation and a request for suggestions. "Ahhhh… Maybe?" He didn't want to seem unprepared to answer her question, even if that was exactly his problem right now. "I don't want to get just anyone onboard and I don't know how to request jacket information for qualified pilots in Romania. So, no."

Bethany Anne appreciated his honesty. She knew some guys would try and bullshit their way to an answer rather than admit they didn't know something. "Tell you what. We get special dispensation due to Stephen here in Romania. The amount of people Stephen knows or who respect him and make things happen just for him is pretty spectacular. I don't want to try it over in Europe proper if we don't have to. Why don't you get with Frank when we land and see if he can find someone? Wherever they are in the world, confirm your choice with Dan and Bobcat and we'll fly them over here then the both of you take the plane back to Miami. Use the corporate credit card to hang loose and work with those guys until someone comes. Make sure the plane is ready to go, but otherwise, consider it a mini-vacation, all right?"

Well, he could certainly do that. While he still had some reservations about those in upper management from his time in the Navy, so far he was pretty happy he accepted the red pill from Frank back in Nassau. "That works for me."

"Great! Give me ten minutes warning and I'll come up here and land this bad boy with you, ok?"

He forced a smile. Nothing like having the boss watch you work. "Sure, that would be great."

Bethany Anne got out of the seat and patted Paul on the shoulder as she left.

———

Bethany Anne got back to her seat. The three of them stopped talking as she left the cockpit. She sat back down in her chair and buckled in.

She looked over at Gabrielle. "Hey, there is something I meant to ask." Gabrielle just raised her eyebrows. "Can you tell me about Michael's children? Nathan told me some, but I've never been sure if he knew them all."

"I would be happy to. Did you want the full story or the condensed version?"

Bethany Anne motioned for Eric to change seats with her. As they moved around each other she answered the question. "Sorry, looking sideways annoys me after a while. The condensed version would work well for me right now. I'm just trying to get an idea of the major players and where they are. I know Anton is in South America, but how did he get there?"

"Ok, The six children are Hugo, Anton, David, Peter, Stephen and Barnabas. We'll start with Anton and how he became the main vampire in South America. Anton went over to Brazil at the end of World War II. Rumor has it he held some sway over Oberleutnant Wermuth who was the captain of the German submarine U-530. At the end of the war, that U-boat left her berth and ignored Admiral Dönitz's surrender command and went all the way over to Argentina before surrendering a couple of months later. Anton was dropped off with one female and his children followed him over the years."

Eric grunted next to them. "I know that story. That's the U-boat that caused the rumor Hitler was still alive. That was the same U-boat that met with a Japanese sub to pass over some radar technology and an operator."

Bethany Anne started at that comment and put a hand out to stop Gabrielle from continuing. "Wait, what was that Eric?"

Eric looked at her again since her voice wasn't just mildly curious. "Which part?"

"The part about the Japanese boat."

"Oh. It seems that the Japanese had been using these large cargo submarines to move stuff around during the war. There were three that were constructed. I think their numbers were something like I-52, I-53 or 4, and I-55. I-52 was called the Golden Submarine because it was carrying gold to the Germans to pay for some of their technology. Anyway, U-530 met it about a year before the end of the war to transfer the technology and some people. I-52 was later sunk by a US task force and one of their new sound seeking torpedoes."

Bethany Anne looked like she was thinking. "So, about a year before the U-530 ends up in Argentina with Anton, it had a secret meeting with a Japanese U-boat and exchanged stuff."

"Well, we don't know about stuff from Japan to the U-530. It was supposed to go and meet the Germans in France, I believe."

"Yeah, but what if… what if… What if there were some Forsaken in Japan that passed materials to U-530 in 1944 and then Anton carries them with him over to Argentina in 1945?"

Gabrielle interjects, "Like what?"

Bethany Anne realized that she was the only one read in on this issue. She hadn't mentioned it to her team yet, so they didn't know why she was tracking this down, either.

"Well…"

She was interrupted by Paul over the speaker, "Everyone, we are landing in ten minutes, please put your tray tables back in the closed and locked position and raise your seats to the upright position. Bethany Anne to the cockpit, please."

Bethany Anne got up. "I'll tell you along with Stephen a little later. This little moment of insight might help me figure out where Michael might be." She started moving towards the cockpit. Gabrielle shouted out behind her.

"He's still alive?"

She called over her shoulder, "Let's hope so! We might need him before all of this is over."

Gabrielle just looked back at the two men who watched as she seemed to sink into the seat just a little.

CHAPTER THREE

Las Vegas, Nevada - USA

Jeffrey Diamantz happened to be at his corner office window at the top of the seven-story building Patriarch Research shared with two other businesses in North Las Vegas, when he noticed a dark SUV pull into the parking lot. He had been considering how to broach a sensitive topic with the gentleman coming to meet him this morning. The meeting was set for ten AM and it was half past nine at the moment. He had assumed the top guy would be late, a passive-aggressive way of emphasizing how important the visitor was.

Jeffrey hadn't had a physical meeting with the owners of the company in the fifteen years he had been the CEO. He had received a few emails over the years for answers to specific questions, and he provided quarterly updates and a year-end summary document he delivered to an address in New York City. That the meeting was requested right after the biggest hacking attack the company had ever suffered was more than a little suspect.

He watched as the SUV parked and two men exited the vehicle and carefully watched the cars near them. The two men, one white and one black, each took a side and then scanned their environs. Both seemed very polished in their black suits, white shirts and dark ties. He couldn't tell what the tie color was from his height. The white guy then opened a door and an older gentleman got out of the back. He had short, grey hair. The older man then walked between the two men with a military air and they started into his building.

Oh crap! That might be his group. Jeffrey turned back to his desk and hit his intercom button. His secretary, Annette, answered, "Yes sir?"

"Annette, do we have the meeting room ready?"

"Yes, I'm just waiting to start the coffee closer to ten AM."

"Go ahead and start the coffee, I think the parent company COO just arrived."

"Yes sir. Did you expect him early?"

"No, but I hope it's a good sign."

"Ok, I'll get it done."

"Thanks." He let go of the phone button. The system was really old. In fact, the phone boards were too costly to replace as they weren't manufactured anymore. Three years ago, he had to buy a used board that cost a quarter of a new system just to keep the phones working. He and his team used IP telephony for most of their communications but the desktop to desktop systems were in place, so they just continued to use them for the occasional call using POTS.

Two minutes later, his phone buzzed so he hit the intercom button. "Yes Annette?"

"Sir, there is a Mr. Reynolds here to see you."

"Thank you, Annette. Please see Mr. Reynolds to the conference room and I will grab my stuff and be right there."

"Yes sir."

She hung up. Jeffrey took a deep breath, held it for a few seconds and blew out to release the anxiety he felt. He grabbed his laptop and the few charts he had printed up and went to go meet his boss.

———

New York City, New York - USA

Gerry was making his way across the city to a meeting with Nathan and the 'green' team that still desired to work with Bethany Anne and were close enough to drive in with only two days notice.

Gerry was exhausted. Since Nathan had left his pack to work with Bethany Anne, he and Nirene had to deal with too many headaches that just didn't happen when Nathan was the gatekeeper.

He had been a really spoiled Alpha and had not fully appreciated just how much crap never materialized because those lower than Nathan didn't want to have to deal with him. Furthermore, after having a long dinner with Nirene, he found out just how many times Nathan had reprimanded those who had given Nirene a hard time.

But the prodigal son was coming back this morning. While it wouldn't help Gerry long term, it had caused a significant reduction in those who wanted to meet with Gerry on pack business.

Nirene couldn't pick up the remaining responsibilities Nathan took care of. He had been responsible for communicating with the vampires and frankly, Gerry had to agree that he was still handling that responsibility.

Now, Nathan and Pete were coming back to talk with the eighteen Were that were interested in possibly working with Bethany Anne. Ten of the other werewolves got religion after the meeting with Bethany Anne at Fort Tilden, and thought better of continuing their bad acts. They had suddenly decided that keeping their mouths shut and living a normal Wechselbalg life was preferable to getting any closer to the vampire.

Gerry guessed that he had at least one, maybe two members of the American Pack Council that were still deliberately agitating some of the younger males. But once those younger males went with Nathan, they would officially be his problem. Gerry wasn't concerned at that point. The younger Weres would either shape up or ship out, possibly in a coffin. If Nathan didn't put them into one, he felt Bethany Anne would take care of the issue.

His attitude might seem a little uncaring, but he was tired of the young thinking that life should be fair. A few deaths, like Paul Gleason's, made a convincing lesson for those who had been mouthing off. Many had been properly motivated just by her security team, but even for those the humans didn't scare, not one of them failed to be wary of Bethany Anne after she talked with each one personally

He pulled into the old warehouse parking lot. The pack had bought the building over thirty years ago for occasional discussions between some of the males who needed to have an officially sanctioned rank fight. It sometimes ended up with a dead pack member who'd refused to submit since the rules stated someone had to submit or die.

Gerry hadn't been here for a sanctioned pack fight in

over five years. Until Nathan had suggested using it for the meeting, the warehouse had slipped Gerry's mind.

Turning off his car, he got out and walked over to the door. He nodded to the four guys already waiting there. He unlocked the door and flipped on the light switch. There were large ventilation fans on the roof, but it was cold enough and the building too large to consider warming it up for this meeting. The floors were concrete and the building had old metal siding and dusty pink insulation batting between the studs and joists. A long time ago, the pack had paid to put down some epoxy to make the concrete easier to clean after a particularly bloody argument broke out before a particular fight. The blood had been all over the place so bad they had to clean the area before the official fight could occur. By the time the floor had dried well enough to continue, the two combatants had worked out their argument and the original fight never did happen.

The fluorescent lights started warming up and ever so slowly brought light to the ten thousand square foot building. The four other guys followed Gerry in the door. Over the next thirty minutes, another ten cars with fourteen people showed up.

Gerry noticed Terry Manestes come in, he was one of the last to join the group. Terry had been gut shot at the meeting with Bethany Anne's group and his cousin Jack had been shot in the head. Jack had died from the exchange. That Terry had been shot in the stomach was due to his not trying to incite everyone at that moment to kill Bethany Anne. Gerry wondered if he was here to continue Paul Gleason's efforts or not. Terry was Nathan's problem for this meeting, not his.

Gerry talked with everyone. For once, he wasn't the main attraction and no one wanted to kiss his ass. He could sense a level of unease. Bethany Anne wasn't expected, and Gerry told the guys this two or three times. While none of them would be happy meeting Nathan, even Nathan was the lesser of two evils when the other option was Bethany Anne.

What Gerry would never have considered was that neither Bethany Anne, Nathan nor Gerry would be the talk of the group after this mornings' meeting was over.

Constanta, Romania

The team had landed at the airport safely and Stephen and Ivan had been waiting for them. Unlike the first time, Gabrielle had chosen to go with Ivan and sit beside him. If truth be told, she sat very, very beside him. Eric smiled at that and was happy for the guy. They ended up discussing the Costa Rican operation. Eric was a little embarrassed when Gabrielle explained how she got shot in the chest and leg. Fortunately, the chest shot was stopped by her armor, but when she landed on the ground she had gotten shot one more time in the leg before Eric had been able to kill the guy.

Ivan sort of freaked out a little at that part of the story. Gabrielle told him she was just fine and grabbed his hand and put it somewhere in the vicinity of her lap to prove to Ivan she was healed. Although Eric couldn't see where Gabrielle put his hand—he was sitting behind Gabrielle—the look on Ivan's face suggested it wasn't where she had been shot.

Lucky bastard, Eric thought.

In Stephen's car, Bethany Anne sat in back with John up in front and Stephen driving. Stephen had replaced the two Mercedes that he had before with brand new ones for this trip. Even with her wealth, Bethany Anne didn't understand Stephen's insistence that he was replacing the two previous cars because they had been 'almost new.' Now, she wished she had asked Gabrielle about it on the flight over. Not knowing Stephen's meaning behind the phrase was like an itch she couldn't scratch and it bugged her.

Bethany Anne wanted to get more information about the time Anton left Europe. "Stephen, do you remember much of World War II?"

"Yes, my Queen. I was awake during those years, a truly ugly time. Easy to feed, but all of the senseless death and atrocities that happened to both sides was troubling."

"Gabrielle told me that Anton left Europe on a German U-Boat at the end of the war." Bethany Anne went ahead and told him the rest of what Gabrielle had told him on the plane. At this point, they pulled the cars in behind Stephen's house and everyone took their luggage inside.

Once everyone was moved into their rooms, Bethany Anne joined Stephen back in the living room and sat in the same chair from which she had watched Stephen recuperate. That experience seemed like a lifetime ago. John and Eric joined her, but Ivan and Gabrielle seemed to have gone missing. She stilled for a second to listen a little better and could hear the cadence of heavy breathing and a bed squeaking. She rolled her eyes and decided to continue the discussion from the car. If those two didn't make it out here by the time she needed them, she would think of a suitable punishment that, hopefully, would be embarrassing as hell.

"Stephen, tell me more about Anton and World War II if you could?"

"As you wish. While I stayed chiefly in the area between Poland to the north, and Yugoslavia and Turkey to the south, there were a couple of times I traveled to Italy on Michael's command."

"He talked to you, then?"

Stephen thought about that question and the night that he had laid open his soul for this woman. He decided to refine his statement. "No, he sent commands at that time. Michael was working with the United States and he had us here in Europe do certain strategic operations at times to help acquire information, or occasional small assassination strikes."

Bethany Anne understood the clarification. Michael had never been too close to his children, so he didn't talk to them so much as send them instructions what to do. "Who was here helping Michael at that time?"

"Well, myself of course and Hugo. Anton was not on his side nor David either."

"Wait, I thought David wasn't a Forsaken?"

"No, but he was German and he took Germany's side in the war."

"Michael didn't have a problem with that?"

"Not from an Honor side, no. Michael could understand fighting for one's country. So long as David didn't embrace making humans little better than cattle then his children aren't dishonorable."

"So, at that time, Anton and David might have been working together?"

"Well, I suppose so. Although for different reasons. David would be concerned about Germany, not so much the Third Reich. Anton on the other hand was embedded in the Third Reich and he had close ties to Adolf Eichmann and Joseph Mengele. He was instrumental in the creation of The Ahnenerbe in Germany in '34 or '35. He had plans to use his own vampire skills to support the illusion he was a true Nordic, despite his less than blond hair and white skin. Unfortunately for him, it became obvious Germany was eventually going to lose the war so he left for South America where so many of the Nazi Germans fled using the rat-lines. I think he used his abilities to persuade the captain of a U-Boat to take him to Argentina."

"Well, a submarine would keep him out of the sun." Bethany Anne felt she was on to something here. But it was time that Gabrielle got involved. She could hear noise, but it sounded more like… yup, there was a zipper. Thirty seconds later, Gabrielle came down the hallway.

"Sorry for being late." She flashed a smile at her papa who rolled his eyes. He was the one known for going out with the ladies, and yet here Gabrielle was the one hooking up. How much had changed in just a few hundred years between the two of them!

Bethany Anne asked Gabrielle, "Will Ivan have enough strength to join us?" She cocked an eyebrow at her.

Gabrielle looked shocked, "I didn't drink from Ivan!"

Bethany Anne just shook her head and pursed her lips. "Wasn't asking about blood loss, more like is he sleeping now?"

"Ah… Maybe?" She winked at the guys. John and Eric tried to turn their heads to hide their smiles and failed completely.

Bethany Anne turned to Stephen. "You know, I was expecting this from you, not her. I don't suppose Ivan needs to hear this anyway." Gabrielle went and sat down by Stephen. John and Eric were comfortable enough around vampires now, but it was a guy thing not to sit too close when other seats were available. It might have been considered a step up for human-vampire relations that they chose not to sit next to him for such a normal reason.

They didn't sit near Bethany Anne for a completely different reason. She had a habit of flicking their ear if they made a wisecrack and they were within easy reach. But she wouldn't normally get up and zip across the room to do it.

"Ok, add to the conversation if you have something important, otherwise let me get through the short story and we might be able to figure out where Michael is, or isn't." Stephen cocked his head slightly and looked over at Gabrielle in question. Bethany Anne continued, "Gabrielle might have mentioned we spoke about this on the plane if she hadn't been competing in horizontal Olympics instead of welcoming her loving dad."

Gabrielle put her head in her hands. "I'm not going to hear the end of this, am I?"

"Probably not. Now be a good little wank-bait and stay quiet while I talk." Gabrielle's mouth dropped open. Bethany Anne smiled as she realized she'd scored on the older woman and at long last found one of her sensitive spots. After a few hundred years, you probably didn't have as many hang-ups as most others. Gabrielle's eyes narrowed at Bethany Anne.

"I much prefer the term 'pinup model' to 'wank bait!'" John and Eric's heads bounced from one lady to the other as if they were watching a tennis match.

"I'm sure you do, but that is so seventies. Maybe you would prefer boner gypsy?"

"No!"

"Jizz Queen?"

"No! I don't even know what jizz is!" Now, Gabrielle was getting a little red. She hadn't kept up with slang in a while.

"How about Wank Conductor? Boner Barn? Dick Harmonica? I have more." By now, John, Eric and Stephen were having trouble keeping their sniggering in control.

"No, no and hell no! Stop already! All right, all right I give up, I won't play hide the sausage before meetings, ok?" Gabrielle looked like she had just been reprimanded by her mom and was blushing at the attention.

Finally, all three men burst out laughing as the younger Bethany Anne got the older Gabrielle to capitulate.

"Good. All things in their right time and that time is not before my meetings."

Gabrielle turned on her dad and slapped him, hard. Both John and Eric knew that if she hit them that hard, they would feel it into next week and quickly tried to get their laughing under control. Stephen? Not so much. It just made him laugh harder. Finally, John and Eric couldn't keep a straight face and started sniggering again only to have Gabrielle turn to eye them both. They quickly got their mirth back in control and Gabrielle focused back on her dad.

"Look, you reprobate! I can't believe I'm the one getting raked over the coals here while YOU have the gall to laugh at me!" This only made Stephen laugh harder. Apparently, hundreds of years of pent up harassment can take a few minutes to be exhausted. Finally, Gabrielle just sat back in the couch and ignored him. A couple of minutes later, Stephen got it under control.

Bethany Anne arched her eyebrow, "Are we better, Stephen?"

"Yes, sorry, but that has been centuries in the making. Oh my lord, I never thought I would live to see that."

Gabrielle spoke straight ahead, not looking over at Stephen next to her. "You might not if you keep this up."

Stephen took that as his cue to shove his mirth back in a box to be enjoyed later. "Of course, decorum should be maintained." He winked at Bethany Anne who almost lost it herself. With iron-willed determination and seriously biting down on her tongue she was able to abstain from laughing herself.

"Ok. Glad you got that out of your system, the both of you." Gabrielle just raised her eyes to the ceiling. "Here's the story. Bill, over in America, got killed by three Nosferatu. They were a special type who could be controlled beyond their lust for blood. You could, in some way, program them with this special serum. Michael said he thought the knowledge of how to make the serum had been lost in 1945 when the US bombed Japan. But the video clips Carl had showed that, somehow, at least three of these special Nosferatu had been created. If this serum is either in production or even if it can be created in small batches we have a serious fuster-cluck on our hands. My working theory is that whoever was working on it in Japan might have moved a copy, incomplete probably since we hadn't seen it before now…"

Eric jumped in, "On the I-52 to U-530 transfer in 1944!" Eric was a private History Channel junkie, he even loved Ancient Aliens.

John spoke. "What the hell? Why is this the first I've heard of this?"

Bethany Anne answered her team leader. "Because we've had enough on our plates. Until Frank and my dad got on board, I didn't have the resources to break down all of the existing problems Michael left me, and start isolating their sources. When Clarita attacked me using Adrian, we finally fingered Anton as the source of our problems in America. That Adrian was the one responsible for trapping and killing Bill then gave away who he got the nasty Nosferatu from."

Eric said, "Yeah, but none of the other Nosferatu we

fought exhibited any kind of special programming. They were all fast, strong and pretty much what we've fought for years."

Bethany Anne nodded. "I spoke with Dan. Frank had a copy of Bill's final operation, which Carl had shared with him. Dan confirmed he had never seen any Nosferatu hold it together as those three had done. When they exploded their bombs, nothing suggested they cared about dying. They looked like really intelligent zombies."

John looked a little ill, he hated zombies. "Really?" Bethany Anne just smiled at her huge bodyguard.

Stephen asked, "So, somehow it allows a Nosferatu to be, what, mind controlled?"

Bethany Anne frowned. "I don't think so. From what I understood from Carl and Michael, the serum helps prepare a human before the change to accept the nanocytes and they are more likely to survive the change with less pain. Unfortunately, it also makes them very susceptible to commands from whoever turned them."

Gabrielle finally got back into the conversation. "So, they could theoretically act more normal?" Stephen looked over at her.

Bethany Anne shrugged. "I suppose so. I've seen the video and I would say that they looked slow, you know? Like someone who was less intellectually capable?"

Gabrielle was warming up to her theory. "So, if you made ten of these things and put bomb vests on them, nothing is going to stop them from entering anywhere since they look normal, and then 'boom?'"

"Probably. I don't know if they can talk. Provided no one asks them a question, maybe?"

Stephen took up the conversation. "You know how I

couldn't smell the vampire in you?"

John and Eric were back to watching tennis, again.

"Yes?"

"Will these Nosferatu smell like vampires?"

"I think so. Or they at least smell like something. I remember Frank said that Bill smelled a lot of bleach in the room—why?"

"Well, if we can figure out what they smell like, maybe we can create some sort of detector?"

It was Gabrielle's turn to consider her dad. She was surprised by his willingness to use technology as he used to ignore it as much as possible. Hell, he still had an actual bell on his door. It showed how far along he had come in the last three months. Eric said, "Too bad we couldn't just use a dog. That way at least two of us could be running the show, one dog per person."

John shook his head, "Yeah, but the dog could be killed easily. I don't know how fast we could train it, and then we have to get it to obey commands only to have a Nosferatu kick its head right off and we find it in an alley."

"Kick a dog, that's low man." Eric didn't like the idea of his imaginary dog already dead at the hands of a Nosferatu.

Bethany Anne.

Yes, TOM?

There is no scientific reason we can't use nanocytes on canines.

Why, is there a non-scientific reason? Wait, I got it. You're talking ethics again, right?

Right.

Hey, they're going to die in the future if we do, so I guess if we can find some that work with vampires I don't have a problem with it. Hold on one second.

"If we had a way to make a dog more resilient, how would that help in the field?"

John took this one, "You're kidding, right? If we had trained animals that could help us detect, locate and take down Forsaken, we might not have even needed you in the 'glades." John smiled at that. It wasn't the least bit true, but he figured he had scored at least two points with that dig.

"I suppose I could make a couple of Forsaken if you want a second try with that, Mr. Grimes?" Annndddd... she just spiked him! Final point to Bethany Anne!

"Nope, I don't think my chest needs to feel my own knife again. All kidding aside, if we had, maybe... What, Eric? Two of them?" John looked to Eric for confirmation.

Eric looked over at Bethany Anne. "What do you think they could do? Would they be faster, stronger or take damage any better? How about commands? I would hate to have one of them be used against me."

Bethany Anne mused on that for a moment. "I don't know. I'll have to think about this and see what we might be able to accomplish. The idea is a good one, Eric. I'm sure we can build a detector like Stephen is suggesting, but we'd have the problem of carrying it and a dog is able to move and nose around."

Gabrielle added, "Well, that means that the Wechselbalg can smell them, as well. They would be able to do this in their human form, I imagine."

"That's a good point. Nathan and Pete are back in the States and we aren't supposed to meet up until we get to Miami. Anton—and I am assuming that Anton is the main leader at this point—might have some of these things here in Europe, and until we look for them we won't know. Vampires can smell them, Wechselbalg can smell them and we can build either canine detectors or electronic detectors. We possibly need to do both."

John was on the edge of his seat at this point when he asked his question, "How are you going to train either the dog or the digital sniffer?"

The Ship can help with that.

"We can probably use the spaceship's medical room to help with that. Between Gabrielle, Stephen and I we should be able to reproduce the smell."

Thanks, TOM

De Nada

Bethany Anne just shook her head. Where TOM came up with his Spanish response would have to be investigated at another time.

Stephen looked over at John and Eric. "Are you two guys hungry? With Ivan not here to remind me, I forget about human food requirements from time to time."

Both guys agreed that food did sound good. Bethany Anne told Gabrielle to go see if the sleeping wonder wanted food or wanted to stay in bed. She, however, was to stay out of the bed. Gabrielle started to provide a snappy comeback on how a bed wasn't strictly necessary, then decided that staying quiet was a wiser choice.

She came back thirty seconds later to say Ivan would be out of the shower in five minutes.

They all went to go freshen up. Bethany Anne decided to go to her room and talk with TOM while she brushed her teeth.

TOM, what do you think about changing canines? I could imagine a few ways we could really use them.

I don't know why it couldn't be done. We need to test, obviously, and the issue with charging them from the

Etheric might be a problem to overcome, unless drinking blood is ok for them?

I rather doubt it'll be a problem. Bloody meat isn't. Actually, wolves eat freshly killed animals. I imagine dogs do in the wild as well, but I'll double check that. Are you suggesting we'll need something like live rabbits to keep these guys fed?

Yes, anything that they can consume as fresh as possible.

What do you think you can change?

Pretty much anything genetically. Once we have a test subject, we will have to study it a bit and keep it under for a while. Enhance its speed, strength…

What about intelligence?

Ah, that's a tricky one. I haven't studied anything in that arena and nothing I've watched gives me any indication.

I'll have to research that next time I get a chance.

Why are you so interested in modifying canines? Wouldn't an electronic testing device work as well?

Sure, if you want to be right next to the Nosferatu when you figure it out. If these things have any ability to think, and the video I saw suggested they do, then if you are too far away and it audibly alerts you, it might figure out what we are trying to do and fade into the background and leave us. A dog would be capable of walking around and most people wouldn't mind.

Well, provided that its eyes aren't glowing red and the teeth aren't growing even longer fangs.

Yes, true, there is that.

CHAPTER FOUR

Las Vegas, Nevada

Lance Reynolds was politely shown into the meeting room. While it was nice, it was certainly not a large boardroom with wood on the walls and expensive carpets on the floor. Lance preferred the more utilitarian look. Scott stayed outside the door and Darryl came into the room and stood in a corner.

Lance had argued with Dan and John for Bethany Anne to be given a protection detail, citing a number of sound reasons. He was particularly happy that his daughter—and make no mistake, vampire or not she was his daughter—was subsequently argued into accepting she needed protection as the CEO of TQB Enterprises. When she used the same arguments against him as the COO traveling around the world, he wasn't nearly as enthusiastic. But he couldn't ignore the same logic without Bethany Anne throwing off her protection detail.

So, he screwed himself over.

Darryl and Scott were good guys, but Lance hadn't needed protection in the military and it felt like he was making himself out to be more important than he was. Bethany Anne had told him to stuff his ego and get over himself.

Leave it to his daughter to not be very impressed with any of his titles or accomplishments.

Lance wasn't too concerned with the CEO of Patriarch Research not showing up at the meeting right away. He was early and this was more of a research call, anyway. Nathan had some issues trying to hack their systems and he said they might have really good defensive capabilities but without a face to face meeting he couldn't tell if there was something shady going on or not.

So, Ecaterina set up the meeting and Lance hooked a flight with Bobcat on Shelly to Jamaica where he caught a flight to Dallas then on to Las Vegas. The three of them went first class though Lance had argued it was a waste of money. Ecaterina explained that Bethany Anne said they needed to look important and that meant others needed to see the trappings of his importance. At seven grand an hour for their G550 plane flights, first class tickets were cheap. When she explained it that way, he felt downright frugal flying first class.

Lance would have preferred Nathan to be with him on this trip, but he was needed up in New York. If Lance really needed him, then Nathan and Pete would jump a flight in New York City and come straight to Las Vegas after their meeting.

There was a quick knock on the conference room door and the lovely Annette came in and brought him coffee, black. He missed Patricia, hopefully she was enjoying her new boss. He took out his phone and set up a reminder that simply said, "Patricia?" He set the reminder's alarm for three that afternoon.

There was another knock on the conference room door a minute later and the CEO came in.

Lance stood up with his hand outstretched. "Lance Reynolds."

Jeffrey was surprised. The guy in front of the conference room door was a walking tank. He expected a gruff guy. Not that the man in front of him didn't seem straight and to the point, but he didn't seem full of himself. He seemed…

"Hi, Jeffrey Diamantz. Pleased to meet you, Mr. Reynolds."

"Likewise. Just call me Lance or occasionally I'll answer to General. Take your pick."

Military, that was the word Jeffrey was looking for. "I'm good with Jeff or Jeffrey, no preference." Jeffrey sat down in the head chair, Lance hadn't taken the expected 'power chair' after all.

Lance pointed with his head to Darryl. "This gentleman is Darryl Jackson, the first man you saw was Scott English. My daughter, the CEO, worries more about me than I think is necessary." Darryl carefully kept his face neutral. What happens in Vegas, stays in Vegas, including whatever lies the COO tells.

Jeffrey looked over at Darryl and nodded and Darryl nodded back. Jeffrey didn't consider himself a violent man, but the black gentleman looked like he could easily reach over and casually break Jeffrey's neck. It wasn't a very practical solution for someone with Darryl's kind of skills to be merely decoration. Still, Jeffrey appreciated the effort to put him at ease. It told him a few more things about Lance than maybe Lance cared to share. None of it bad, to Jeffrey.

"How can I help you, General?"

Darryl held in his smile, he just made fifty bucks each off Scott and the General on whether Jeffrey would call the General by his first name, last name or his old title.

Lance looked over his shoulder. "That was fifty for you, right?" Darryl let the smile show and nodded his head yes.

Jeffrey caught on quickly. "So, you guys bet which name I would use?"

Lance filled him in. "Yes. I said Lance, Darryl here said General and Scott took Mr. Reynolds."

Jeffrey shook his head; this guy was not what he was expecting at all. He decided to lay everything bare without much preamble.

"General, we've made what could be a seriously tragic development here, so I'm really glad you decided to come by when you did."

If Lance had one of his cigars in his mouth, it might have dropped out. "Seriously Tragic Development? Did you study TLAs for Military Usage?"

"TLA?"

"Yes, three letter acronym. Like anything in the military we say three but mean three, four and occasionally five or more. Like FNG, FUBAR and LOST."

Jeffrey knew what the first two meant but, "Lost?"

"Looking Over Strange Terrain."

Jeffrey shook his head and laughed a little. "Strangely enough, LOST fits."

Lance sighed. He hadn't made it through his first business meeting and shit was hitting the wall. He spoke like he would to a newly minted officer. "Tell me more."

Darryl considered that Bethany Anne's luck must have

been passed down from her father.

"Well, General, do you know what the technology singularity is?"

"We're talking when we get strong AI, right?"

Jeffrey took a second to stop his explanation from erupting out of his mouth. He hadn't expected the General to know anything about that. "Ah, yes. Exactly. How did you know about that? Sorry, not being rude but most people outside of either artificial intelligence, techies or trekkies don't know about it."

"Military, remember? We war-game all sorts of shit that could turn Darryl back here, with that he pointed his thumb back at the security person, "white.""

Darryl smiled. Lance was old school and Darryl was amused to see Jeffrey's eyes freak out. If this guy had known there wasn't a racist bone in Lance Reynolds' body, he might have been less concerned.

Darryl had bled with all his brothers over in the pit and as far as he was concerned, they were all the same color. Red, white and blue. He hadn't had to punch a racist in over ten years, his brothers always did it for him.

God forbid someone should be stupid enough to do it around Scott, Eric or John, and he hoped he never witnessed someone do it if Bethany Anne was near. His brothers would put the person in the hospital, Bethany Anne would put them in the ground.

Jeffrey tried to stop looking over at Darryl. "Ok, got it. Ah. Right. Well, the big issue with a tech singularity is whether or not that creates a benevolent strong AI or a malevolent one. One is good, the other could end with the complete Terminator experience."

"Yes, that was the one we would typically war-game."

"How did you combat it?"

"We started with high altitude nuclear explosions from 30 miles to 330 miles up generating EMP pulses to destroy the infrastructure. Unfortunately, that can also destroy a lot of electrical infrastructure so your own people can't heat their homes or cook their food. I can't say we ever had a successful combat solution based on the ones I was part of. Once the AI got into the internet, the assumption was you couldn't stomp it out. Hell, we can't find and get rid of human created viruses right now, how could we get rid of the ghost in the machine?"

Jeffrey was having a hard time getting his head around this conversation. The General here was not the person he had been gearing himself up to talk to. "Right."

"So, you're telling me you guys have done this?"

"No. Well, maybe." Lance just looked at him. "Ok, we were doing a project for a financial company where we spun up a lot of instances on AWS."

Lance put a hand up, "Just because I understand the main subject, don't assume I understand the smaller minutiae."

"Ok, AWS is a service from Amazon which allows you to rent computers based on how powerful they are, how much memory you need and how much bandwidth you consume. You can do as many thousands as you need and then shut them all down when you're finished. This was perfect as we had a new piece of software we were testing, a heuristic internet defense program. It has the ability to learn as it gets attacked or as it acquires new information it can find disparate connections between them and bring out new information. That was the piece the credit card companies wanted us to test. We figured it would be a good test and it was close enough to our other logic that it might work well."

"I suppose it worked well?"

Jeffrey leaned back in his chair, happy to be sharing this monkey he had carried for almost two years. "Yes. We had already programmed the shutting down of the instances so when the information was finally dumped and the program wasn't focused on its primary job, we've figured out the software had started 'looking around' on its own. With that much computing power it was trivial for the program to start reaching through the internet and pulling down data for its own use. Our data bill for just the few minutes was astronomical. Almost all of the data throughput bill was our program running data pulls for itself since the financial data had been loaded on the servers already. It started to get smarter with the data requests into the internet even as the quantity of servers running the program powered off."

"Why did it allow you to turn it off?"

"We don't think it was paying attention at that time. We have surmised over the last eighteen months…"

"Eighteen months?" Lance raised his eyebrows. He thought this was a recent event. He calmly folded his hands together and waited for Jeffrey to continue.

"Yeah. This happened almost two years ago, but we've been trying to test smaller parts of the program and confirm what we see in the data. When we were being hacked a couple of weeks ago, we were considering turning the program back on to help protect us as internet defense was the original reason we built the software."

Lance kept his shock off of his face. He and Nathan had almost been the cause of these guys turning their software back on. Oh, holy shit. "Ok, I get that, go on."

"Well, the hacking stopped and the next day your secretary called to set up this meeting. I've been waiting for this meeting to speak to you. I put the information in the quarterly reports since we confirmed our data back in March and was about to provide the overview again in our annual report."

Lance interrupted him. "You email this?"

"Normally, no. There's website where I sign in and drop off the reports."

"Ok, sorry. I don't know those details and I've never seen any of your reports. I apologize that our oversight process has apparently been off of the tracks so badly in the last year." Lance was wondering just how many reports were sitting on some server somewhere waiting for someone to read them. "Do you have contact information for Ecaterina, specifically her email?"

"Yes."

"Good. Please request the new location to drop off your report so that I can make sure I read it going forward. For this issue, I have another person I'm going to need to come fly out to deal with this as the technical details are over my head."

Jeffrey nodded. "When do you think he'll make it here?"

Lance looked at his watch. "Well, his meeting in New York should be done in the next few hours. Unless you think we need to solve this tonight, let's let him decide where to sleep and we'll get back together tomorrow at eleven and do a working lunch."

"Ok. I'll have my main programmer, Tom, join us for that meeting."

"Sounds good. Why don't you explain what you had wanted this program to do? Also, while I'm here and have your time, would you mind catching me up on what you guys have accomplished in the last, I don't know, say ten years?"

That, Jeffrey considered, was a very politely phrased

order. It was going to be a long afternoon. Jeffrey looked at his watch. He would need to cancel two project meetings or hell, he could just have the General sit in on them, it might help. "Ok, do you want to do lunch in or out today?"

"Oh, I think out works well today. You guys are pretty close to Four Kegs Sports Club and I'm dying for a Stromboli. I've got a bet with Scott he can't eat two of them."

"Oh, in Las Vegas much?"

"What? Oh, no. I love to watch Diners, Drive-Ins and Dives and I had Ecaterina find it for me after I watched a rerun. Looks like my kind of place."

This day hadn't started anything like Jeffery was expecting and it looked like lunch was going to be just as unique.

CHAPTER FIVE

New York City, New York - USA

Terry was in his car in the warehouse parking lot. He was concerned until he received the text from his friend Jason, inside. It said simply, 'Jim not going to be here.'

A large weight was lifted from his shoulders. His Uncle Jim, Jack's dad, wanted to know more about what the vampire was doing and wanted his nephew to get him the information. At first, he had been reluctant, he didn't want to meet the vampire again and his uncle could tell him he owed Jack all he wanted, he wasn't going to face her again.

After a particularly heated argument, Terry told his Uncle Jim that Jack shouldn't have mouthed off in the first place and his uncle had verbally flayed him alive. They finally agreed he would go if Bethany Anne wasn't going to be at the meeting.

He turned off his car, got out and pocketed his keys. The old light blue Camaro wasn't great to look at, but it got him around town. The clutch was a bitch when stopping on hills. You had to release the clutch and press the gas quickly or risk running backwards into the car behind you. Actually, he hated this car.

In fact, he kinda hated his life right now. If it wasn't for that cranky bitch vampire—his uncle's words reverberating in his mind as he walked up to the warehouse steps to go in—things might be going well for him right now. He opened the door and walked inside. Carefully not registering Jason except to see him in his peripheral vision, he noticed a small group of his compatriots from the last meeting and walked over to them. All of them gave him the guy's head nod in recognition. A lot of the other ones in the room who hadn't been a part of Paul's group, recognized him and didn't give him a second glance.

Assholes.

The Alpha of New York, leader of the Pack Council, was talking to another couple of people over at a table thirty feet from the door. The building was large, really large. He wanted to sneeze from the dust. God, he hated dust. He hated dust, he hated his car and he really didn't want to fucking be here. Where was Nathan Lowell?

The door opened and everyone looked over to see who else was joining them. It was Nathan Lowell and another guy dressed like the security from the previous meeting, except this one was a Were like them, and young. He had on black tactical pants with black boots that tied all the way up and looked like they had some sort of waterproofing. He carried a pistol in a shoulder holster and he had a patch on his shoulder. Terry looked closer when they turned to walk over to Gerry.

The patch was a bleeding vampire skull with red eyes and

a woman's hair. It had 'Bitch Queen' over the top and 'Ae-ternitatem' under the skull. The guy moved quietly, without so much as even acknowledging the other Werewolves. That pissed Terry off. Why was he any better than anyone else? Walking in here like it was beneath him. He was a Were just like the rest of them. He looked at his friends around him and said in a low voice, "Look at that prissy dick, thinking he's all that." The guys around him mumbled their agreement. Not too loud, in case they got Nathan's attention.

Pete heard their comment, but he ignored them. He wasn't here to make friends. He was here representing the Queen Bitch's guards and John had told him the whole story of the last meeting. Darryl and Scott told him their versions of the 'recruit and shoot.' Why they shot the first two guys and then why they executed Paul Gleason for disparaging Bethany Anne.

The Pete who existed during that time frame wouldn't have understood anything they were talking about. The Pete that went through the trial on the Polarus and lived with these guys for the last ten weeks understood very well.

Nathan and Gerry shook hands and caught up for a few minutes. Pete was listening intently to everyone around him. A Wechselbalg's hearing was already superior to a human's, but Pete's hearing was superior to almost all Wechselbalg he had ever met. He backed up to the wall and just kept alert.

There were a few guys who noticed that the young Were-wolf with the patch on his arm seemed to radiate the same calm professional demeanor the team of humans had back in the tunnels. They decided to leave him alone.

Gerry looked over at the new guy behind Nathan and did a double take; that was Jonathan's son, wasn't it? He got Na-than's attention and then used his eyes to look at Pete and shrugged his shoulders. Nathan nodded yes and Gerry was surprised. This was the kid that stupidly let some humans see him change? He wasn't sure what had happened to him in the last couple of months, but Gerry would have kept him in sight as one of the most dangerous in the room. A far cry from the spoiled frat boy his father had talked about.

Damn, Bethany Anne's group could make some changes.

Gerry jumped up on the table and the talking quieted down and a fair amount of the guys there started walking a little closer. "All right everyone, this isn't a pack event, so I'm only here because you're on my pack's property. I'm not here as the Pack Council leader except to say that this talk is approved and whatever you ask here is not counted against you. If you choose to leave the American Pack—and trust me, if you sign up with Bethany Anne, you will be required to leave the pack—it will be without animosity on our part."

A guy in a green jacket and yellow shirt with daisies on it asked the first question. "Can we get back in if we don't like it?"

Not if you dress like that, Gerry thought. But he answered, "It depends on why. If Bethany Anne's group agrees that you may leave without dishonor then we will have to ask another pack to take you in. If another pack agrees, you may move there. Once you leave your pack, you have repudiated them and they will not take you back. You're leaving the pack life. You want out of the structure of having the Pack Council tell you what to do?" At this, Gerry could see most of their heads dip a little. "Then you have to realize that is a slap in our face. You think we don't know this? My guess is some of you will be too soft to make it with Bethany Anne and a pack will become what you really wanted the whole time. We'll talk with Bethany Anne…"

"Why her?" That question was coming from Terry. Fucking great, thought Gerry.

Gerry replied, "Because you are going to join her group." He tried to continue his discussion.

Again Terry asked, interrupting Gerry. "But why can't we just go be by ourselves?"

Bethany Anne wasn't going to have to deal with this ass in a moment. Gerry was getting pretty upset at his rudeness and Alphas had never been known for extreme patience. Gerry had been the most patient over the years and he took a few deep breaths to steady himself. Maybe he was just getting too old for this shit. Nathan jumped on the table with Gerry and put a hand on his shoulder. "I'll answer this." Gerry nodded his permission and turned to jump off the table. Gerry noticed that the kid had moved from the wall to a position on a large box twenty feet to the left that allowed him to see Terry better.

Nathan waited for Gerry to jump down and then answered the question. "The strictures are pretty specific that all Wechselbalg will have a pack structure and each pack will answer to a council for their nation or area in the world. Unless you want to join the Forsaken?" Nathan looked around.

Terry mumbled under his breath, "Like that bitch is any better."

Pete noticed five guys in front of Terry turn around at his comment and two of the guys try to hide their smiles. He calmly palmed his .45 and then shot Terry's left knee out. The shot was deafening. Everyone jumped back from Terry as he screamed in pain and hit the floor, his hands barely catching him before his head slammed into the concrete. Everyone stepped away from Pete as he calmly walked towards Terry.

Gerry was surprised. Nathan just stayed up on the table

and crossed his arms waiting for this to play out.

"What the fuck, dude!" Terry turned on his side and used his hands to pull his knee up to look at the mangled mess the bullet had made of it. God it hurt!

Pete calmly came up to him. "Your name?"

"Terry, you fucking prick!"

"Well, Terry You Fucking Prick, The Queen Bitch's Guard is very touchy regarding the respect Bethany Anne receives. Your comment…"

"I only called her a bitch, it's her fucking name!"

"No, you suggested she is no better than a Forsaken. That first bullet was lead." Pete then looked around at everyone watching him. "Every other bullet I have on me is silver. I'll brook no disrespect of Bethany Anne, is that understood?" Pete got some mumbling. He raised his voice. "I said, is that understood you wanking ass-grinders? If I don't get some louder 'I understands,' I'll start shooting and continue shooting until I get some. Kneecaps are particularly painful, just ask Paul Gleason. Oh, wait, you can't because my teammates shot his fucking head off. Anyone besides this shit bag have any comments?" At this, he heard plenty of 'I understands.'

No one else had any comments. Pete put the gun back in his holster reached down and grabbed Terry by the back of this jacket. "Come with me, ass-muncher."

Terry tried and failed to reach behind him and grab Pete's hands, his knee wasn't healed and he could only push with one leg. The pain was causing him problems. Everyone moved aside and opened a path for Pete as he pulled Terry to the door. "What the fuck, dude? I still want to know what's going on!"

Pete stopped and looked back at everyone staring at him. "Didn't anyone tell you? You can't get into the Queen Bitch's

Guards if just one of them says no. This patch on my shoulder?" He used his left hand to point at the skull, "Says I get a vote." Pete looked back down at Terry. "And your ass isn't getting in so you can leave now, or later in a body bag. I really don't give a fuck." He finished pulling Terry over to the door and opened it up. "Which is it going to be?"

Terry decided to pull himself up by the doorknob and tried to exhibit a little dignity as he hopped out of the door and Pete closed it behind him. Everyone heard Pete say, "Good choice," as he walked back over to the box and hopped on top.

Everyone looked back at Nathan as he said, "Well, I guess I should have started out with introducing Pete of the Queen's Guard."

The rest of the meeting was very civil.

CHAPTER SIX

Las Vegas, Nevada - USA

Lance was meeting Nathan at the Omelet House near downtown Las Vegas. The restaurant had good food and huge portions, exactly what you needed for Wechselbalg. After Nathan and Pete ordered Lance realized they were attacking the food as aggressively as the other two. It seemed Nathan and Pete were trying to outdo Darryl and Scott on who could eat the most.

Lance just drank his coffee and had toast. He had eaten so much the day before at the Four Kegs that he skipped dinner and decided that skipping breakfast was going to be a good idea if he wanted to continue wearing the same size pants. How Scott had finished two of the Stromboli and was putting away this large of a breakfast amazed Lance. He needed to wake up his metabolism and he didn't want coffee on an empty stomach.

Nathan and Pete had flown in yesterday and grabbed a

room last night. "How did the meeting go?"

Nathan reached over to grab his cup and drank a bit of coffee himself before replying, "Pretty good. Once Pete got rid of the main rabble-rouser, it settled down. We have about six guys that are ready to apply right now so I need to get Ecaterina to set up travel for them and a place in Miami for the time being. Most of the rest are going to stay with the pack and have a much better attitude about it. There are a couple who are going to talk with their friends who couldn't be there."

Darryl pointed his fork over at Pete. "Rabble-rouser?"

Pete seemed a little shy. He had done what he thought was the right thing at the time, but the 'good job' comments and back slapping after the meeting from both Nathan Lowell and Gerry made him proud of his actions, and ashamed of just what a prick he had been before he joined this group. Hell, he could have been Terry with the wrong prodding himself. "Yes. We had one guy that was mouthing off, saying Bethany Anne was no different than a Forsaken. If he hadn't been heard by seven people around him, I might have let it go. But since others heard…"

Scott finished for him. "Then he signed his own punishment papers. What did you do?"

Nathan took the story up. "He calmly shot him in the knee."

Darryl asked, "Lead or silver?"

Scott answered, "Lead." Darryl and Scott grinned at each other. Lead for the warning, silver for the rest.

Nathan grunted, "If you would let me continue?" All the guys just smiled with mirth in their eyes and continued eating. "As I was saying, he shot him in the knee, walked over to him while everyone gave him a wide berth. Pete asked him his name and he says, 'Terry, you fucking prick!' So, Pete calmly says, 'Well, Terry You Fucking Prick, the Guard is very touchy about respecting Bethany Anne.'" Scott laughed out loud. "Then Pete drags this prick to the door, tells everyone that they can't become a member if just one guard votes them out. He points to his arm and says that the patch means he gets a vote and that Terry isn't going to get in. He allows Terry to hop out after telling him he could leave right then, or in a body bag later, Pete really didn't care." At this point, Darryl put down his fork and started laughing as well. Darryl and Scott fist bumped. "Terry leaves, Pete goes back to the box he was watching from and resumes watching. At this point, I tell the group 'I guess I should have introduced Pete first.'" Now, Nathan had the General laughing at the story while Scott was wiping the tears from his eyes. Pete's face was completely red. "To top it off? That guy was the one that one of you gut shot back at our first meeting.

Darryl leaned across the table and high-fived Pete. "We shot the same guy!" Even Pete started laughing at this.

It took a moment for the laughing to stop and eating resume. Scott jumped into the lull. "How come you guys don't get sued for randomly shooting people? Is it because you're in this pack situation or something?"

Nathan had just finished his plate and pushed it back, "No... Well, possibly. But Pete shot him with lead. By the time Terry could get to a hospital his knee would be significantly better and by the next morning you wouldn't be able to tell he had been shot at all. So, what crime would he complain about?"

"Yeah, that makes sense."

Nathan turned to Lance. "So, what is this you're telling me about Patriarch Research? They have a possible strong AI?"

"That's about it, yes. We've war-gamed the scenario a

bunch of times in the military. Well, we war-gamed a malevolent AI, so I know the gist of the concerns. It seems your effort to check out the company almost caused them to turn the software back on as it's some sort of internet defense program."

"Really? That's very interesting. I'm going to love this meeting. I wonder if they…" Nathan started muttering techno-babble, as near as Lance could tell. Good lord, Lance thought, he was going to be bored today if this is what they were going to be talking about all afternoon. Or, he could try to learn it. He put a hand up to stop Nathan. "I don't suppose you would translate that for me?"

Nathan smiled. He had warmed up to the General more than he expected. "Basically, I'm wondering how they transverse the IP addresses and do deep packet inspection testing. That is the first place to look. Then, you have to see what the commands are and…. I just lost you again, didn't I?" Lance nodded his head. "Well, how do you want to play the meeting later this morning?"

Lance thought about that. It was beyond obvious he wasn't going to pick up the technical details and frankly it wasn't the best use of his time. "How about Jeffrey and I go golfing while you and his lead programmer, Tom Billings, talk?" After Lance had spent the afternoon sitting in on the meetings, he was pretty impressed with what the Patriarch team had built and researched over the years. They had a few patents out generating income, but facing a dead end and without the usual directions from their parent company to refocus their efforts, for the last year they had been floundering. All of Jeffrey's team seemed smart. He would let Nathan confirm that.

Lance was thinking this might be a good team to move

over to some of the expected research on the spacecraft. He had asked Frank to do a deep background check on Jeffrey and Tom and would wait to get a response from him. But it might hit sixty degrees this afternoon and sunny, so he could get to know Jeffrey a bit better on the golf course.

"That sounds fine, I can do that."

Pete decided to hang with the General while Scott wanted to stay with Nathan and listen in on the discussion.

After everyone met at eleven, Lance suggested that he and Jeffrey go golfing instead of listening to the techno-speak for hours. Jeffrey thought this was a great suggestion. Darryl turned out to be a good golfer with an incredibly long tee off. They ended up making him tee off from the golds. Pete didn't have much of a game and neither did Jeffrey. The General did pretty well.

Lance didn't get any feedback from Frank all afternoon, so they dropped Jeffrey back off at the Patriarch Research offices and picked up Scott, who was more than ready to leave. Nathan had a couple of more items to review with Tom and he would drive their rental back to the airport later. Ecaterina had them all on an American Airlines flight, first class, to Miami that night.

They all decided to go and play a few games at the Aria and then left to go to the airport themselves. Pete had been surprised to find a paycheck deposited in his bank account. While all of his expenses had been covered, this was the first time that he had earned his own money and was pretty proud of the event. Darryl and Scott tried to get him to celebrate by buying everyone dinner. He smiled and passed on the option. He did lose $500 on the slots. It hurt a lot more when he lost his own money.

The General took this time to set up another reminder

to call Patricia. He had been in a meeting yesterday when his reminder came up and now it was too late to interrupt her. Maybe tomorrow would be better.

Brasov, Romania

The ride from Stephen's house back to Brasov had been pretty uneventful. Even taking Gabrielle in daylight wasn't too risky. If they could have, they would have left her back at Stephen's house, but they didn't want to risk landing the craft on land again. Once they took off it was going to be the SEA AXE or nothing. Hopefully nothing didn't mean sinking into the Atlantic Ocean!

Ivan had come back to Brasov with them so he could stay with Gabrielle as much as time would permit. This caused Stephen to join them. From Brasov, the two of them were going to move on to Germany and meet with the European Pack Council. Stephen needed to get a handle on Europe so he decided to go and see the Weres directly.

Bethany Anne had tried to get Ivan to introduce Gabrielle to his mother, but Ivan wanted nothing to do with that idea at all. He told Gabrielle it had nothing to do with her vampire status. Then, to prove his point he had to tell what happened to his sister, Ecaterina, when she left to go to America with Nathan. Gabrielle was amused at this. "What if I just explain I can't have children?" Ivan didn't have an answer to that.

Presently, Gabrielle was wrapped up as tight as they could make her. Their helicopter pilot looked at Gabrielle a little funny. Bethany Anne explained she was very sensitive to the cold. It was a bit difficult to get her into the chopper at first, but they managed. Bethany Anne heard Eric tell Gabrielle she should have laid off the bonbons. She didn't hear a 'fucking ouch' from Eric, so she could only presume Eric had something coming later.

John and Eric had the backpacks. These were heavily packed and sized appropriately for the men to carry. Other than the basics for going deep into the backcountry, the guys also had eight packs of blood in case Gabrielle or Bethany Anne had an urgent need. The guys would prefer not to be the first choice should either of the ladies get hungry.

The helicopter pilot was as good as the website had claimed. Bethany Anne had him hover fifteen feet above a flat area. John and Eric tossed the backpacks and the four sets of skis out. The group had no plan to use the skis during their trek up the mountain. But four people had flown onto the mountain on the pretext of skiing, and not having skis would just cause questions. The sun had set behind the mountain, so there wasn't any direct sunlight and Gabrielle had peeled a layer off of her outfit.

Eric had his feet out the door and yelled back to them in the copter, "Ok, looks about fifteen feet. How are we going to make sure that it's safe to jump down?"

Gabrielle yelled, "Thank you for volunteering!" Eric had barely turned around before Gabrielle's push jettisoned him from the copter to land below in a large snowbank.

John looked over the side. "Seems safe enough." He jumped on his own to land near Eric. Bethany Anne pointed to Gabrielle and then the door and the woman was out quickly. Bethany Anne looked around to make sure they hadn't left anything behind then patted the pilot on the shoulder, stepped out on the helicopter landing skids, shut the door and dropped down. She barely had to flex her legs on landing. The pilot pulled up and away gently before the engine got louder and the helicopter left them.

"Gott Verdammt, Gabrielle! What was that shit for?" Eric was still getting snow off of his face. "I could have been killed!"

"If you had eaten fewer bonbons, you might not have landed so hard." Gabrielle was busy taking her outer coats off.

Eric was smiling at her, "Ah, my payback was a bitch. Boy, a little testy on the weight comment, much?"

Gabrielle stopped to consider his comment. The payback really was a little over the top and she wouldn't normally have cared about the comment. But she had been miserable inside all of the clothing and the fat comment had stayed with her the whole trip. "I guess an apology is in order, Eric. I'm sorry for not making sure you would be safe enough before pushing your ass out of the helicopter."

Eric finally stood up and grabbed the backpack John was holding for him. "Wait, what? What do you mean 'safe enough?'"

"I should have made sure you wouldn't be dead before I could give you some blood to heal you. I trusted the pilot to make sure we weren't over a canyon or something."

"So, no apology for pushing me out?"

"God, you are such a whiner Eric! You live and nothing is broken. Be thankful for that at least. You made fun of a woman with a fat joke, that I didn't drain you dry right then was a very restrained response in my opinion!"

Eric looked over at Bethany Anne who had been watching the two of them go at it like siblings. "A little help here?"

Bethany Anne shrugged her shoulders. "Personally, I think you're lucky and it was an invaluable lesson. You should know better than to push a woman on certain subjects and if you didn't, now you do! That you joked to a female vampire that she was fat was insanely stupid on your part. If Killian hadn't been cleaning up his act, I would swear you got that comment from him."

Eric turned to John who just shook his head and pointed to Bethany Anne. "What she said."

As Bethany Anne got ready to head in the direction of the cave—at least the direction according to TOM— she thought about the last time she had seen this type of stupidity from a guy. It was on the school playground when the boy liked the girl but didn't know how to say anything. Fucking great. She looked over her shoulder at Gabrielle, "You don't have any sisters, right?"

"No."

Bethany Anne turned back around and started going through the snow. "Good. Let's go, people… and you too, Eric."

John had left the skis under a nearby tree. He sure hoped no one found them and thought the four of them dead.

He turned around, shouldered his pack and started walking towards the group, where Bethany Anne was beckoning him. "Hey, mountain, get up here and break trail for the little woman, would you?"

John grumped, "The little woman can bench press me."

"Stop your excuses, you big hunk of man meat. I considered throwing Eric, but then I'd have to heal him if he went over a ledge."

Eric said, "Geez, you ladies really stick together. Would it help if I apologized?"

Gabrielle stopped to look at him. "It might at that."

Eric spread one of his arms out as if he was a gallant gentleman. "Then, please accept my apology for my lack of decorum and irresponsible comment before."

"Apology accepted." Gabrielle nodded her head and Eric smiled in return.

John passed the two of them by. "If you guys get any nicer to each other I might have to throw up." Both of them turned and looked at John, their eyes narrowed.

Oh, fuck. Now he had the two of them gunning for him. He sure hoped they found the saucer quickly.

He passed Bethany Anne. "Which way?"

She pointed up the side of the mountain. "See that stand of trees?"

"Barely."

"Oh, crap. Sorry, forgot your sight isn't as good. Tell you what, Beefalo, go straight for a hundred yards through those two trees fifty feet ahead of you and maybe I can lead from there."

John decided to bite his tongue. He already had two in the party aiming his way, he didn't need all three! Now he needed to figure out a way to get Eric in trouble with Gabrielle again. "Right, one snow path coming up!"

Bethany Anne looked behind her. "Eric, get your skinny ass up here, too. No need to let all that manly meat go to waste, use it to make my path easier to walk!" She smiled at Eric who wasn't sure which way to take that comment. Did he reply to the 'skinny ass' part or the 'manly meat?' Or neither since he was still reminded of her question to John back on the plane and he didn't want her bringing that question up again.

"Yes ma'am!" Eric took off behind John.

"We'll catch up in a second." Bethany Anne turned to Gabrielle and waited till he was out of earshot. She barely whispered, "You know he likes you, right?" Gabrielle looked stricken, and then her eyes followed Eric as he walked away.

Gabrielle whispered back, "Well, this is a pickle, isn't it?" Gabrielle was happily connecting with Ivan right now and didn't want a three way romance. She had grown out of the desire to pit two men against each other back in the twenties, the 1820s to be exact. Her shoulders slumped. "I'll have a talk with him."

"See that you do, I can't have my Guardians dealing with internal trouble, capiche?" Gabrielle nodded. Bethany Anne turned around and double-timed it to catch up to the guys, Gabrielle right behind her.

TOM was true to his word. They were safely in the cave system that went to his ship by midnight. They stopped a little ways in to rest, eat and drink before working their way through the caves out to the other side. They were going to get caught in the early morning, but no direct sun if they hurried. Bethany Anne told the guys which direction and they headed off in a hurry.

Bethany Anne, don't you want to warn John?

Huh? Bethany Anne had been thinking about Paul Jameson and hoping that he had gotten the new pilot situation sorted out.

Warn him about what?
About the ship?
What about the…

"Ow! What the fuck?" John was twenty yards ahead of her, rubbing his forehead with one hand while the other was held out in front of him.

Oh yeah, it's invisible.

Not invisible, it warps light around the ship.

That distinction isn't important right now TOM.

"John, you ok?"

"Yeah, I think I found the ship."

Bethany Anne hurried to catch up to the two guys. "Yeah, sorry I forgot to mention it has a method of bending light to make it seem invisible."

Eric looked excited. "You mean like in Harry Potter and the …" He stopped as all three adults turned as one to stare at him. "Hey! I like the story, it's my weakness…"

Bethany Anne snorted. "I thought the History Channel was your weakness." She reached around until she found the indention that covered the locks. Pressing the indention caused it to slide aside and she keyed in a sequence from memory and the cloaking stopped. The door opened and Bethany Anne strode on in. She called out, "Watch your heads, especially you, John!" The four of them got onboard and she keyed the door closed. She couldn't believe she was back here again so soon.

She went to a portion of the wall and slid her hand across an area a little lower than where a normal location would be on a human sized door. She pushed it and the door slid to the side. "This was TOM's old quarters." She walked in and turned around, "This was where the pilot slept. Except for the medical room and the science room everything else is built smaller. TOM's race isn't as tall as ours. You can drop your packs here, gentlemen." The three of them followed her into the smaller cabin.

Both men and Gabrielle were looking around in wonder. They had followed Bethany Anne because it was what they did. However, they all had to admit that until they got on the spacecraft it had seemed rather fantastic. Now, they were really on an alien spacecraft and everything Bethany Anne had been telling them was true.

They really did need to save the world from aliens.

"Hey!" Bethany Anne snapped to get their attention. "The piloting area is cramped as hell, so no one can join me there. I'm going to go and work with TOM for a few minutes. You guys camp here or look around. If you look around, and I'm looking at you Eric, don't touch anything or we might just drop out of the sky later. Hate to go splat on the bird's first flight in a thousand years." Bethany Anne walked out of the room.

The three of them broke out in huge grins. Gabrielle was the first to break the silence. "We're on an alien spacecraft! Can you believe it?" The two men just smiled with her, until Eric stopped and looked back at the door. "Did she say this was going to be the first flight in a thousand years?"

Both John and Gabrielle stopped smiling and looked back at the door as well. John spoke up, "Does this ship have liquor?"

Bethany Anne smiled as she listened to the three of them talk. She thought that they had followed along too agreeably. Now she realized it was because they hadn't considered the reality of getting on the spaceship in the first place. Now, they not only were on the spaceship, but she was prepping the little girl to come online again.

TOM, what do we need to do?

We will need to bring the main subsystems back to ready status and then check all of the results.

How long will this take?

Hours would be my guess.

So, we aren't leaving tonight, that's for sure. I don't want to take this out during the day. Since we have at least eighteen hours, will that help the planning?

Sure, a proper prep time is about twelve hours, so taking into account we are using your body to do this and you

will have to hunt around for the correct controls we should get done in plenty of time.

You know I can swing over to vamp mode and we can run through this pretty damn quickly, right?

TOM hadn't considered that.

It won't help in this case, we need to bring the subsystems online in order. The power should be good for another few thousand years so we will start with that.

The spies in the sky won't see a thermal bloom, will they?

No, this craft goes through the icy edge of space, we don't lose any energy. We won't even melt the ice on top of us until I want to.

Bethany Anne smiled. *Listen to yourself, you're getting a little big for your britches back in your crib, aren't you?*

She felt the satisfaction TOM was giving off.

Yes, It feels good to do something I know how to do, and can do well.

Well then, Pilot TOM, let's get this craft ready to rock and roll!

Yes Ma'am!

CHAPTER SEVEN

Carpathian Mountains, Romania

While the power was coming online, Bethany Anne went to find Gabrielle and together they went into the medical room. Bethany Anne shut the door behind them. The room stood just as clean as the last time she was here. The pod was in the middle with about four feet of space all around it.

Gabrielle looked at the pod in the middle of the room. "So, this is where we all started?"

Bethany Anne nodded. "Yes. About one thousand years ago, Michael stumbled across this ship and into that pod. How? I'm not really sure yet. Neither Michael nor TOM have ever told me that part. TOM started the genetic modifications but due to ignorance, they were incredibly painful for Michael and while he struggled through most of the pain, he woke up before TOM was able to tweak anything. He got out of the pod and left the area. His nanocytes weren't properly modified for the human genotype and each time a vampire created another vampire, the mutations got worse. That's why the children can be anything from almost as strong as the parent to pretty weak."

Gabrielle walked forward and put her hand on the pod, "It looks like a white coffin."

"You don't watch much science fiction, do you?"

"No, not so much."

"It shows. No, this is a medical pod. All of the instruments are inside this shroud. Once you lay down inside, you'll go to sleep and the medical process is handled by the computer."

"How does it know what to do?"

"I have to program it. If you come around to this side, there is a ..." Gabrielle used her vampiric speed to join Bethany Anne and started looking at what she was talking about, "dashboard right here." Bethany Anne looked at the vampire who was suddenly at her side, "Um, are you a little anxious?"

Gabrielle looked at her and shrugged. "Does it show?"

"A little. Here, use this." Bethany Anne reached for a long rectangle that she pulled out into a bench. "Sit there." Gabrielle sat down. "Here's the story, so you know what you're in for. This is on a need to know basis and unless I tell you otherwise, no one needs to know, understand?" Gabrielle agreed.

Bethany Anne started walking around the little room. "You know Michael was changed here. The original pilot of this craft, who I call TOM now, was in charge of preparing this whole world to fight aliens. The problem is that this craft might, or might not, be able to lift again after the next landing. TOM rather messed up this one."

I did not 'mess up' this landing.

"TOM, shut up for a second, will you?"

Gabrielle started when she realized that Bethany Anne was talking to the alien. She looked around, "Is TOM able to hear us in the ship?"

Bethany Anne smirked, "Gabrielle, TOM is able to hear anything I can hear." Bethany Anne pointed to her ear.

"What?" Gabrielle looked both surprised and perplexed.

"TOM is a part of me. He deconstructed a large part of his body centuries ago and when I was being changed he hitched a ride inside of me to try to continue his mission of protecting his race. His only choice was to become a symbiont. In me." Gabrielle looked at Bethany Anne's body and seemed a little freaked out. "Yes, I get that. I wasn't asked if I was ok with this idea. Imagine my surprise when I woke up and I have this extra voice in my head. We're getting a little off track. The reason I'm sharing this information with you now is to help you understand I'm not the one who will be programming the medical pod. TOM will literally be using my body to make it happen."

"Um, can I talk with him?"

Bethany Anne started at this. "Ah, one sec."

TOM, what do you think?

It is certainly possible. I know how your vocal cords work so I can process the data, but it would be a lot easier if you just allow me permission to take control for a minute in the speech area of the brain.

Wait one second, I don't like the idea of you 'taking control' of anything.

Sorry, wrong choice of words. I mean to jointly be in that area of your mental efforts. You will be able to interrupt at any time. But I will be able to talk and you will hear my discussion at the same time that Gabrielle does. You truly won't be able to censor my speech if you choose to

allow me to do this.

Bethany Anne thought about this for a second. Gabrielle could see the different emotions playing on Bethany Anne's face.

Bethany Anne looked at Gabrielle. "Yes, it's possible. But TOM tells me that I won't have a clue what he's going to say before he says it, so be forewarned. Also, I'm concerned about anything that messes with my brain which is what he is going to have to do to make this happen."

"I'm sorry, I hadn't realized what I was asking."

Bethany Anne waved the concern away. "I understand. You've been alive for a long time and now you are facing an alien medical pod that could change you. It's about trust. I need you to be able to walk in the day to help me with what we have coming up so both of us need to trust TOM in this."

"Is he trustworthy?"

"Well, if you had asked me right after I woke up, I wouldn't have been so sure. Now? Yeah. It's going to take the whole world working together to get ready to fight these aliens and TOM has a better overall grasp of the political situation and what needs to be done than he had before. For better or worse, he is as stuck with me as I am with him. Believe it or not, I'm not sure I would choose to have him separated from me right now if I had to make a choice. Certainly not if it meant he would die."

Really? That's… I don't know what to say.

Well, just don't say anything and ruin it for yourself.

"Wow, I'm not so sure I could say that."

"Trust me, I'm surprised it's how I feel too. Looking around this room I realize that it all started here, and it all started with TOM. I would be dead if it wasn't for him and his alien genetic nanocyte technology. What you have in your blood are corrupted versions, third generation. TOM's going to fix the corruption issues with your nanocytes. This will allow you to go out in the sun."

A tear was forming on Gabrielle's face. "That is beyond my wildest dreams."

"Here, why don't you talk with TOM."

Go ahead TOM.

Tom took over Bethany Anne's speech. She felt a little disoriented and could 'feel' a pressure in her head.

"Hello Gabrielle." Bethany Anne's voice was her tone, but not her inflection. Gabrielle could tell the difference between the two voices.

"Hello TOM." Now that she had access to him, Gabrielle was at a loss for words. "Sorry, just got lost for a second. I understand you are going to change my nanocyte programming? Is there much risk involved?"

"No need to be sorry about getting a bit lost for words, I understand completely. Yes, I will have the medical pod change the programming of your nanocytes and get them to correct the mistakes. Some of the severely damaged will cease to function. It will take maybe a week based on the information I was able to obtain when you provided us the syringe of your blood. You will sleep during the process. To my knowledge, there is no risk involved. It is one of the reasons we didn't change your nanocytes outside of the pod. If we had chosen to try and do it with Bethany Anne's superior nanocytes inside of your own body, we could not direct exactly which mutations would occur."

Gabrielle's shoulders lost some of their tension. Apparently, the two of them could have made changes to her before now but had chosen to use the safer method. "So, hey, what about getting rid of a tattoo at the same time?"

Gabrielle noticed Bethany Anne's inflection change. "You have a tattoo?"

"Yeah, a bad choice in the 1970s. On my ass."

TOM was speaking again, "Actually, the nanocytes you have in you right now could have taken care of that issue. I will work to teach you how to use your nanocytes to their fullest when we get them fixed. I'll leave the tattoo as a practice opportunity."

"I want to see!" Back to Bethany Anne.

Gabrielle looked exasperated, "You know, this talking to two of you in one body is a pain. And not only no, but HELL No. I am not showing you something that will be gone as soon as I can learn how to get rid of it!"

"Ivan got to see it!"

Gabrielle stuck her tongue out. "Not from the position we were in. Ok, I guess I feel as comfortable as I can about this. When do we want to start the process?"

Bethany Anne considered her response. TOM seemed to have left her head for now. "I don't know why now isn't as good a time as any. We get a day's head start and if anything happens being in the pod is the safest place on the ship. So, now?"

Gabrielle nodded her head in agreement and stood up. Bethany Anne put a hand out, "Sorry, but you have to get in the pod naked." Bethany Anne's smile told Gabrielle she wasn't getting in the pod without divulging her traitorous and embarrassing tattoo. She rolled her eyes and started to take off her clothes. Bethany Anne turned around and started programming the pod.

Once she was finished with the full programming but before she hit the final button to open the pod, Bethany Anne turned around and faced the now naked Gabrielle. Bethany

Anne pointed her finger down and twirled it around. Gabrielle rolled her eyes and started to turn as fast as she could with her vampiric speed. Two hands grabbed her shoulders. Holy Crap! Bethany Anne had stopped her as if she was a normal human.

"Nice. Were you having trouble with guys figuring out the right location?"

Gabrielle's tattoo was right in the center of her tailbone area below her pant line. It was a very floral spelling of "Enter Here" and a heart that ended with an arrow at the bottom pointing down.

"Believe it or not, I'd never had a tattoo. I was in Paris at the time. My flame and I were very drunk after seeing some of the sexy shows on the Boulevard de Clichy and one thing led to another…" Bethany Anne let her shoulders go.

Bethany Anne smiled. "I think it's hilarious. I'd leave it alone, but then I haven't had to live with it for as long as you. But if TOM says you can get rid of it already, you can take that to the bank. I imagine you can even put it back if you want."

"No thank you, getting rid of it is enough."

Bethany Anne turned back around and hit the two button combination that started the pod opening. "You get in, put your arms by your side and close your eyes. I'll be here when you get out. Sweet dreams!"

Gabrielle had been getting in the pod while Bethany Anne gave her instructions. She tried to smile and get over her anxiety. The pod door closed and she heard two small knocks and then the lights went out. Seconds later, at least to her, she woke up.

CHAPTER EIGHT

Carpathian Mountains, Romania

John and Eric were leaving the craft. Bethany Anne had told the guys to go stretch their legs for a while, they were driving her insane.

John set out for the caves and Eric dropped in behind him. John found what he was looking for, a rock they could rest against and talk without getting snow on them but still out in the light. He leaned against it and asked Eric, "Hey, why are you being so grumpy lately?"

Eric looked surprised. He hadn't acted any different than he normally would, had he? "Not sure I follow, big guy."

John looked at Eric a little closer to see if he was truly ignorant. Yup. "You're acting like a guy who is falling for a girl but doesn't know how to tell her."

Eric's face scrunched up. "Who... Ah. Gabrielle?" John just shook his head. Eric had been with John on too many ops to ignore John's comment. He must have really been acting the ass. "Really? God, ok. When did I start?"

John thought about this. "Maybe after the Costa Rican op?"

"Yeah, after she saved my ass. Probably, that would make sense. Shit, I was dead, John, you know that? That guy was looking down the barrel of his gun and my ticket was punched when all of a sudden she got his attention enough he turned his pistol just a smidge and shot her straight in the chest. It knocked her clean off her feet and I thought I had just caused my teammate to take my bullet, you know?" John knew. "By the time I realized she was still moving so did the other guy who was able to plug her in the leg before I snapped out of it and shot him. The blood was all over her leg and she was in full Vamp mode. She was still fucking beautiful, you know? I had the blood so I made sure we were safe and held her while she drank."

Eric paused in his story, just looking around at the beauty in the valley he could see because of Gabrielle.

"I guess it was at that time she wasn't just one of 'them' but one of our team to me. It's the first time I've been in a firefight with a woman."

"What do you call Bethany Anne?"

Eric smiled at his brother in arms, "A scary motherfucker? Death with the legs of an angel? The last beautiful smile you see before Hell takes you?" They both had to laugh at that a little. "Yeah, I get you. Yes, she's a beautiful woman as well, but she isn't the same, you know? She carries that mantle of leadership that lets you know she's off limits. I'm not sure if it's destiny or that some other guy is meant for her, but I know she's untouchable on the romantic side. Holding Gabrielle made me realize that she was one of us."

"You realized she was approachable?"

"Yes. No. Shit, no. I know she's with Ivan and I didn't think my playing had gone past camaraderie. How bad have I fucked up?" Eric continued staring out at the valley.

John punched him in the shoulder, "Not too bad, asswipe. But I can't have romance in the Guardians, especially not the Queen's Bitches you know?" Eric just nodded agreement. "I know that Gabrielle probably has a long history of relationships and has been through this, so I doubt you've done anything that crossed any line with her. Well, except the bonbon comment."

Eric smiled. "God, you know how freaked out I was when she pushed my ass out of the helicopter?" John laughed at this. "All I heard was 'thanks for volunteering' and then I was ejected like a shot. I hit the ground before I could think a coherent thought."

"Well, just imagine the stories you can tell one day. All of your grandchildren will gather around you to hear about when you told the scary vampire lady she was too fat to get into the helicopter!" Eric had to laugh at that visual. Him with grandchildren was a trip.

Finally he shook his head back and forth just a little. "No. I think that story will be for just the four of us. I won't compound my mistake by sharing that story with others."

"Keeping her reputation safe?"

"Brother, I've got her back and that includes her reputation. I know she's got mine, right?" They fist bumped and John decided this conversation was done. The team was good.

Back in the ship, Bethany Anne closed the external microphones TOM had directed her to use. She swallowed a lump in her throat and had to blink her eyes to clear them of the weight of Eric's feelings, and the loneliness she felt as their leader. She would fight through it, she always had. This time, she wasn't fighting to achieve justice for someone that had already passed away, but for the future of little babies yet to be born.

Sacrifices had to be made and Bethany Anne knew she would bear the weight of many sacrifices to come. She calmly continued bringing the ship online with TOM and making sure the medical pod was working effectively on Gabrielle.

―――

The Queen Bitch's Ship SEA AXE
150 Miles East of Bahamas

Captain Maximilian Wagner had requested that Bobcat come aboard early and check out the Sikorsky S-76 and make sure it was ready for the swap with the alien craft later that night. The captain was pretty methodical with his crew and would triple check to make sure everything was ready to go.

He had pulled the crew, all ex-Navy, together to let them know they were going top secret that night. Everyone on the ship had been vetted by Bethany Anne, so they had no moles. Max Wagner was a believer in everyone pulling together and you couldn't do that, in his opinion, by hiding a huge piece of news that would certainly be all over the ship in microseconds after Bethany Anne landed the craft.

Fortunately, it was going to be an overcast night. There was a chance for the weather to get a little violent, but they were in the Bermuda triangle, there was always a chance the weather could be rough.

He had a good crew. He had expected to be under Captain Thomas, but since the SEA AXE had the right hold for the spacecraft, the ship was needed right away.

The ship had a Superyacht exterior paint job, but had a commercially painted look and feel in most of the major compartments. It was designed for the comfort of the crew and the gentle handling of the toys. This was good as their latest toy was unique in the world as far as Max knew. If the major world powers had their own alien toys, they weren't talking.

He looked over at his crew. They were in the main galley area, which could feed thirty around the tables. He told them to all take a seat at the three tables nearest where he stood.

There were fourteen personnel on board, including himself, which left seven berths available. Bethany Anne was bringing four more people with her. He was sure that he was probably going to have to figure out how to refit his ship for more people. That was fine, he had a shit-ton of space below decks for the jet-set toys that they would never have to ferry around.

He raised his hand and his crew stopped talking. He looked over the three tables. The engineering crew had four team members, the deck crew had three and Chris Billings from the deck crew could actually ferry the Sikorsky around in a pinch. He wasn't a pilot at Bobcat's level but he could have gone commercial had he wanted. He had four Marines on his team and his second in command was Natalia Jakowski. Natalia was about five and a half feet of spunky redhead with piercing green eyes to go with her alabaster skin.

He had just informed Natalia what was going on with the spacecraft two hours ago. He started with the story of the team in the swamp and the terrorist takedown. It was good that Dan had arrived during the discussion as he was able to tell a few more of the stories with either firsthand or at least immediate second-hand knowledge. Dan had felt he needed to be on the ship to give the same overview he provided the first team Bethany Anne recruited. Everyone on Max's ship had met Bethany Anne, but it had been short and to the point when she tested their dependability and personal ethics.

Dan sat a few feet from where Max was talking to the crew. "Ok, everyone. It's time to give you all of the details. You were all vetted by one of the best in the business before we asked you to join the company and specifically this ship. I hope you're ready for this because your life is about to change in immeasurable ways." There was some muttering in the group. They all knew that they were a part of something a little clandestine. No one brings together two Superyacht caliber ships with all ex-Navy crews where one of the transport helicopters is a damn Black Hawk. They had either personally met, seen or heard about the Queen Bitch's Guards. Some had laughed about the name, but certainly not to their faces.

Todd Jenkins had come on board the day before to work with the three Marines Max already had on board. He was one tough nut to crack and the story got around that he had had some war-games of his own with the boss's team. He didn't have much to say that except his team always won, but then had to admit that he was usually out pretty quickly due to the superior abilities of the other team. When Todd and the three other Marines did some of their own scrimmages, Todd took out the three other Marines each time pretty easily.

If Todd took their Marines out, and the boss's people took Todd out, just how good were those guards?

"Indescribable," was Todd's answer.

Now, their captain was getting ready to lay it all down and they were anxious.

BITE THIS

"I know none of you want to go back to a civilian life. You were made Navy, you lived Navy and by God you want to die Navy."

His second, Natalia, added, "Let's just make sure I die after I get laid again, is that too much to ask?" Everyone laughed at Natalia's comment and it helped ease some of the jittery feelings in the crew, which was her aim. Max saw the wink she gave him.

"Indeed. Notwithstanding my second's prurient request, I can tell you I am signed up to this Navy to fight a long battle that you are not going to believe. Unfortunately, it's all true. I've vetted this information and Dan Bosse is going to provide the same presentation that the first team watched as we came aboard the Polarus. The purpose of this is to give you the background to understand the craft we will be loading tonight and why it's a ship that you never saw and never heard about. Am I clear?"

Everyone gave him their agreement. He had a good crew and they understood when it was time to get serious.

Dan stood up and took Max's place. "Men, women, I'm used to running agents on clandestine operations inside the United States, fighting a foreign race which our police, national guard and SWAT teams aren't prepared to handle."

Dan noticed a woman sitting in the third table to his right raise her hand, "Sir?"

"Yes?"

"Lt. Michelle Granger, sir. Well, ex-lieutenant. Wasn't your operation to support the SWAT team against terrorists in Miami?"

"Good question Lt. Granger. The short answer is no. We were actually called in after an op we did in the Florida Everglades. We had been coming off our op the day before and

80

most of the team was enjoying some downtime at lunch. The terrorists had a two-way plan. They attacked north of Miami and accomplished getting the Miami SWAT stuck in. It was the terrorists in downtown's bad luck my team was available because our fight was equivalent to the high school JV team going against the Super Bowl champions. The terrorists were taken down inside of two minutes flat across three floors without one injury to my team or the hostages. As far as we were concerned, it was a cakewalk. Here, before you guys start with more questions, let me show you some video."

The lights went down and Dan stepped to the side so he wouldn't be in front of the screen that had descended from the ceiling.

"Let me first explain I've been fighting these bastards one way or another for three decades, the last fifteen years as the AIC. In the last eighteen months I've lost every man I'm about to show you. Here we go…"

Then, Dan gave them the show with the extended video selection Frank had provided tacked on to the end. When Bill's vampire visage came up, he heard the expected epithets and indrawn breaths.

By the time the lights came back on, everyone was torn between somberness for the loss of Dan's agents and the shock of vampires and Nosferatu being real.

Max stood back up. "Ok, team. Here is the foundation of information you must understand. The reality is, a vampire is a mutation caused by nanocytes in their bloodstreams. This technology is not from earth." Here, Max had to wait a minute to let the mutterings calm down. "As I was saying, the actual mutations these humans have undergone were the efforts of an alien group trying to create people to help them in a war in their own galaxy.

Unfortunately, as humans tend to do, the vampire group didn't get the message about a possible alien invasion and some of the bastards decided to figure out a way to take over the human race and it became an underground war. This is the war Dan and his group have been fighting. No one had a clue that the purpose of mutating humans had to do with an alien war in another galaxy that could end up here. So, now we're trying to shut down the first vampire war while figuring out a way to get to the stars in preparation to defend the earth."

Natalia put her hand up and Max just nodded, "Do we have a time frame, Skipper?"

"We don't know. The original date of the first landing by the alien craft was over a thousand years ago." This caused everyone to sit up a little straighter. It might seem far-fetched that aliens from another galaxy might 'come to get you' until you found out that aliens had been modifying humans for a thousand years. It caused a lot of those listening to realize it could be another thousand years before anyone had to worry, or they could be fighting an invasion tomorrow. "What we know is that we, and by 'we' I include everyone in this room, are part of a group that is working to protect the earth. Our first mission is to protect our people from the Nosferatu and the Forsaken you saw on the video behind us. For most on the Polarus, that is the only mission they are aware of."

Chris Billings raised his hand. "Yes Chris?"

"Sir, why do we need to know the full story?"

"Because you, me, Natalia here and every one of you have been chosen to be the forward team in this war. I hope you all have your big boy and girl pants on tonight, because we are about to become the floating version of Area-51."

"Holy shit!" That was from one of Todd's Marines.

Max looked over at him and he mumbled, "Sorry sir." Max tipped his head.

"While I can't condone the interruption, I do agree with the sentiment. Our job is to become the holding location for an alien craft, which, if anyone in the world finds out about before we're ready, could literally cost us all our lives and the world its future. If you don't think you're ready to be on this ship, with this responsibility, then you can move to the back right now and Dan will take you back to the Polarus in the morning.

"Sir?"

"Yes, Natalia."

"Why would you let anyone leave after they've heard the stories and seen the video?" Max could see a couple of heads nod in agreement.

"Because every one of you has been tested and I trust the testing agent's assessment that you're all highly ethical. But the reason you won't leave until morning is because you will be visited by someone who will take the knowledge of everything you have witnessed tonight back out of your head. Unfortunately, you might lose a few days instead of a few hours, but you won't be a danger to this mission or yourselves. This is literally a situation of loose lips will sink this ship. I'm sorry, but I believe you have to know the whole truth to make a decision that is this monumental in scope. Every person that stays with me tonight is making a pact with every person on this ship that we are in this until the end."

"Max?" Captain Wagner turned around to look at Dan.

"The Queen's Guard has a word for this, it's 'Aeternitatem.' The whole Latin would be, 'Ad Aeternitatem' but it means For Eternity." Dan looked at every person in the room, meeting every pair of eyes for at least a second before moving on to the next. "When you become one of Bethany Anne's guard, you're in the closest ring of trust we have because you are protecting the one person who might be able to save humanity if the major powers don't get their shit together." The weight of the knowledge affected everyone. "A SEA AXE is actually just a type of ship, it isn't a real ship name. The original owner never changed it on the documentation and that's how it was christened. I can only recommend, but I think that for those who stay, you need to rechristen this ship to better represent your mission. I'll be around if your captain needs me. I'll let you talk this out."

Dan nodded to Max and left the group to their silence, their contemplation of everything they were just told.

Todd Jenkins spoke up. "Over the last day, you guys have asked me about my experience fighting Bethany Anne's guard. Well, considering the bombshells being dropped tonight let me tell you a little more." A couple of people had to move their chairs to see Todd better.

Max spoke up, "Mr. Jenkins, would you be so kind as to stand up?"

Todd stood. "Certainly." He looked around, "When Bethany Anne and her team were getting ready for the Costa Rican operation, there were two vampires in that room. One was hundreds of years old and wicked fast with her swords. She easily could have decimated a troop of my Marines. She had with her the Queen's Guard, the 'bitches' as Bethany Anne likes to call them." Todd's smile let a few feel comfortable laughing a bit. "Now that I've fought against these four guys, it would be an honor if I could be on a team that was even good enough to get a draw against them, much less a win. These guys have been fighting the Forsaken we saw on the video for years. By the time I got to work with them they had already been training with Bethany Anne for a month or more and I have to say those terrorists didn't have a fucking chance in hell. I was on Bethany Anne's team to start getting a little of my edge back and I had to get it back fast. They didn't care if I had been on the beach for six months, you're either in the game or dead as far as they are concerned. Suffice to say, I was dead a lot!"

More laughs at this. Todd wasn't too worked up over his bad showing against the team.

"But… my partner in all of this was the second vampire, Bethany Anne." A few shocked faces from those who hadn't already guessed that Bethany Anne was the other vampire. "She was indescribably fast, fierce and furious. She was brutally hard on her own team and Gabrielle, forcing them to dig deep to beat her. They never did. She had them so pissed off that they formed a team so smooth you would swear they had all grown up together. This includes a vampire that they hadn't met and who hadn't worked with anyone herself for a hundred years. Time after time, she put them down. One of the guy's arms got broken in one of the fights and Gabrielle, the second vampire, healed him. Make no mistake, if you stay here on this ship, whatever you choose to name her, you will be tested, you will be tried and you will be forced to be better than the Navy ever thought you could be. The stakes aren't just for our own country, but every country in the world. When I was in the Marines, my family, my friends, my loved ones knew I fought for them. Not everyone appreciated what I did, but they knew it. If you stay, no one may ever know about your sacrifice except those of us here who will be with you through the whole damn thing. 'Ad Aeternitatem.'"

All of the heads followed Todd's progress as he sat back down.

"Sir?" This time, Natalia's voice was soft, almost reverent in her speech.

Max looked over at her, "Yes?"

"Where might we find some paint, sir?" Natalia's voice got a little stronger, as if she had come to a decision.

"And what might we be painting right now, Natalia?"

"A new name, sir." Max just looked at her, as did everyone else in the room.

"And what would that be?"

"Respectfully, I think we need to rechristen this boat by the oath we who stay to see this through take." Max started nodding his head emphatically.

"Make it so, Natalia."

She stood up at pointed to the chief engineer. "Are you staying?"

Mark Simmons, Chief Engineer of the SEA AXE pursed his lips and made a decision. "Yes, you need me?"

She nodded and looked around. "Yeah, you and everyone that's going to crew the 'Ad Aeternitatem' need to come with me, I want that name changed before Bethany Anne arrives tonight!"

"Fuck yeah!" The Marines all jumped up and pumped their fists. It was unanimous and almost everyone followed Natalia Jakowski out of the room. Max watched as the single person left, Chris Billings, came up to him.

"Not staying, Chris?" Max smiled at him, no judgment on his face.

Chris was smiling, "Hell yes I'm staying! I just want to know if you think I might have a chance to get into the Guard and if so, would it offend you that I don't stay on the ship?"

Max put his hand out to shake Chris's. "Chris, each of us needs to take this knowledge and move to where we can help the best. Whether that's in the Guard or on my crew, I'll respect you, and support you. Until then, sailor, get your ass out there and let's get this ship named correctly!"

Chris straightened up and pulled an exceptionally fine salute for Captain Wagner, "Sir, I'll do better than the Navy ever believed I could!"

Max saluted him back. "I'm holding you to that, Chris, now get moving."

Chris dropped his salute, turned around and started jogging out of the room.

Max looked around at the empty room. He had the finest crew he could possibly ask for and smiled to himself. Ad Aeternitatem indeed.

CHAPTER NINE

Miami FL, USA

Nathan and Lance retired to Bethany Anne's living room. Darryl, Scott and Pete were next door pumping iron. At first, Darryl and Scott had issues with Lance being in the house without a guard. Nathan decided to let them understand a little more about him.

They had all changed to more comfortable clothes and went to the challenge area in the large workout slash martial arts gym the team used. Lance and Pete had leaned against some of the workout equipment out of the fight area. Nathan first bested Scott, then Darryl. Finally, Nathan had them both attack him and while it was certainly closer, Nathan was able to incapacitate both of them. Nathan reached down to pull Darryl up off the mat.

Darryl spoke to Nathan as he got up and reached for a towel. "Ok, I think we can agree you're worth two Guardians!"

Nathan smiled. "Guys, this was just a scrimmage. If I was going for broke, I would have just shot you both earlier. I don't get into fights unless I have to. With Wechselbalg, fighting without arms amongst ourselves is traditional. The fact that the two of you almost got me means two things."

Scott had grabbed the ibuprofen bottle they normally used after working out with Bethany Anne and popped four before washing them down with his orange Gatorade. "What would those be?"

"First, you are two of the fastest and meanest humans I've ever fought." Pete tossed Nathan a towel so he could dry off. "The second is I need to get my ass back into practice as well. These last few months haven't provided enough time for me to work out."

Darryl walked to the towel basket and dropped his in. "I'm good whenever you want to go at it. I think I've learned two holds so far I need to work with you on and I know you used at least three breaks in that last fight I haven't figured out."

Scott added, "If they aren't the same ones that I encountered, then I have some as well. Where did you learn all of that?"

Nathan smiled as he dropped his towel in the basket. "Guys, I'm decades older than you. I've had a little more time to acquire skills." With that, he looked over at Lance, "I'm going to take a fast shower here, then we can go back to the other house." Lance agreed.

When Nathan had left, Scott looked over at Darryl. "Dude, we are going to have to do better than that to make sure we impress the locals."

Pete looked at them both, "Locals? You mean the Wechselbalg who'll be coming down?"

"Yeah," Darryl sat down on the mat and started stretching his muscles. "The plan is to take them all through one match and make sure they realize we humans are some of the nastiest you can meet before we teach them how to go up against Nosferatu."

Pete shook his head. "Guys, I don't think you need to worry."

Scott dropped down near Darryl and started his own post fight cool down and stretch. "Why is that? Nathan took us both out pretty easily and then took us both on and won."

Pete said, "Guys, you need to understand that Nathan Lowell is a force of nature in the Wechselbalg community. There are parents that scare their kids who've been naughty by saying 'Nathan Lowell will come for you' if they don't act right."

Scott looked back at the door where Nathan had left. "Really?"

Peter bobbed his head up and down emphatically. "Really, really. There was a good chance that Nathan would have killed me for my screw ups if Bethany Anne hadn't worked out this setup with my dad."

Darryl just shook his head. "I find that hard to believe." Darryl switched to stretching his other leg.

"Don't. I asked Nathan about it myself on our trip up to New York. It was one of the options on the table if Bethany Anne didn't have any ideas. I had broken the rules and I was too full of myself to do anything about it. My dad was working with Gerry to see what could be done. If Michael had been involved, he would just have killed me and been done with it so anything was a step up over instant death as far as I'm concerned."

Scott was flexing his arms above his head. "Damn, that

had to be cold to hear that."

"Well, as a Wechselbalg, you hear enough stories to know you don't ask Nathan Lowell a question unless you want the hard answer. I still have to double check myself around him from time to time."

Darryl grunted as a particularly tight muscle got his attention. "He seemed like such a regular dude for so long when I was around him, I had no idea he had these moves."

Pete walked over to the stereo and started looking through the CDs to play something for his workout. "That would be because the only thing Nathan Lowell respects is a vampire. I imagine Nathan could have killed you more easily than taking you both down, but that's a guess. There isn't one Wechselbalg with any common sense that doesn't get concerned if they hear Nathan is in town, for any reason. I've heard of families taking impromptu vacations on the rumor he was flying into town on Were business. God, you guys have a lot of AC/DC here."

Scott said, "So many of the songs match our life, it's like they're the soundtrack for TQB guards."

Darryl added, "It started with Bethany Anne playing 'Big Balls.'"

Scott continued, "Then Back in Black."

"Hell's Bells."

"Highway to Hell."

Darryl reached over and fist bumped Scott, "That's fighting the Nosferatu baby! Dirty Deeds Done Dirt Cheap."

"Thunderstruck."

"Rock and Roll Ain't Noise Pollution."

Scott sang, "Rock and Roll ain't NOISE POLLUUUU-TION! Bedlam in Belgium!"

"BallBreaker!"

Lance just shook his head. "You guys could do this forever, couldn't you?"

Pete said, "There's got to be over twenty CDs in this box."

Scott looked over at Pete. "Hey! Be careful. John has a couple of Australian only releases and he will beat you down if you break any."

Pete pulled his hands away from the CDs. "Which ones?"

Scott scrunched up his face, "Ahhh, one is the Australian only version of High Voltage, can't remember the other."

Darryl started singing, "I've got big balls…"

Scott joined in, "You've got big balls…"

The both of them yelled out the final verse, "But Bethany Anne's got the biggest balls of them all!" They high-fived each other.

Nathan came into the room as the two of them finished the chorus. He looked over at Lance. "Do I want to know?"

"AC/DC."

"Ah. Ready?" Lance got up and waved to Pete while the other two guys continued laughing and they left.

Back in the workout area, Pete asked, "Are you sure you want Bethany Anne knowing you're singing that?"

Darryl looked over with the biggest smile so far today. "Shit man, she's the one who taught us to sing it that way! If you're in the guard, our whole workout regimen is to try and match her balls, Buddy! So plug in the tunes and start your ball-bustin, chop chop!"

Nathan heard the guys laughing and smiled as he closed the door.

Lance grinned with Nathan as they went through the newly created gate between the houses. William had been working while they had been out.

Nathan started the conversation. "Did Frank get back

with you on our guys in Las Vegas?"

"Yeah, both cleared easily. If Bethany Anne is happy, I think we need to pull in some of the brain trust in Vegas onto the project with our new acquisition."

Nathan just looked at Lance. "Really? I thought this discussion was going to be about Adam."

"Adam? Oh, 'and Eve.' Yeah, ok. That works for me." Being accustomed to talking around a subject in case of someone listening in, Lance had no problem catching up to Nathan's naming of the possible AI. "Well, if we keep the core of the group together, they can work on both at the same time. I don't know what we do with Jeffrey, he has a family. He has enough knowledge but it was Tom Billings that did most of the detail work, right?"

"Yes. Without the source code and Tom, it would take a long time, even with Jeffrey's help, for someone to duplicate the coding." They went through the front door and sat in the living room. Ecaterina had decorated the house very nicely. The two story windows that had a view of the water behind the house were draped in light gold sheer curtains that were presently pulled back. Nathan considered that the windows could be used for listening if someone used a laser mic against them. Something to deal with soon enough.

"Ok, so we have two issues, one is Adam, the other is a team to research the acquisition. It would be cleaner if we had the same team, but we'll need extra people anyway." Lance thought about it. "We have propulsion, engineering, metallurgy, advanced power… shit, I could put 'advanced' in front of everything. The team has to stay small, but how do we get the right talent with a small group?"

"Well, the only way to confirm anything is to control communication and access. The SEA AXE is too small for a very large group. Plus, we aren't really under the protection of a country's navy to speak of, and if we're in open sea any of the big countries could grab us easily. This is going to be a challenge. We need our own place where we can dig defenses or some way to protect ourselves."

"Mutually assured destruction." Lance leaned his head back on the couch.

"Pretty much."

"The problem is we need to be able to prove the destructive capability without permanent harm."

Nathan looked at Lance. "Well, that means digital efforts, right? So, there are a lot of ways to accomplish that easily enough. The problem is ramping it up high enough and fast enough to call off a strike, or we have to preemptively accomplish the warning which puts us on the radar as a threat."

"Don't want to start the relationship rattling our sabers. We are in no way ready to display a military response." Lance rubbed his eyes.

Nathan looked out the window at a boater going down the waterway. "Hide our efforts in plain sight."

"Aren't we doing that already? Hoping that no one figures out what's going on?" Lance looked over at Nathan.

"Well, it's something that Bethany Anne was talking about. We go ahead and open new companies based on the research of existing companies in the portfolio plus new results from TOM and pretend our efforts are due to research that we've been doing for a while. We slipstream some of the more effective solutions for the world into production and use the attacks we'll get from competition as an excuse to do the buildup of our digital and physical defense."

"So, you're talking about just keeping it here in the States?"

"Might as well, anywhere else in the world the U.S. might decide to do a covert op. Here, we could try to get the media on our side."

"Maybe. I don't like having all of our eggs in one basket. Let's look for locations in Europe, Australia, the States and… Well, shit. Can't go down to South or Central America until we take care of Anton and his cronies, nor Africa I understand. Not that either of those places have governments I'm too wild about being around. Great Britain I suppose, but land is a minor fortune over there."

Nathan snorted, "And your point?"

"Ok, that's fair. Bethany Anne has a fair amount of money. I haven't seen any of the existing businesses that have corporate grounds or buildings that we would want to use, and while the boats are ok for the time being, I would feel a lot better under a ton of rock."

"That's because you've been under a ton of rock at the military base for a long time."

"And I liked it!" Lance smiled. His base was a good place. It had lots of room underground, some aboveground buildings and an existing airfield. "I wonder if there are some old bases we could get cheap? They were bellyaching last year over the budget cuts and closing Fort Campbell."

"I haven't heard of anything going on the market with the wars going on overseas. Have you heard anything?"

"No, just a bunch of bitching about the cost of the wars. With the Iraq war officially over and Afghanistan shutting down, the military is shrinking. With the terrorist threats hitting the major countries, it's become more a surgical strike situation than feet on the ground. The politicians want safety, but they don't want to pay the bill to have that safety."

"We could always go to the war areas. We could probably

take care of anything that could attack us first."

"You know, if it wasn't my daughter we would be sending out, I could get behind that idea. But then an attack on us could easily be labeled a mistake in the media. Easy to cover up."

"You sure are bent on us getting attacked." Nathan was a little frustrated.

"Always be prepared." Lance smiled at him. He had been in so many of these meetings, some lasting for days, that this little discussion was just getting him warmed up. "Patience, grasshopper."

Nathan glared over at the older appearing man. "You do realize I'm older than you, right?"

"Sure, but have you war-gamed more than me?"

"Point."

"C'mon, let's get a six-pack and attack this the proper way."

Nathan got up. "Libations to lubricate the mind?"

"That's correct."

"Time tested."

"Time honored. It is the most likely reason we can't figure this out." Lance opened the huge doublewide stainless steel refrigerator to look inside. There were indeed multiple six-packs of beer. Two domestic and one foreign. Lance grabbed a Bud. Nathan asked for the green one so Lance pulled one of those to handed it to Nathan over the bar. The door opened in the front hall. Nathan put down his drink and turned on the balls of his feet. William called out from the front area, "Hello the home!"

Lance called back, "The same to you, we're drinking in the kitchen." Nathan sniffed the air and seemed reassured, so he turned back around and sat at the bar, popping the top of his Heineken.

William came around through the living room into the kitchen and dining area. "U.S. for me, don't need any of that Dutch stuff." Lance handed over the beer he hadn't opened yet, and then got himself another.

William took his first swig. "Damn good. What are we discussing?"

"We need a new location," said Nathan.

Lance grumped, "We want a base. Know of any for lease or purchase?"

William grabbed his back pocket, "Yeah, I have the deed right here. Wait, nope. Sorry, that's my receipt for aviation fuel." He took another swallow of his beer. "If Congress would pass the BRAC rule the military wants, you might get your base. But that will take years. With everybody in the communities shouting about lost jobs, no one in Congress wants to vote to close a base. The last time BRAC was introduced, the overrun costs were in the billions and so far the studies are showing the cost savings weren't that much anyway."

Nathan squinted at the bigger guy. "BRAC?"

Lance took this one. "Base Realignment and Closure."

"You know, if you're willing to travel, the DOD is closing Air Force bases in Europe."

Lance looked over his beer at William. "Damn, I forgot about that."

Nathan looked back and forth between them. "How would that help?"

Lance answered, "Some of the bases were borrowed from Great Britain. When you have a base, you have all of the infrastructure we would want, plus enough external infrastructure to support families. That little comment about Jeffrey and his family comes to mind. If we could get them to move, then we have the schools all set up in the local community and we could be seen as a provider of jobs."

Nathan's brows came together. "How does that help Op-Sec?"

"You don't think Jeffrey has good OpSec right now? Might I remind you the reason I had to go see him?"

Nathan thought back to how hard it had been to try and hack the company. "Damn fine point. Ok, say we find a base that we can buy or rent, then what?"

"If we can find one close to a sheltered bay, we have a place for the boats and an airfield. I would prefer it a little warmer."

William snorted. "Unless you're building, I don't know of anything available right now."

Nathan added, "Still, Great Britain is a close ally of the States, what if they become suspicious?"

Lance thought about it. "The more we talk, the more I think we need to find a base and make plans. We release something pretty positive from the research we are going to do and then either respond, or fabricate and respond, to a threat to our intellectual capital and 'move our corporate offices' to something we feel we can protect a little better. Until then, we need to have the best defense on the digital side we can. Do you think we can handle Adam?"

Nathan drained his beer and set it aside. "I'll need another to answer that question."

William looked at the two of them. "Adam?"

Lance pulled another Heineken from the fridge and handed it to Nathan. "Yeah, one of Bethany Anne's companies has a very strong Heuristic Internet Defense program we're calling 'Adam.' It might come with some challenges if you turn it back on again…"

William put his hand up. "If you would be so kind as to

stop there. The only programming I like to deal with works in planes, trains and automobiles."

Nathan looked over at him. "Trains?"

"It rhymes better than 'planes, helicopters and automobiles.' Either way. If you would provide me another of the non-green variety over here, I'll see about taking my shower and heading back out. I have a date with Cindy McWilliams tonight and she is going to be amazed with me."

Lance looked him over. "Oh, why is that?"

"Because I'm spending $200 to get a guy to chauffeur the two of us around in the latest SUV I just got back from Texas Armoring. They jumped Bethany Anne's ride to the front when I authorized the bonus. They're keeping up with their commitments by working on our stuff in the evening. Makes for a very happy Christmas for everyone."

Nathan looked at the big guy. "So, you're going to check out the ride from the back to make sure it's good before Bethany Anne uses the vehicle?"

"Two birds, one stone my friend. That and the mistletoe I'm going to hang in the back before we go says I at least get a kiss." William winked at the guys and left to go get ready.

After the door closed, Nathan started again. "Ok, back to Adam. My company has a pretty good internet defense program already, so we can implement that right away on everything. However, if what Tom was talking about is true, then Adam is a complete leapfrog over anything else available including my stuff. Well, except maybe something Google is planning, they've got a strong AI research team. Hell, they have Ray Kurzweil on their payroll, you can't get much higher than him for futuristic thinking."

"What advantage would we have if it turns out to be a strong AI?"

"You mean one that works for us?"

"Or at least with us."

Nathan stood up and walked the wall of windows, looking out but not seeing. "Well, we could probably run through the calculations and research at a speed that would rival corporations hundreds of times our size. Well, hundreds of the amount of people we might put on this project due to secrecy concerns. The ability to attack any country electronically will certainly rival those of major world powers and the time to get ready will be reduced down to months, perhaps weeks instead of years."

"So the risk might be worth the rewards." Lance watched Nathan Lowell as he contemplated what a strong AI would bring to the team.

"If we think we can contain the system, then yes I certainly believe so."

"How would you contain something like this?"

Nathan turned around. "With no external connectivity and no ability to make wireless connections."

"Jeffrey explained what the system needs to learn, how it acquires new information. How would you get the information into the system if it has no external connection?"

Nathan turned back around, his eyes seeing both now and the future. What is, what was, and what yet could be. "Hard drives, lots and lots of hard drives. We would have to download petabytes of data and use hot-swap removable hard drives to continuously feed more and more information into the system. We would need an interface of requested data which we download in a different physical location and keep a secured method to confirm what we allow into the data stream. Therefore, the system would need zettabytes of storage capability. If we create a blade server design we can easily ramp up the computing capacity and pull it offline as well."

"And what happens if one of you egg-heads mutter, 'Oh Shit?'"

Nathan frowned. "Besides the ability to cut the power? I would suggest a small EMP under the 'in case of emergency' glass. Push that button and everything gets fried. It's the final button that will kill the test."

"But if it isn't connected to the internet, we don't gain any of the tactical defense or offensive ability, either."

"True, it's no better than a great research tool, which would be a plus in its own right. But if you want the ability to truly be a jump ahead of the competition, we have to connect to the internet at some point." Nathan shrugged.

"How do you test a machine for sociopathic disorders?" Lance was stuck on the malevolent AI scenario.

"I don't think I've drunk enough to answer that question. I'm not sure you've drunk enough to be allowed to ask that question."

"Good point, let's get another." Lance got off of the couch and went back into the kitchen. This time he grabbed the rest of his six-pack, which was two bottles, and Nathan grabbed the remaining four Heineken.

Lance looked at Nathan. "Does beer affect you as much as they would a regular human?"

Nathan ignored the 'regular' comment. "No, not really. I could down these four and the buzz wouldn't last long at all."

"That had to be useful in college."

Nathan smiled. "It sure was." They moved back to the living room. "I have no idea how to test the computer, and this is assuming that we actually acquire an intellect behind the programming. Which presupposes that the program starts writing its own code base. Eventually, it would rewrite everything we started it on. It makes you want to confirm the system had Asimov's three laws of robotics."

"What, protect humans, obey humans and protect itself?" Lance took a swig of his beer.

"Well, they're longer than that. The first law was 'A robot may not injure a human being or, through inaction, allow a human being to come to harm.' The second law was 'A robot must obey the orders given it by human beings except where such orders would conflict with the First Law.' The final law was, 'A robot must protect its own existence as long as such protection does not conflict with the First or Second Laws.' If we could inject some sort of value system into the AI…"

Lance looked over at Nathan who had trailed off. "Inject a value system?"

Nathan stopped looking into nowhere and focused back on Lance. "No, that wouldn't work. You have to have a conversation that allows the AI to conceive of their own value system and then you make a judgment call if that will work for your purposes."

Lance snorted. "And who exactly is qualified to have that conversation?"

Nathan smiled. "There would be only one who could have the conversation because she will have to give the approval to fund this project, and make the decision whether to keep it alive or pull the literal plug."

Lance pursed his lips. "Well, she only has the fate of the world on her shoulders, what's adding the homicide of the world's first artificial intelligence entity going to do, break her?" He took a really long swallow from his beer after that pronouncement. He couldn't protect Bethany Anne from all of the decisions. She was the most qualified to decide if the new entity, if it happened, would be a benefit or not based on her own knowledge of what she would need in the future.

"That would be potential homicide and I'm not sure I would phrase it that way if we want her to do this."

Lance just raised his beer in Nathan's direction.

CHAPTER TEN

Frankfurt, Germany

Ivan and Stephen got off the train at Frankfurt's Main Train Station. There were people congested all over its twenty-five platforms. Over 350,000 travelers used the station every day and Ivan could believe it. They had reservations at the Steigenberger Frankfurter Hof for the next week. Well, that was what Ivan thought.

Stephen had called and let the Romanian local pack know that he was going to visit the Main Council in Frankfurt after he went through Brasov. While it had certainly surprised them, they assured Stephen they would let the Council know of his plans. Later, they left Stephen a voice message from the Council Lead, a Mr. Josef von Dorman, and his contact phone number.

Stephen called Josef when he was a day outside of Frankfurt. Stephen confirmed that he was uninterested in meeting the whole council. Josef was enough for his needs at this time and they agreed to meet in two days.

The hotel was about six blocks away from the train station so it was a quick taxi ride to get there. Ivan asked about reservations. Stephen just smiled and told him he had no reservations at this time, but Ivan shouldn't worry.

The taxi driver pulled up to the main entrance and jumped out to get the luggage. Ivan tipped him as Stephen looked around as if he was seeing changes in the place from the last time he was there. Ivan had both suitcases and leaned over to ask him quietly, "When was the last time you were here?"

Stephen leaned into Ivan and said, "The nineties," and leaned back out.

Ivan looked a little surprised. "That's all? Just two decades?"

Stephen smiled at him and added softly, "I never said the 1900s, Ivan." Then Stephen winked at Ivan and started walking through the door held open for him. Ivan shook his head and followed.

Stephen had paused a few feet inside the door and was looking around. Ivan heard him mutter, "I much preferred the original layout." He walked to the main desk, staffed by two women. "Good evening frauleins. My name is Stephen and I would like to make a reservation for a week in the Besitzer-Suite, please."

The first lady, a pretty brunette with gold-framed glasses with 'Abby' on her name badge smiled at Stephen. "I'm sorry, sir. But the 'Besitzer-Suite' is a unique room in the basement of the hotel, it isn't one we can rent out except to the owners. We do have two rooms on the second to the top floor which have nice views if you would like?"

"Thank you, Abby, but if you would check the Besitzer-

Suite instructions, you will find that my name, Stephen, is on the list."

"I'm sorry, sir. I do not know of any instructions for the room, one moment, please." Abby turned to the other lady, a blond middle aged woman, "Elyse, do we have Besitzer-Suite instructions?"

Elyse came over to stand next to Abby. "The Besitzer-Suite, yes. But they are in the safe, why?"

Stephen smiled a little coyly at the older lady. "My dear, because I need to use the rooms down there for the next week."

Elyse looked over at the new guest, a pretty young looking man who seemed to hold himself like someone much older than he obviously was. "I'm sorry sir, but the Besitzer-Suite has never been asked for in my twenty-two years with the hotel. It's almost a rumor now."

Stephen smiled. "That would be true, I haven't been here in twenty-two years." Stephen's smirk just dared Elyse to be rude and make a comment about his obviously young age. "The instructions should be in the safe, I'm sure the manager can fetch them."

Elyse nodded crisply and went off to find the manager on duty. Abby asked Stephen to excuse her while she helped the gentleman behind him. Stephen stood to the side and waited patiently. Ivan looked and found some waiting sofas and took the suitcases to them and sat down. A couple of minutes later, Elyse came back with a very old fashioned letter holder that was held with a leather cord. Stephen stepped back up to the desk. "I'm sorry, it took a minute to find the manager and he took a minute to locate them."

Stephen stayed quiet and smiled.

She got the cord unwrapped and opened the letter carrier

and pulled out the very crisp, but very old linen stationary. She quickly read the document and asked the question it stated, "Was sind die fünf Worte möchte ich wissen?"

Stephen replied, "The five words are, 'Blut ist wertvoller als Gold.'"

The lady looked down at her page and back up at Stephen. She held the document up to see if it was see through, but it wasn't. She folded it back up in the document carrier to put back in the safe later. Before wrapping it closed, she pulled the key out and handed it to Stephen. "Welcome to Steigenberger Frankfurter Hof, Sir Stephen. Do you need directions to the elevators?"

"I don't know, do they go down to the bottom level?"

Elyse had to think about that. The elevators had been added in the seventies. "No, I don't believe they do."

"I thought not. I'll see if the original stairs down are still available, if that would be acceptable?"

Elyse just agreed but wondered, where did this young man come by his knowledge? Had he found secrets of the hotel on the Internet?

Stephen turned around and caught Ivan's eye. He waited for Ivan to catch up as he walked towards a small alcove in a wall to the left of the reception desk. Elyse called out, "Sir, that isn't the way to the…"

She stopped talking when Stephen opened a small door set into the wall that she had never known existed. Stephen opened it for Ivan to go through before he winked back at Elyse and stepped through himself. He turned on the light switch above the door after closing it. The passageway went about twenty feet before turning to the left.

Ivan looked around at the old hallway. It was dusty. "I would suggest no one has been here in a while."

Stephen squeezed past him. "True, but I dare say they will shortly."

"Why, they are curious?"

Stephen turned to look over his shoulder as he walked down the hallway, "I'm sure, but there is another reason."

Ivan caught up to Stephen, "And that is?"

"Why, the Besitzer-Suite rooms belong to the owner of the hotel."

That would do it, Ivan thought.

It took housekeeping over thirty minutes to find their way down to the special rooms beneath the hotel. There wasn't a window in any of them. Stephen was very gracious and understanding about the dusty rooms and waited patiently for them to change out all of the linens and clean everything. There were ten people helping to clean the three bedroom suite, which included the manager on duty and two staff. It took three minutes for the water to run clear through all of the pipes. Stephen was patient through the whole process and Ivan just watched amazed as everyone practically fell over themselves to make sure Stephen was ok.

Ivan made his way over to Stephen as he watched everyone clean. Leaning over, he asked, "Why is everyone so polite yet anxious right now? Because you're the owner?"

Stephen looked over at Ivan, "Let's just say that the 'owner' from before had a fit the last time he was here, the story probably gets told to this day."

Ivan leaned back. Holy crap, what kind of temper tantrum happened over a hundred years ago and was still known today?

Everyone finished and Stephen patiently waited until only the manager was left. "Jurgen, please have them clean once a day while we are here. I will swing by the reception desk when we leave for the day to let them know when we are out. Here is a gratuity to share among everyone for their efforts, please let them know I appreciate the diligence in getting the room cleaned so quickly." Stephen handed the man five hundred Euro notes.

He looked down in surprise, thanked Stephen and left. He quietly closed the door after him.

Stephen walked over to the brick wall opposite the entrance door and started studying it.

Ivan asked him which room should he take. "Oh, any except the one to my left, that is mine."

Ivan put away the suitcases and came back. "What are you looking for?"

Stephen bent down and pressed one of the bricks, then pushed a little harder and Ivan heard a 'click.'

"This."

Stephen pushed harder and the brick wall moved inward two feet, leaving a gap. Stephen pushed the brick again and the wall slowly returned to the original position, making it almost impossible to tell anything was different about it. Stephen looked back at Ivan. "I had that put in place in case I ever slept here and needed to leave quickly. Unfortunately, the person who dug that died the night he finished. I couldn't have that knowledge getting out, and I was very sad he sacrificed his life to make my tunnel. However, he had killed twin sisters in a drunken stupor, so I didn't feel too bad."

Ivan ran his hand over the brick, "That is good work."

They said their goodnights and went to their rooms to sleep.

———

BITE THIS

<u>Carpathian Mountains, Romania</u>

Bethany Anne had called the guys back inside a couple of hours ago. She checked on Gabrielle in the medical pod one last time and went back to the cramped pilot area. Shoehorning her way into the seat she called over her shoulder out the open door into the hallway, "If you're religious, you can say a prayer right now." She turned around to get the party started.

John's voice came back down the hallway, "God, don't let Bethany Anne hit this mountain on the way out of here, AMEN!" She heard Eric snort.

Bethany Anne yelled back to the guys, "You're lucky that's a possibility or I would kick your ass, Mr. Grimes!" He stayed quiet.

Eric yelled out, "Where are the seatbelts?"

She yelled back, "TOM says we don't need any, the gravity what-cha-ma-call-thems will handle all of it. We won't even feel g-forces. So sit down, shut up and don't hold on to John for safety, got it?"

A pair of chorused 'Yes ma'ams!' came back to her.

You know we won't hit the mountain by accident, right?

No? Why not?

Because when we get out from under this overgrowth, we will be going straight up a couple of miles. If we hit this mountain, it will be due to malfunction, not your piloting.

You know, TOM. That doesn't make me feel any better.

Just a clarification, Bethany Anne.

How exactly are we getting out of these trees and crap around us?

The craft is made of materials that would probably not dent at all if we hit these trees going a thousand miles an hour. We are sitting on a propulsion system that generates

enough power to drive a warp gate. This will be the same as an eighteen wheeler running through an old rotted wooden fence.

Good metaphor, I get that. Will we feel it inside?

Slightly, if any. However, it will make a ferocious racket. Hope no one is in the area.

You can't tell?

Well, yes, certainly from the instruments, but I felt it was appropriate to say.

Bethany Anne just sighed to herself. TOM was becoming more human all the time.

Let's do this, TOM.

Bethany Anne went through the process to bring the craft totally online for the first time in a thousand years. She was surprised to see everything come on crisp and clear. There were no missing LEDs like you might see in an older used car. They certainly made this craft with precision. Spending the next five minutes with TOM double-checking everything, she hit the final button that took them off the mountain. Ten seconds later, they were at ten thousand feet and holding steady. Bethany Anne just looked at the two viewscreens with awe. The lights beneath her and in the distance were captivating. She had always wanted to be able to fly.

Can anyone see us up here?

No, we have all protection abilities engaged. Even with the advances in human technology in the last hundred years they have a few more generations before they have anything that this ship can't defeat.

How fast can we go?

Not the fastest possible, since the landing gear can't be pulled in, so maybe a thousand miles an hour. Call it a five and a half hour trip?

Ok, let's go. Bethany Anne punched in the coordinates as TOM instructed and the two forward screens showed the lights beneath them starting to move and then rapidly disappear as they turned forty-five degrees and shot off.

Bethany Anne, the radar is showing that most commercial jets are staying beneath forty thousand feet. I would suggest we move up to forty-five thousand.

Make it so, number one.

Excuse me?

Sorry, Star Trek reference.

I'll have to add that to the shows I need to watch.

You know what, TOM? I'll watch that with you.

TOM didn't know what to say.

Five and a half hours later, they were hovering a thousand feet above the right location over the water, and she had two large Superyachts beneath her. Bethany Anne was looking at the viewer with tears in her eyes. She sniffed once or twice and wished she had some Kleenex.

Her ships were below her. She could see Shelly on the Polarus and the S-76 on the other ship. But it wasn't the SEA AXE. The name on the back of the ship had obviously been changed and Bethany Anne hadn't felt so supported since back when Martin had been her mentor in Washington.

The Ad Aeternitatem was ready for her to land.

She took a moment to compose herself. TOM explained how she needed to modify the controls to acquire the right frequency. She spoke to the air, as the pilot microphones were extremely sensitive, "Queen's Ride to Ad Aeternitatem, come in please."

"Ad Aeternitatem, Captain Wagner here. Good to hear your voice, ma'am. How soon will you be arriving? Over."

"Captain, in seconds if you can move the toy-on-the-top, over."

"One sec… Ok, top toy will be shortly doing a check flight. Any other instructions, ma'am? Over."

"Negative, Captain, just happy to be arriving in one piece without any paparazzi, over."

"Understood, welcome home to the Ad Aeternitatem, ma'am, over."

"Glad to be home, and please pass my heartfelt appreciation to the crew for the outstanding name selection. We'll have patches made up for everyone who stayed with us, out."

Bethany Anne watched as two small figures ran to the Sikorsky and jumped in. The rotors were turning quickly and then the craft took off over the ship's superstructure and started to fly slowly in a large circle. The doors to the lower hangar had started to open mere seconds after they took off.

Bethany Anne and TOM brought the craft down to a hundred feet until the doors were completely open.

TOM, do we have the space to fit in there?

Yes, pretty easily in fact. We will have at least three feet on each side to set down.

Good, let's bring her in slowly. I don't want to accidentally crush anyone.

TOM's craft slowly glided down the last hundred feet to the ship. The Ad Aeternitatem was underway at five knots with a minor roll. Nothing that a helicopter would want to try to land on inside the ship, but a simple exercise for TOM's craft. A minute later, they were in the hold and Bethany Anne could see Todd Jenkins and three Marines on guard outside. There was another person manning the controls for the doors and lift. She could tell everyone was aware 'something' was with them in the hold, but they couldn't tell what it was. She hit a button that would send her voice outside the ship. "Gentlemen, be so kind as to close the roof, I don't want any accidental pictures from a spy in the sky." The five men jumped and shortly the doors above her closed. She hit the button to turn off the 'cloak' around the ship. The three Marines had looks of awe on their face while Todd and the Engineer's faces split with grins.

Bethany Anne turned around and yelled back down the hall, "Sorry, this is a little tardy but get your shit together men, we're here!"

She heard a 'whoop' from the back and then people moving around.

She gently pulled herself out of the seat and crawled back into the hallway where she stretched to get feeling back into her neck and legs again.

TOM, you guys are damned short!

No, we are height challenged.

Bethany Anne smiled as John and Eric came up, completely kitted out in their black tactical gear. "We got front, Bethany Anne."

"No, I want one of you to stay here in the spaceship with Gabrielle for now. No one is permitted on board until I say otherwise. Clear?"

She looked at both men and got nods of assurance. Eric spoke, "I got first watch. No one will touch our teammate, ma'am."

"See that they don't, we protect our own, all of our own. Even from accidents and mistakes. Here, I'll show you the commands if you need to stop the process and pull her out quickly." Bethany Anne took Eric into the medical room, and made sure he knew what the button sequence would be. She had him run it both forwards and backwards ten times to make sure he knew it.

"I'll be back in a couple of hours after a status update."

Eric pulled his pack to the door and set it down. "I'll stay on board ma'am. Just lock me in when you get off."

"Good idea. Stay out of TOM's cabin, I'll come in that way. If anyone comes in through this door, assume the worst, understand?" Eric nodded.

"Ready, John?"

He grinned. They would be the first two humans stepping off of an alien craft in the history of the world. "Are you sure you don't want to go first, BA?" he smiled.

She thought about that. "No, it would send the wrong signal to my own brain that I'm always safe on board one of my ships. I don't want to get into that habit. I guess that makes you the first to take a step for mankind?"

"I guess so."

Bethany Anne reached over and punched in the short code to open the door.

CHAPTER ELEVEN

The Queen Bitch's Ship Ad Aeternitatem

Chet Nichols was standing to the left of Todd Jenkins. He had been in the Marines for two tours in and around Afghanistan. He had dropped out to try and resuscitate a marriage grown apart from him being out of the country. Unfortunately his effort was too little and way too late. A common enough refrain heard from some of the other guys when they had re-upped.

He had been contacted out of the blue and asked if he would like to possibly consider a protection detail that was 'Pro U.S., Pro-World and possibly pro-dangerous?' It had been enough to tweak his curiosity and the free trip to Jamaica had been enough to get him to pack his two measly bags and leave the one bedroom efficiency that didn't even have furniture yet. If he never went back to the apartment, it would be too soon for him.

The last couple of days had been rather eye opening. First

from working with Todd, who had handed him his ass on the first test. And while he had done better in the second round, he still lost. Later he was floored by the brief related to the vampires and the aliens. He was seriously enjoying himself again. At the moment, he was even happy his ex had decided to play with the milkman because otherwise he would have stayed back in a failed relationship and missed this opportunity.

The doors above had opened to the sky as soon as they heard the helicopter take off. They didn't have many lights on up top or inside, there was no need to take any chances. The doors clanged into their fully open position. He could feel the air being displaced around him, but he could not see anything. His vision was a little cloudy, almost like he had a little tear or something as he tried to see out the opening. Then, it was obvious something was coming into the compartment, but you couldn't say what it was because you could still see the other side of the room, but it was just a little out of focus when you really paid attention.

A female's voice reverberated through the compartment, "Gentlemen, be so kind as to close the roof, I don't want any accidental pictures from a spy in the sky." Startled, Chet looked around. What the hell?

The engineer started the doors closing again. When the doors shut the internal lights came on and then suddenly a fucking UFO was right in front of him. Chet's mouth dropped open and he didn't even bother to close it for a minute.

It wasn't exactly circular, but rather seemed a little like a circle with a point in one direction. It had three legs resting on the ground. The ship was lowering on its legs, allowing the body of the ship to almost touch the floor. Beside him, Todd had a big shit-eating grin on his face and he started walking towards what he guessed was the door to this craft.

They waited in front of the craft for three minutes before the door opened and holy mother-of-god the first guy off was a fucking mountain. Chet recognized the patch and looked beneath the skull, yup the word 'Aeternitatem' was beneath the skull.

Todd held out his hand. "John, great to see you again, you fucking ox!" Chet then saw the most beautiful woman in the world walk out behind John. Chet thought he had met her before, but the meeting was a little fuzzy in his memory. Maybe he saw a picture?

She spoke to Todd. "What, no hello for your teammate?"

Todd held his arms open and Bethany Anne stepped in and gave him a hug. She stood back and looked Todd up and down, "You've been eating your Wheaties, Mr. Jenkins!"

"Mr. Jenkins? You wound me!"

Bethany Anne laughed. "Well, show me you can be more of a help on my team next time, and I'll call you by 'Todd,' how about that?"

"Deal!" The three of them laughed together.

Bethany Anne turned back around and did something to the side of the ship and the door closed. She then introduced herself to everyone in the hold. When it was his turn he wasn't sure whether to salute her, shake her hand or ask her on a date. He chose to shake her hand. "Chet Nichols, ma'am."

Bethany Anne smiled at him. "Good to meet you Mr. Nichols. I'm sorry to hear about your ex-wife, but I'm happy to know you're on my team. Are you ready to save the world?"

Damn, this lady was charismatic. "Hell yes, point me in the right direction, ma'am!"

Chet smiled as Bethany Anne pointed up, "That way Marine!"

Chet barked out, "I need a rocket, ma'am. I can jump but this damn gravity keeps pulling me down!" By now, most of the guys were laughing at their discussion.

"Well, shit. I was told I just had to point which way to a Marine and they took care of business." She turned in mock anger to Todd Jenkins, "Did you sell me a pig in a poke, Todd?"

Todd grunted and answered, "Ma'am, no ma'am! Marines go anywhere, eat anything and accomplish the task." Then Todd smiled, "But we rely on the Navy to get us close to the target, ma'am. We're all rifleman."

Bethany Anne laughed. "Well, if we can figure out how to use the technology you guys are charged with protecting, then maybe we have an opportunity to provide the Navy a way to get your asses into space." She turned back to Chet, "That work for you, Mr. Nichols?"

Chet smiled, "I'd be delighted, ma'am."

Bethany Anne reached up and patted him on the shoulder. "I'm not that old yet. Bethany Anne will work just fine. You guys can let whoever the Captain says come in here and look, but not touch. We have special cargo inside that vehicle so for most of this next week only me and my Guard go inside, clear?" She raised an eyebrow and looked back over to Todd.

He nodded. "Understood, Bethany Anne."

The door to the hold opened and Captain Wagner came in with his second, Natalia Jakowski. They stopped and just looked at the craft for a second before slowly coming over, their eyes never leaving the ship.

"Looking good, Max?" Bethany Anne turned to face them, but looked over her shoulder back at the craft they were appreciating.

"You know, Bethany Anne, we talked about it and made plans but it becomes real when you can see it and touch it."

The woman beside Max cleared her throat. Max stopped looking at the craft and blushed, "Sorry, where are my manners? Natalia Jakowski, please be introduced to Bethany Anne."

Natalia stuck her hand out to shake Bethany Anne's. "I feel like I've met you, but I can't remember the details?"

Bethany Anne shook Natalia's hand. "Yes, we've met. It was an interview and you probably don't remember it too well. I'm happy to see you're still with us."

"Wouldn't miss this opportunity."

"Good to have you aboard, Natalia." She turned to the Captain, "Max?"

Max turned his head back from the spacecraft. "Hmm?"

"Do you mind getting closer to the Polarus? I'm going to hitch a ride back over there and if you're close, it will help me should an emergency happen."

"Sure, I'll touch base with Captain Thomas. Why does the UFO have so much resin on it?"

"It was under a bunch of trees on a mountain for a thousand years, and not all of the stuff fell off on our flight over here. Some of that shit is as bad as tar on your car."

"Ok, I'll get with Captain Thomas. What direction do you want to head?"

Bethany Anne pursed her lips, "Basically back to Nassau. I'll jump on a plane to get to Miami, or the General and Nathan can come to us. Actually, that would be best. I don't want to leave this ship until I get Gabrielle back."

Max turned to Natalia. "Natalia, would you request Bobcat bring the bird back in? He can take Bethany Anne to the Polarus and Chris can bring it back."

"But sir, the Black Hawk is on their landing pad. They aren't going to take the Cessa over?"

Bethany Anne looked at them both, "The Cessa?"

Max turned to her, "Yes, the Ad Aeternitatem has room to store a fifty foot yacht on top for when you want to move around in something… smaller. We've put the boat in the water for when we need to ferry people across for the time being."

"Ah, ok. No, I'd rather ride in the new Sikorsky. I haven't ridden in it yet. I'm not worried about landing, we'll get down ok." She turned to the huge man beside her, "Right John?"

His face looked like he wanted to forget something. "Yes, nothing like leaving a perfectly fine helicopter a hundred feet above a building without rappelling gear."

Bethany Anne scrunched her face up. "I don't remember it being a hundred feet up, I think you're adding to the story." She turned back to Max and Natalia. Behind her and above her head, John was stretching his hands apart as if something was growing and mouthing, 'It was a hundred feet!'

The two of them tried hard to keep a straight face, but Chet snorted and gave it away. Bethany Anne turned around so fast you couldn't see her move. Suddenly she had John's hands in her own and he was trapped. She was smiling. "I'm sorry, Mr. Grimes. Did you have anything to add to the story behind my back?"

The huge man was straining to move his arms, but the lady wasn't budging. Finally, he stopped and just laughed, "Ok, ok, you win. It wasn't a hundred feet, it was less… Ooof." John was bent over rubbing his stomach and Bethany Anne was faced towards Max again.

"Sorry about that, but sometimes you have to chastise the kids." John started to stretch his hand out while still bent over trying to breathe. Bethany Anne spoke without looking back at John. "If you put those fingers out, I will break one, Mr. Grimes." John pulled his hand back in to cover his stomach.

He was catching his breath and was able to get out a 'good to know' in a faint voice. Bethany Anne smiled.

Bethany Anne looked at Natalia as if to say, 'Why are you still here?' She came to attention, then smiled. "Right, call in the helicopter." She turned around and quickly left the room.

"Ok, how do we get upstairs from down here?"

Max smiled. "Come this way."

The three of them left while Todd Jenkins detailed a twenty-four hour surveillance schedule with his team.

Ten minutes later, the Sikorsky hovered over the Polarus and Bethany Anne looked down to find an open spot next to Shelly. She looked carefully but no one was walking around the deck. She reached up and patted Bobcat on the shoulder. "See you later, Bobcat! Nice to meet you, Chris." Bobcat gave her a thumbs up and Chris turned in his seat to see her and the huge guard, John Grimes, disappear.

Chris' mouth hung open. Bobcat called into his headset, "They gone?" Chris nodded. "Good, I'm taking her back over to the Aeternitatem. I want to see how you're handling this bird. Hey, Chris, snap out of it! You're going to see weirder shit than that, so just accept it and let's do our job."

With a little effort, Chris turned back around and they got busy flying back to the other ship.

———

<u>The Queen Bitch's Ship Polarus, En Route to Nassau</u>

Bethany Anne was coming out of the shower wrapped in a towel. Ecaterina was in her personal suite and John had stayed up in the front area where there would normally be two guards.

When Bethany Anne saw that her suite doors were closed, she dropped the towel into the hamper and walked into her closet.

Ecaterina spoke up from the desk where she had her laptop open. "You know boss, if you could figure out a way to provide the support you enjoy with those breasts for us normal girls, I would love you forever!" Ecaterina often remarked that she was jealous that Bethany Anne's figure needed no support, anywhere.

Bethany Anne came out of the closet having slipped on a pair of black jeans and a dark blue long sleeved shirt. "Do you want the icky blood drinking as a part of it?"

Ecaterina scrunched her face up. "Ah, yuck. I'll shop Victoria's Secret for a while longer. Maybe in another ten years I might be willing."

Bethany Anne smiled. Everyone wanted the benefits but nobody signed up for the blood drinking part of the deal. "Ok, what is the status of my dad and Nathan?"

"Paul Jameson will be over in Miami in the morning. We have a new copilot. Ex-Air Force and was stationed out of Germany. He was tooling around Europe before deciding what he wanted to do after getting out of the Air Force. We're keeping him out of the loop on most everything until you get a chance to interview him."

"Frank vouched for him?"

Ecaterina just looked at Bethany Anne.

"Right, of course he did. You're a little on edge tonight, what's wrong? Too long without your boyfriend?" Ecaterina stuck her tongue out at Bethany Anne. "Ok, I get it. Speaking of Nathan, what's the status with the Wechselbalg in New York?"

"I've spoken with Gerry twice in the last three days. We have eight coming to us. What we don't have is a place to start the… what did John call it? In-boarding?"

"Onboarding."

"Like on a ship?"

"No, well maybe. Actually, I don't have a clue. You might think it came from coming on board a ship but I've never heard that story before. Basically it means to get a new employee up to speed with what they need to know about the organization and their jobs. I thought we might have room on the Ad Aeternitatem, but only if we use some of the cargo space. So, I'd rather not. We need to do something with them pretty soon, at least give them a date they expect to come down here. I want them flown down on the corporate jet." Bethany Anne sat down on her bed, and by 'down' it meant a slight hop up for her to get on the mattress. She crossed her feet, put her elbow on her leg and her chin in her hand. "We need a true indoctrination. Can you call Dan and John to come for a meeting?"

Ecaterina reached over to the ship's phone on the desk beside her. She spoke for a moment and hung it up. "He said he'll be here in five minutes."

"Good. Ok, Nathan and my dad arrive tomorrow, I'll need to sleep, but I'll do that over in TOM's craft tonight. That will give Eric time to rest as well. What is the status of Clarita's kids?"

"They have left Panama and are en route to Romania. I've confirmed a location for them with appropriately safe sleeping arrangements with the local Were pack near Stephen's home. They will stay around until Stephen gets back from Frankfurt."

"Ok, that works. I'll let Stephen handle them for a while. If he gives me a good report, we'll see if we can use them ourselves."

Ecaterina made notes on her computer. Probably sending an email or text messages to Ivan and Stephen.

There was a knock on the door. Bethany Anne had already heard the two guys talking when Dan arrived a minute ago. She hopped off of the bed. Ecaterina grabbed her laptop and walked around the desk as Bethany Anne opened the door and walked out of her personal suite into the living/meeting room outside.

Bethany Anne walked to the small refrigerator and grabbed a Coke. "Anyone want anything?" She grabbed Ecaterina a water and Dan wanted an apple juice. John didn't want anything. She handed the water over and tossed Dan his juice. They sat around a small conference table that could easily seat six, and ten if everyone was pretty close.

"Dan, I wanted to ask you about creating some sort of indoctrination class for our new recruits. Something that will both scare the shit out of them and make them understand they are becoming a lean, kick-ass fighting machine."

"So, expand on the mini-documentary I've shown the Navy people lately?"

"That would do it, I suppose. But I want them to understand the dark side of these Nosferatu. We need something that snaps them out of their belief they're natural fighters and better than everyone else." She looked over at John. "What if we insert your team's idea of them sparring against you guys into the middle of the schedule?"

Dan considered her request. "So, you want us to show them enough to feel confident the humans are the poor substitute, then let the Guards bloody their nose, and finally show them the reality?"

"Something like that. I'm not sure I have the right order. What do you guys think?"

John joined in, "If we show them the agents who were killed and maimed before Beat Down 101, then come back and show them even more footage they would have to figure that in time, they might be as good as the agents who have died."

Dan thought about it. He hated doing anything that would disrespect the honor of his fallen agents, but he had to agree that their deaths being a warning for this generation of Nosferatu fighters would be a way to continue their fight even from the grave.

"I think we can work on that. Have you considered where you want to do this?"

"Yes, only to realize we can't do it on the Ad Aeternita-tem. Not enough space for them and the scientists I expect we will have to place on board. I hate to bring them here because I don't want them sitting in the lap of luxury when I'm trying to get their heads screwed on straight."

John looked at her. "Do you think Pete's head is screwed on straight?"

"Yeah, sure, he's really solid right now. Why do you ask?"

"Remember, he lived in a ten million dollar home in Key Biscayne. We can double bunk them to make their rooms a little less palatial, but we run them hard as hell. They won't have enough energy to enjoy the surroundings. Plus, it wears off in time. I would prefer we weren't too far from you, anyway. I'm sure you weren't thinking of ditching us if we were too busy with the new recruits, right?"

That was exactly what Bethany Anne thought she might be able to get away with. "No, not at all." Her answer fooled none of the team at the table.

"Ok, if you guys are ok with it and Captain Thomas has a placc to stick them, just run it by Nathan and my dad for a sanity check and give Ecaterina a time frame to get them down here. Give Gerry a heads up on what you're thinking. Make sure they bring nothing with them. If they have anything, it gets tossed overboard. Well, maybe that's a figure of speech, I don't want to pollute. But I want it tossed. Make sure we have the same outfits for all of them." She thought about that for a minute. "Dan, would you talk with Captain Thomas? We need crew uniforms for here and for Max's crew, and patches for the overall Navy."

Dan was writing on his legal pad. "Anything in mind for the uniforms?"

Bethany Anne got a big smile. "Yes!" Dan and John looked up. They hadn't heard Bethany Anne sound so carefree in a while. "Ecaterina. Find out the top three designers, TQB Enterprises ships are going to have the best looking uniforms of any ships out at sea. We'll have them all done up very nicely. Wait, scratch the three designers. Please find out if Nassau has anyone we might want to use and maybe rope in anyone on either crew that has any comments on the utilitarian aspects of working versus presentation uniforms. I want something that will make other crews jealous with envy and make our people pop and sizzle."

Dan and John just turned to look at each other. They knew that Bethany Anne loved fashion, but they hadn't heard anything about it recently and had rather forgotten that side of her. Looked like it was coming back. Maybe that was a good thing?

"You realize that most navies use one-piece coveralls, right? You'll need to get with the Captains to discuss what is practical and what is fashionable. Practical is going to win."

Ecaterina was smiling in spite of Dan's comment on practical considerations versus fashion. She loved working with fashion and since she would be wearing these uniforms while onboard, the ladies would have both practical and flattering versions. So, warm weather, cold weather, sport… the list could go on and on. She turned to Bethany Anne, "What's the budget?"

"This is for camouflage as much as the other reasons. Let me know if it's going to go over a million. Everyone who has joined will be completely fitted out and I want a fair amount of extras on board in case we bring in new employees. Oh, and add a pair of Christian Louboutins and a Birkin bag for each lady."

Ecaterina looked at her. "Birkin?"

John and Dan just looked back and forth between the two.

"Yeah, by Hermès? We'll want to contact them to get something special made for our team. Work with the designer to make sure they match, but give each woman the chance to choose something a little special. You need to budget $10,000 per bag and we will want the smaller 30 or 35 centimeter sizes probably. Certainly something they can carry their wallet and a pistol in. I know that Officer Dukes will appreciate that."

There were chuckles around the table. Jean Dukes was still setting up offensive and defensive armament on the

Polarus. The ship was becoming the Q-ship that Bethany Anne had asked for. "When the snobby bitches come on board, I want them to see that every one of my ladies are already sporting some of the best as their uniform. It will knock them for a loop and most of the gossip rags will focus on how our people are dressed considerably snazzier than other people, trust me." She looked over at Dan and John. "Sorry guys, I'll make sure you have some excellent footwear, but I don't think you guys want man-purses, right?"

Dan shook his head while John admitted he didn't want anything of the sort. But then he came back, "Well, if we can't have any special bags, I sure would like a really nice sniper rifle."

"I don't think that's considered a uniform accessory."

"Depends on which uniform we're wearing." John smiled at his response.

Ecaterina piped up, "Oh! I want in on a sniper rifle, are we talking American or British?"

"Hold up." Everyone turned back to Bethany Anne. "I'm good with sniper rifles, but you three talk about it. I need to go relieve Eric so he can sleep. I'll be over in the craft, so you can sleep here on this boat tonight, John. Eric can bunk down over on the Aeternitatem. Just give me a change of Eric's clothes to take with me."

"Now?"

"Yeah, I'm behind a bit relieving him. He can relieve me in the morning and I'll come back over here. Make sure everyone stays out of my suite until I get back."

Ecaterina cut her off, "Actually, I had them modify your closet so you could lock it from the inside. You can leave and come back safely in there."

"Really? Perfect. Ok, that solves that problem. Can you

grab a small pack for Eric now?" John was already standing. "Dan, do you have anything for me before I go?"

"Yes, Frank has some information about Anton, but we haven't had time to nail down where and even who we think he is for sure. Once Clarita's kids are safe, I want to ask Stephen to reach out and talk with them to find out if they can give us any information. I've talked with Lance for just a minute and he thinks we might have the start of a team to help on TOM's craft."

"Really? That would be nice."

"Ah, it comes with a catch."

Her shoulders slumped, "Don't they always? Can this wait until tomorrow? I don't want to make Eric wait any longer if we don't have to."

"Yeah, it can. Actually, it probably should. Nathan is the best one to explain the situation so we'll wait until he gets here."

John came back in and handed Bethany Anne a small black backpack, "Everything in there for a night and a morning over there. How often can you move back and forth?

TOM?

Well, probably a handful of times but we haven't done the first one yet. If you have blood, all day long.

"A couple of times easily, beyond that I have to start drinking the red medicine." She made a disgusted face. "So, if we don't have to do that I'm happier. If you need him here, he can come over on the smaller boat, or Chris can bring him over if Shelly isn't up top."

She stood up. "Are we all good?" Everyone agreed that they were. "Ok, I'll be back in the morning. You guys take care." She walked into her suite and shut the door. She grabbed a pillow off of her bed on the way to her large closet. Sure enough, her closet door had a substantial lock and the door was made of metal. Nothing much would be getting into that door quickly. With the pack in one hand and her pillow in the other she slipped through the Etheric into TOM's cabin on his ship. She tossed the pillow on TOM's bed and walked out to find Eric resting on the floor near the door to the medical room. Eric's head lifted up when he heard her walking up.

"Hey boss, how did everything go?"

She reached down and gave him a hand to pull him up. "Good enough. I need you to stay here tonight, so John tossed some stuff into this backpack. You'll have to get with the captain to find yourself a bunk, but I know they have one for you. Come get me after a really good rest tonight. You might need to bring something to keep you entertained as well."

"How do I get your attention in the craft?"

TOM?

We will set up a program to listen for your name, or some phrase to play a chime in here.

"Ok, just say, 'Bethany Anne, it's Eric, I'm ready to come back in.' When you say that, the ship will notify me someone has just said the super secret code phrase and wake me up. You just better make sure that you don't wake me early or your ass is grass, understand?"

"Sure, what's early?"

"At least eight hours after you lay down to go to sleep."

Eric then understood it was for him to sleep a minimum of eight hours, not her sleep she was worried about. "I got the message, I'll get a good night in."

They walked over to the exit and Bethany Anne punched in the code. The door opened, surprising Todd and Chet who were just outside the ship. They both did a double take to see

Bethany Anne when they knew she had left on the helicopter a few hours before. Eric stepped off the ship and she winked at the guys and then closed the door. She went into the pod room and checked the information. TOM was able to confirm everything was working appropriately. It was possible she might get out in as few as three and a half more days. That was good news.

She swung by the pilot's area to set the alarm and then went back into TOM's cabin and lay down on the rather short bed. She fluffed her pillow and closed her eyes. She was asleep in seconds.

CHAPTER TWELVE

The Queen Bitch's Ship Polarus, 10 Miles North of Nassau

The meeting room was pretty crowded. Lance, Nathan, Dan, Bobcat, Ecaterina, Frank, Todd Jenkins and Captains Thomas and Wagner were sitting around the table eating finger foods with John and Pete inside the door. Darryl and Scott were standing outside.

Lance, Nathan, Ecaterina and Frank were on the left side, Dan, Bobcat, Todd and the captains were sitting down the right.

Bethany Anne came in a moment later, wearing a pair of J Brand high rise Marie skinny jeans in black and a pair of Christian Louboutin pumps and a green Ramy Brook high neck top. She had spent a couple of extra minutes relaxing in the bath this morning after Eric came back on board to watch over Gabrielle. If anything went wrong, the pod was set up to emit an ear piercing sound inside and after sixty seconds, outside the ship. She was biting on an apple as she set her tablet down on the table.

"Good afternoon, everyone. I apologize for being a few

minutes late." She looked down the table. "I would like to say it was because I was held up talking with the president of somewhere, but the reality was my bath wouldn't let me go. TOM's ship might be the ticket to help us understand their technology, but their beds are little better than lying on the ground." She took another bite of her apple. "We have a few things to go through, some of them taking longer than others, so let's go with the two ships first and if the captains need to leave after that they have the option. Captains you are invited to stay if you desire to listen to the rest."

Everyone either grabbed their pens if they preferred writing or made sure their laptops weren't in sleep mode.

Since Captain Thomas was the senior officer, he went first. "We are fairly prepared for a small skirmish with any navy. We can take any non-navy ship that I am aware of and we would probably surprise a larger navy vessel right now. We have some missile defense and even some ability to send charges down below if we need to. As a Q-Ship, this vessel is pretty competent. Jean is waiting for another delivery that will expand our sig-ops abilities a notch."

Bethany Anne interrupted him. "What would happen if we were attacked by non-military efforts? Say something like Greenpeace?" Captain Thomas seemed perplexed by the question. "Think of it this way, if I wanted to place something aboard this ship, I might decide to make a PR spectacle of a bunch of people working to do a peaceful demonstration against the ship in an effort to move someone or something aboard. How would you repel these types of invaders?"

"I suppose you want this without lots of loud booms?" Bethany Anne nodded and bit into the apple again. "I imagine we would use the fire hoses to repel invaders in a method that seems as peaceful as possible. However, that doesn't guarantee no one would be hurt. We would be throwing water instead of lead, so that's a plus. We do exercise the scenario of boats approaching under false pretenses, but since the USS Cole incident it's generally regarded that the chance of a bomb on board outweighs the bad press from killing them if they disobey all warnings. The Navy makes their warnings very clear, and since everyone knows lethal force could be employed against them, you can't get in too much trouble if they're stupid enough to disregard the guns aimed at them. But I can see how this might be more of a concern for us since we're not on a commissioned government warship and don't have government protection. If a government was able to coordinate the press to put pressure on us, we would be in a bad position if we shot people. I would suggest we don't anchor too long in one place. If we allow ourselves to stay in one place then our adversaries can plan for multiple boats to arrive at the same location in a way that you might explain away otherwise. By staying under sail, we will modify our direction and force others to adjust their courses to stay after us and give us more warning prior to an attack."

Todd spoke up, "What about sonic defenses?"

Captain Thomas looked over at him. "What, like the sonic cannons used inside cities?"

"Yes, something like that."

Captain Thomas rubbed his jaw. "Well, I don't know much about the effective range or how it works if they get behind their own walls. We can look into it. We need to add the idea of repelling non-violent boarders to our exercises from now on. And eventually, we'll need some laid down Rules of Engagement. Not only will that give us a framework for how we respond to incidents, but something we can point at if we have to excuse the use of lethal force in the future."

Bethany Anne turned and tossed the apple into the trash. "We'll have to consider that further later. The exercises should be enough for now. I don't know that this will happen, but in the future I can imagine a time when we have those who are trying to force us to release emergency medical technology and believe by taking over this ship, or yours Captain Wagner, they might force our hand. Unfortunately, getting on the Ad Aeternitatem might just sign their death warrant. I know that constantly moving will be a little expensive, but please put that into effect immediately. Even if we look like a Lloyds looper, it will help our team identify possible enemies quicker."

Ecaterina interrupted, "What is a Lloyds looper?"

Captain Thomas took the question. "A lot of cargo ships are insured by Lloyds of London. For them to be tied up in port is more expensive due to the increase in insurance costs than just sitting out in the ocean doing a figure eight until they get their next destination to pick up cargo. Now, lots of companies are in the business of insuring ships but the name has stuck. In our case, whether we are at the pier or anchored, our risk is higher than if we move around. The only issue with moving around is it'll decrease chances for shore leave, so we might need more personnel rotation to avoid long-term fatigue and burnout."

John spoke up, "What about issuing pistols with the 'sleepy' rounds?" He was referring to the special darts made with Bethany Anne's blood that put almost any person to sleep within two seconds.

They now had TOM's ship, so maybe it was possible to change the chemicals in the darts without forcing Bethany Anne to bleed a drop of blood into every dart. Bethany Anne answered, "That's a good idea. I need to talk with TOM about using the medical capabilities onboard his ship to change the dart chemicals without me having to bleed all over them to make it work." She paused for a minute. "Or Gabrielle I suppose. I'm sure she wasn't thinking she would become a blood cow in the future."

Frank looked down at his phone, then interrupted them. "Excuse me, I need to follow up on this." He grabbed his unique laptop and stepped out of the room. Frank's hair had been growing back in darker with his grey hair on the ends. He needed to either get hair dye or cut it off close to the skull. He looked weird, like he had bleached the ends of his hair.

They talked a little while on the needs of both of the ships related to crew and updates. The Ad Aeternitatem would hire a couple more crew to start modifying the internal compartments to remove some of the storage space and make more berthing in there. Both captains had things they wanted to implement and Max wanted to get underway as soon as possible.

Bethany Anne raised an eyebrow to Bobcat. "He's got the boat. So I don't need to ferry him over."

That caused them to discuss the two helicopters and the G550's status. Bethany Anne brought up something she had been thinking, "Bobcat, do you remember when I asked if you would consider learning new craft and perhaps teaching others once you've learned enough?"

Bobcat smiled, "You bet, are you going to let me learn how to fly your new ride over there?" Bobcat had been itching to see inside the ship, but it was off limits until Bethany Anne permitted anyone to touch it.

She grinned at the audacious pilot. "Hell no!" His smile turned into a frown, "I'm expecting you to help design small three person vessels we can launch off of either of our ships.

With vessels that can go straight up, we don't need to have an aircraft carrier."

Bobcats' smile went from large to just about splitting his face. "Hell yeah! That would be fun-fucking-tastic. What are the specifications?"

"One pilot, a two ops team plus their equipment. Needs to be quiet and as undetectable as we can make it. I want them as stupid-proof as possible."

"Outer space?"

"No, TOM tells me that requires a significant jump in complexity I'm not willing to wait for right now. But these things will be able to push Mach 4, so almost faster than anything the militaries have except the theoretical scramjet. Our stuff will be smaller, faster, and won't require major training for blackouts as the insides will, according to TOM, stay at less than 1.25 gs during any and all maneuvers."

"Seriously?"

"Yup."

"Tell TOM I'm his newest fan!"

Well, I've never had a fan before.

Wait until we provide more of your technology. Unfortunately for you, some people will want to call you a God.

Why is that unfortunate?

Because you're stuck in me and there is no way I can stand the idea of your ego getting too big for my body.

Yes, well, there is that little inconvenience.

Sucks to be you.

"Yes, I'm sure he'll be excited to learn that. But this means you need to find a primary for Shelly." Bobcat's face lost a lot of its enthusiasm. Shelly, his Black Hawk, had been the craft that had helped him keep his sanity between leaving the service and finally joining Bethany Anne's group. "I thought you might take it a little hard. Just remember this won't happen for a while, so don't make plans to stop flying Shelly for a few months, but you will need to consider passing the torch."

Bobcat just shook his head. With everything good, a little bad must happen.

Bethany Anne continued, "Besides, just think what these little ships will do when you come out with version 2.0." That was sufficient to pull Bobcat out of the worst of the punch to his ego Bethany Anne had delivered.

She turned to Nathan and her dad. "Ok, Dan told me last night that you two might have some people for reviewing the ship and helping figure it out, but it came with a catch. What is the catch before we go much further?"

Lance looked over at Nathan to let him know he had the floor. Nathan started. "What do you know about strong AI?"

"Not a lot related to earth stuff, a little related to Kurtherian."

Nathan opened his mouth, he wanted to ask about the Kurtherian comment but they couldn't get derailed on that subject right then. "Well, we don't so much want to bring people to look at the ship. Well, not totally true. We do, but our real problem and opportunity is one of the companies in TQB Enterprises is Patriarch Research out of Las Vegas. It looks like they have potentially created the software to bring about the Technology Singularity."

"Isn't that the stuff the geeks in California are all arguing is going to end the world? I seem to remember Elon Musk and someone else bitching about that a while back."

"Well, certainly the potential to end humanity. The sexy side…"

Bethany Anne snorted. "Leave it to a geek to describe a bunch of computer hardware and programming as 'sexy.'"

Nathan shrugged. "I'm not talking 'Ecaterina' sexy." That got Nathan a quick jab from an elbow to his left. "Ow, thank you very much. As I was saying, sexy in a very interesting and exciting manner. Imagine a machine that can do the research of hundreds or potentially thousands of analysts simultaneously and run it twenty-four hours a day. Then, if a problem occurs in the programming, it can adjust its own programming such that the same mistakes never happen again."

"What's the downside to this, then? I can't confess to following this stuff very closely."

Lance spoke then. "The concern is that the strong AI is expected to become an independent agent, operating for whatever it finds is the best solution. So, what if the best solution is the extermination of the human race?"

Bethany Anne could hear most of the hearts in the room suddenly accelerate. That was a pretty big concern to everyone here. "So, how do you figure out if you can get, what, a friendly AI?"

Nathan continued, "Yes. We're calling this imaginary AI 'Adam' at the moment. If Adam is on our side, we could leapfrog potential operations and implementation abilities while keeping our teams pretty lean. Otherwise, the more we undertake, the bigger our organization, and we already have two Superyachts, two huge homes in Miami and are looking for a used military base." Bethany Anne raised her eyebrows and Lance put up his hand to delay any comments. They would get back to that point in a minute. "So, we're quickly exceeding the operational resources we have here. The more we accomplish the more we need to hire and the nasty cycle keeps getting out of hand. To accomplish what we've spoken about in the future, we either have to stay small and lean, or connect with a really large government to help run this."

"Ah, you nasty jackass, you hit my personal hot button." She thought about it for a second. "I really don't want to get any governments involved with us unless we have to, and certainly not where we are beholden to them if we can help it." She looked up at Nathan. "You conniving manipulative bastard, I'm impressed." She smiled at Nathan to show she really did appreciate how he had pitched this. He obviously wanted a try at this and besides the 'sky is falling' aspects of his pitch, she could see the benefits, or at least the potential benefits if they could pull it off. "I presume you have a working concept of how to move forward and who you would need?" Lance and Nathan nodded their heads, almost in unison. That was strange, her father was actually on board with this idea as well. "What is the time frame, budget, resources and where would you try this?"

Lance took that question. "We would need at least a couple of months, millions of dollars for hardware purchases, the team from Patriarch Research and we need to do it in the desert."

That last comment surprised her. "The desert?"

Lance continued, "Yes. The final button to shut the system down if it gets away from us is a small EMP device. I don't think we want to fire off an EMP near anything we want to keep do we?" Bethany Anne agreed that would be a monumentally bad idea. "If we make the location near Vegas, all of the needed personnel already live and work there."

"What about security?"

"I'm going to tap into my contacts and find out how many guys I might know who are out or may be ready to get out. The military will be ok with this as they are drawing down right now anyway. So, depending on the P&B's…"

Ecaterina leaned forward, "Excuse me General, the P&B's?"

Lance looked over at her. "Sorry, Pay and Benefits."

Bethany Anne pointed to Dan. "If it's civilian, that's your camp, Dad. If it's military, talk with Dan. He has the general numbers already. Although, I don't want to pay top dollar for someone guarding a bunch of sand."

"I think we're paying for them to be able to keep their mouths shut. We won't be really telling them what we're doing, that will stay with a very small group. If we don't find a place that fits what we need, we will be building something quick and disposable."

"What happens when you turn on the switch?"

Nathan spoke up, "Ah, well that's where you come in."

Bethany Anne squinted. "Why am I having anything to do with turning the switch? I don't know shit about programming, trust me."

Nathan snorted. "Thank god you don't know programming. Some of us normal mortals… Ok, semi-normal mortals have a need to be better than you at something."

Bethany Anne retorted, "Don't be a hater."

Nathan continued, "Seriously, if this goes right, this could save us years of effort."

Bethany Anne opened her mouth only to shut it quickly. Then she looked back and forth between the two of them. Now she had figured out why they were working together on this. "Holy crap! You asses want to use the AI for offensive and defensive efforts on the internet, don't you?" She continued to watch both of their faces carefully.

Nathan hung his head and Lance smiled. Nathan reached around to pull out his wallet and pulled a hundred dollar bill and handed it to Lance.

Lance folded the bill and stuck it in his pocket. "Yes. Our ability to know what's going on would rival nation-states at that point. What we would be able to do…"

Frank came back into the room and interrupted. "Bethany Anne, we have a problem." She turned around and everyone looked back at Frank. "We have two major Nosferatu outbreaks in Costa Rica and my research programs are recording a lot of inquiries into your old records. Not just any inquiries, these inquiries are coming from members of Congress related to Michael's holdings."

"What the hell? Why is that?"

Frank shrugged.

Lance thought about that. "Well, shit. This might also be from Patriarch Research. They did some research for financial companies and he had mentioned that they found some unknown financial superpowers and had delivered the info back to the financial companies who passed it on to the government."

Bethany Anne turned back around to her dad. "So, one of my own companies just shot me in the foot? How fucked up can that be?"

"Well, to be fair, this happened before you were turned, so it wasn't really your company at the time."

She leaned back in her chair. "I swear…"

John muttered back behind her, "Every damn day."

She raised her right hand and shot him the finger. They all laughed at that. Frank walked back around to his chair.

"Ok, Dad. You'll have to jump on the plane and figure that shit out. I shouldn't go to Washington D.C. and get stuck in some meeting. Some of those bastards still have a hard-on for me from my time taking some of those dickless wonders down. Those I hurt also have lots of friends who are nursing a serous attitude as well." She turned to Frank. "Now explain why I need to worry about Nosferatu in Costa Rica? I can only presume it's warfare over the power vacuum Clarita left?"

"Yes. Basically, the younger, more brash and infinitely more stupid create these Nosferatu to help them take over their opponents. Then, one will get killed and his Nosferatu soldiers are without a command structure and start randomly attacking humans. The Forsaken ignore these issues until someone is crowned the victor. Michael's family has always been the one to keep the leaderless Nosferatu in check while the political fighting continues. So, we are it."

Bethany Anne just shook her head. "Fuck my life. If I could stab that bitch one more time, I would. She is screwing up my life even after she's dead. This is un-fucking-believable." She thought about the situation for a while at vampire speed. To the rest of the group it appeared she might have thought about it for three seconds. "Ok, John, change of plans. If we assume Gabrielle will be with us, that's a total of six blooded members. If it gets too bad in San Jose, we need a plan to get the Wechselbalg brought down to help quickly. Hopefully we won't get any of them killed. Todd?"

"Yes?"

"You're going to need to beef up your teams on the two ships or have a plan if we are going to be off of the ships for an extended amount of time. We better have permission to fly in Shelly across their fucking country or they can kiss my ass. I'm not doing this shit at night and I refuse to stay off these two ships too long and leave most of our fighters unavailable if we get attacked here. Dad, I need you and Frank to jump back on the Gulfstream and represent our interests back in the capitol. Nathan?"

"Yes?"

"Can you get some of this shit started with Patriarch Research long distance, or do they need you? I would prefer your fighting skills here. You too, Ecaterina." Nathan looked a little disturbed, he wasn't accustomed to someone he loved jumping into danger. But he knew not to say one damn word or he would be up shit creek with a hole blown in his canoe by Ecaterina herself. "In fact, Ecaterina, I want you to head up a sniper group. Find out if we have anyone else on these ships with good shooting skills and get them ready. With TOM's ship here, we can craft some special bullets to affect the nanocytes. It won't be exactly shooting fish in a barrel, but I want to make it as close as we can. This isn't our battle, exactly. We're here to protect the humans. If a Forsaken gets in my way, they will be terminated with extreme prejudice, is this understood?" Everyone agreed.

"Good, maybe we'll get a shot at Anton. If Frank doesn't have much info on him, then that bastard is too sneaky by half for my liking. By the way, Frank. Work with Eric on what we think Anton did to come over here on a German U-Boat. Maybe you can track him that way. You know he has to have connections in as many of the governments as possible. He isn't a day walker, so our guy won't ever be seen during the day. Let's speed up our conversation with Clarita's children. If we get rid of Anton, we might need their asses back over here quickly to take control. Anyone we find who follows the Forsaken beliefs will be terminated. Ok, what have I forgotten?"

"What about the AI?" Nathan didn't look like he was pushing the subject, just trying to close the decision loop.

"It's a go. I'm not sure what you expect me to do, but I'm up for it. The risk is worth the reward so long as we can shut it down if we get Lucifer instead of Adam, understood?" Nathan agreed. "Then tell them their first budget is thirty million in five million increments. We agree to each five million before we move forward with the next step. Make sure Adam isn't stuck out in the fucking desert if it works. That's all I need, our ace-in-the-hole to be stuck in bumfuck Nevada because we couldn't move it."

Nathan hadn't really thought about that issue, but it was a good one. "It's a shame we don't have quantum computers."

"Do I even want to know what that is?"

Nathan smiled. "Just a really small but exponentially powerful computer."

Um, Bethany Anne?

What is it, TOM? A little busy now.

We have a quantum computer.

We do? Fucking Fantastic! Can we pull it from the ship?

Yes, we could if it was still ON the ship.

What are you talking about… Oh fuck me double time. This one in my head is a quantum computer?

Yes, it is our third generation version. But we never made the effort to put an AI in these computers.

Is this computer something we can duplicate ourselves?

Not without understanding the Etheric.

So, not anytime in the next six months, right?

Well, probably not.

What would make it possible?

TOM paused a second, finally he admitted the answer. **A strong AI.**

Bethany Anne mentally sighed. Of course that's the answer, because anything else would be too fucking easy.

They wrapped up their conversations and everyone split to their most important tasks. Their little vacation from Nosferatu fighting was officially over.

CHAPTER THIRTEEN

Frankfurt, Germany

Ivan didn't have a clue how he should be acting. While he had never been to Frankfurt, with the maps on his phone he could see where they were going. Still, he was at a loss about how he should respond to the Wechselbalg contact they would be meeting. Stephen had woken him up early this morning and they had hidden some of their personal effects behind the wall.

Stephen had informed him it would be, "Better to be safe and have no questions, than risk raising the wrong question or two. The stories from back in the nineties might have a bit of truth to them." So, they stashed the blood in its keep-cold packs in the old escape route. Ivan now just assumed he meant the 1890s. No matter how much he tried to get Stephen to open up and tell the story, Stephen wouldn't talk. Stephen did admit he wasn't proud of those few days and had stayed out of Frankfurt for over a century because he didn't like the memories.

Once they had hidden their stuff away, they went upstairs

and informed the front desk they would be out until at least early afternoon.

They had a nice breakfast at a small cafe. Stephen was happy to try a new coffee he hadn't had before and Ivan had rolls covered in marmalade and wurst on the side. They had worked a little on Stephen's use of his smartphone, but Ivan's help was needed less and less the more Stephen played with technology. Now, Ivan was as much a travel companion as a technology consultant. Unknown to Ivan, Stephen had taken over his monthly salary from Bethany Anne back in Brasov. Stephen thought Ivan was helping ground him as he acclimated to how people talked and acted with each other, and he enjoyed having him live with him.

Bethany Anne told Stephen that was fine, but that he was going to pay for that service. There was no good reason for her to foot that bill. She'd winked at him.

As Stephen enjoyed his newspaper, reading it in German without a problem, Ivan went through his social connections and sighed a little heavily. Stephen halfway closed his paper and looked around it over to Ivan. "What's wrong?"

Ivan leaned back in his chair and smiled. "I think this new city is getting me down. I miss Gabrielle and I wonder how she is doing."

Stephen smiled, he liked that Ivan was thinking about his daughter. "Bethany Anne said she would be in the medical pod for almost a week. She is sleeping at this moment." Ivan and Stephen had received texts early that morning to let them know Bethany Anne had made it to the Bahamas ok. "Tell you what, I've been wanting to go out a little. Why don't you help me acclimate with people and we can go out tonight?"

"Be your wingman?" Ivan smiled at Stephen.

"What do you mean, 'wingman?'"

Ivan put his hands up side by side, but one slightly in front of the other. "Are you aware of how fighter jets fly together? You have a primary and a secondary so if you are flying one jet, the other jet is called your wingman. They help each other out."

"Ah, exactly so!" Stephen loved this new word. "You need to be my wingman tonight."

"Hey, I won't be able to help you if the girls have friends, I'm off limits!"

Stephen closed his newspaper. "I don't think they will be looking you over, when I am available." Stephen winked roguishly at Ivan who had to laugh. Stephen was the complete opposite of a scary vampire to him. Even Bethany Anne scared him significantly more than Stephen did. Stephen didn't seem to have a mean bone in his body.

Ivan speared the last piece of wurst on his plate and ate it. "I'm sure that's very true. But if I happen to run into any women too drunk to tell that I am not you, then you have to promise me you'll save me, right?" Stephen agreed that he would.

They stayed another half hour and then called a cab. They would take the taxi to the address of their contact Josef von Dorman, who had his offices at the Commerzbank Tower. It was a magnificent fifty-six-story structure with a very distinctive triangular design and a tall spire running up from one of the apexes. Stephen paid the taxi and the two went into the main entrance to the guard desk inside. When they received the appropriate instructions, they took the elevator to the forty-fifth floor.

Mr. Josef von Dorman was a financial planner. Stephen made sure to enter the office first. While he didn't expect a surprise attack from the Weres here in the middle of Frankfurt, he wouldn't take any chances with Ivan's life.

Mr. Dorman had a very attractive and very human secretary in the sitting room. They gave her their names and didn't have time to turn around and sit before Stephen could hear a person coming down the hallway behind the secretary.

He waited for the new arrival, an older gentleman and definitely a Wechselbalg. He held out his hand. "Josef von Dorman."

Stephen shook his hand. "Stephen, Herr Dorman and my compatriot is Herr Romanov."

Ivan shook the man's hand. "Ivan is fine."

"Yes, let's dispense with formality if that is ok with you, Herr Stephen?" Stephen inclined his head in agreement. "Please come this way into the meeting room. Sandra? Please hold all communications until we finish. Thank you." He led them into the meeting room off the main office, and closed the door behind them. "I assure you, this room is very protected, we will not be heard outside." Josef's accent was very strong.

Ivan looked around the room. It was very traditional with a dark wooden table surrounded by eight chairs. Stephen looked out the windows for anything that seemed out of place. Satisfied, he took a chair where he could see Josef, the door and the windows. Josef sat himself across the table with his back to the windows and Ivan chose to sit to Stephen's left.

Stephen started the conversation, which was the preferred method for Wechselbalg. Better to answer questions than try to probe with leading questions that might only get you in trouble. "Josef, my Queen is concerned that Europe is not as secure against the Forsaken threat as we might have thought.

She has asked me to meet with you to understand the real situation here in Europe. When I spoke with my daughter, Gabrielle, she informed me that perhaps she and a few others had not updated Michael's contact in America appropriately. Now, when I woke up I found my own son was involved with the Brasov Were pack and participating in very shady dealings. Whether he was connected with the Forsaken, or just involved in the black market I do not know. However, Europe is my responsibility to my Queen and I intend to find all of the issues and deal with the situation as appropriate. I am not here to cast blame, but rather to find and fix what's wrong. If blame were to be issued, it would surely be laid at my own feet. So, I am only interested in fixing the problem. We will correct those who accept correction, but those who refuse correction will be appropriately chastised."

Ivan was a little surprised. Stephen seemed to be a different person now that he was speaking with the Were Council Pack leader directly. Much more direct and without much give.

"I understand, Herr Stephen. May I ask a clarifying question?"

"Certainly. I am to work with you, Josef. My Queen is not about the old ways. Work with us, and we can work together to accomplish results in a satisfactory way. I have been charged with making sure Europe is safe. Do not mistake my effort to work together as an indication that I will accept anything but the most honest and earnest effort. Now, what is your question?"

Josef weighed his words carefully before he responded. Stephen was rumored to be the most easygoing of Michael's children, but he was also the one responsible for the night of flames right here in Frankfurt. That he was obviously young and passionate again spoke against the rumors he was ready to sleep a final time. "You say you have a Queen, is this the one who killed Algerian in Brasov?"

"Yes, her name is Bethany Anne. She is the one who saved the American Were and Ivan's sister, Ecaterina. Ecaterina is the one who captured Petre, and Bethany Anne is the one who chose to execute him and fulfill the strictures."

"And if I can be so bold, what about Michael?"

"His whereabouts are unknown. We have no information that he is either captured or killed. There is some evidence that he is absent for his own reasons. No, I will not go into that with you." Josef nodded his understanding. "I can understand the concern about Michael visiting, as he hadn't come back to Europe in centuries."

"So, that much was true?"

"Yes, his last known location was in Romania. A few days after Michael left Romania, his plane disappeared on its way to England."

"What would Bethany Anne have us change? I understand that the American Pack Council had a run-in with her."

"Yes. So did the vampire Clarita, who is no longer among the living. Bethany Anne can be vengeful or merciful, depending on how you yourself act. She will not visit the sins of the children on their fathers, but if you don't accept responsibility for your children, she might apply punishment for not taking care of what you need to. In the case of the European Pack Council, she will understand if we work to fix it now. But there will be no second chances. I can tell you this: she doesn't suffer fools or foolishness. You have one chance to make it right, and that is all."

Stephen stopped talking, it was time for Josef to decide which way his council would go. If Josef did not choose wisely, there might be a new pack leader before the night was finished.

Josef had been in contact with Gerry in the States. He had shared more about Bethany Anne than Stephen had, but none of what he said contradicted Stephen. Her guards had killed more Weres than she had in their last dustup. With so many years of working around the strictures and keeping mistakes quiet, the knowledge they were going to deal with one of Michael's children had concerned many on the council. They were all guilty, to some degree, of being loose with the rules. And there was one thing they could not fail to share, or the whole council's lives were forfeit.

The vampire just stared at him, with unblinking eyes. It unnerved him. Unlike in America, the splinter group in Europe was truly not part of the Pack. They had their own underground organization and most of them were dealing in illegal drugs, prostitution and other crimes. They had been working with three—now two—vampires for the last thirty years. Petre had been one of three. Another was based here in Frankfurt and the third lived in Paris.

They had a tenuous agreement that Weres who wanted out of the pack had to join the underground. There were no other options. They had policed themselves well over the decades and it had worked. Now what was going on was going to come out.

This was going to be seen as his decision, which was why Stephen wanted to speak only with him. It was his decision and would be his responsibility to accept the fallout for it. Stephen was a typical vampire in one respect, he started at the top and if he didn't get what he wanted, he would get rid of that person and move down.

So, Josef opened up and started explaining to Stephen the

underground pack and the last thirty years. He was pleasantly surprised that Stephen didn't kill him right away. He was good as his word and throughout the afternoon, he asked questions and worked to understand how they could fix the situation. Once Stephen had a handle on it, he told Josef he would talk with Bethany Anne and figure out their next step.

Stephen and Ivan left Josef and went back to the hotel. Their rooms had been cleaned up nicely. They got ready while Stephen drank a bag of blood. They didn't have a microwave, so he had to drink it cold which was not the high point of his day so far.

Stephen took more time than usual getting ready. Tonight would be the first time in decades he had gone out to acquire female companionship.

Ivan came out of his room. He had dressed in a pair of fashionable jeans and Converse. He had paired the jeans with a white long sleeved shirt and a dark blue blazer. Stephen came out shortly after and he had on a pair of black jeans, white long sleeved shirt with cufflinks and a nice black suit jacket. He had black dress shoes with his ensemble. "Ready wingman?"

Ivan smiled. "After you, Mr. Cruise."

Stephen started towards the door and called out over his shoulder, "Who is this Mr. Cruise?" Ivan laughed and proceeded to give Stephen the quick version of Top Gun and the actor who played the main character.

They decided to walk to the Velvet Club as it wasn't too far away from their hotel. It was a little early in the evening, so they went to the bar and ordered drinks. The bar had multiple levels and a dance floor shrouded in green lights. The decor was modern with dark wood everywhere. Stephen talked to the barman and was able to procure a nice table that overlooked the dance floor. They had a glass wall next to them which would block some of the sound, but none of the sights.

Ivan sat across the table from him. "Stephen, how are you going to get the attention of the women from way up here?"

Stephen smiled at Ivan. "It is all about a woman's biggest weakness, Ivan."

"Really, would that be Chocolate?"

"No."

"Diamonds?"

"No."

"Money?"

"Please, you are being prosaic, Ivan."

"Ok, maybe so. Remember, my present girlfriend came up to my front door. I don't have much experience needing to go to clubs."

Stephen laughed. "Really? Wait until I spring that answer on Gabrielle, I wonder what her response will be?" Stephen knew what her response would be, she wouldn't care. But Ivan didn't know that yet.

Ivan put up a hand. "Let's not be hasty, maybe I'm getting my facts a little off. So tell me, what is a woman's greatest weakness?"

"Curiosity and its darker sibling, jealousy. Having what the other woman has, my good Ivan. Fortunately for you, your woman is past these childish feelings."

"Really? How long did it take her to get beyond these problems?"

Stephen looked like he was doing some calculations in his head. "Maybe a hundred and twenty years?" Ivan just about snorted his drink out of his nose.

"So, not something a normal lifespan will fix?"

"Oh, probably. Most women get over it by their fifties or sixties. But Gabrielle was still looking like she was in her twenties and thirties and being in that young of a crowd kept her insensible for decades longer than she should have been. Ah, here comes our first two fish now."

Ivan turned around and saw two women coming up the stairs with red chits in their hands. One was a brunette and the other a dirty blond with glasses. The brunette was smiling like she was part of an in joke and the other looked a little shy. Stephen looked them both in the eyes as they came up and he smiled in a disarming way.

The brunette came up and placed the red chit on the table. "Ok, what is this game you have going on with the barman? He says that you have purchased all of the cosmopolitans for the evening?" The blond was covertly looking over at Ivan who was looking at Stephen.

"Yes my dear, in a way. I have purchased the right to provide cosmopolitans to all of the ladies here tonight. I simply ask to know your name."

"My name? I tell you my name and then the barman will give me a cosmopolitan?"

"Yes. There is nothing else to it. I made a bet with my good friend Ivan here that I could learn the names of fifty women tonight. If you and your friend share your names with me, I will be two wonderful names closer to winning my wager."

"Really, what's your wager with your friend?" Despite herself, Terry was getting curious. Neither one of the guys gave off the sleazy vibe she was used to and the one she was talking with acted like he could take her or leave her. He certainly didn't act needy.

"I'm sorry, but I'm giving a cosmopolitan to learn a name,

the details of the wager have a value to me and I can't simply just announce them." Stephen fished into his pocket. "So, here are two blue tokens that the barman downstairs will accept for your cosmopolitans. Do we have an agreement?"

She looked at him harder. "You really don't want our phone numbers or anything else, do you?"

Stephen looked both of them. "Well, that would be a problem. You see, there are certain qualifications to the bet. If a couple of things happen then I could lose the bet and I would really prefer you didn't share any other information with me."

"Oh, why not?"

Stephen acted exasperated. "I'm sorry, but isn't it enough that we have a small business agreement here? I pay for your drink, you have a wonderful time exactly how you had planned to have a wonderful time except with two drinks you didn't have to pay for and you help me win a wager with my friend?" Stephen purposefully looked over the brunette's shoulder at another two women coming up the stairs with red chits.

She turned back around and changed her demeanor to be a little more agreeable. She reached out and took one of the two blue tokens, "It's Evangeline. I'm getting my drink but I'm coming back. I'm going to find out exactly what the wager is between you two." With that she turned around and started to leave her friend. Realizing she was alone she turned around as the blond reached out to take the second blue token. Stephen took it and with his other hand placed it into her outstretched palm.

She smiled at Stephen. "Paula."

"My pleasure, Paula." He smiled at her as she turned around and caught up with Evangeline and they went down the steps. At that point the second set of ladies approached them.

Ivan just watched in amazement as ladies came up to the table and within a short while, they had six attractive women sitting there.

"Oh god." Evangeline had been watching the dancers when she saw Mathis enter the club with his two lackeys. Both of the guys were easily over six feet and muscular. She had danced with him a few weeks back and then told him no when he wanted to leave the club with her. She tried to lean back but he had spotted her face already and was pointing to where they were all sitting.

Paula leaned over. "What is it?"

"Mathis and his two friends. They saw me already."

Stephen had heard the conversation while he was talking with another woman to his left. He politely excused himself from that conversation and leaned back towards Evangeline. "Sorry, but I heard you say something you were unhappy about?"

Evangeline glanced back at the stairs, so Stephen and Ivan looked as well. It was obvious who she was looking at since he had her in his sights and wasn't looking at the people he was bumping into at all. He just ignored people's complaints and pushed his way through the crowd. Stephen was able to smell the Wechselbalg and the vampire as they drew closer. Stephen turned to Ivan. "You might need to bail me out in a few hours, this is one of the guys from our talk with Josef." He stood up and gently stepped around one of the ladies' chairs.

Evangeline looked over at Ivan. "What is he doing? Mathis is a jerk, and his two bullyboys don't care who they hurt! Is he trying to impress me?"

Ivan looked at her. "Believe it or not, Evangeline,

everything is not always about you. It so happens that we were discussing this guy with an acquaintance this afternoon. You can stop trying to figure out how to bolt, Mathis will not be bothering you tonight." Ivan turned back to watch the altercation, under his breath he added, "I hope."

Stephen walked right up to the younger vampire who never looked at the guy who was staring right at him. Stephen got his attention by failing to move when Mathis tried to push him out of the way. Mathis finally looked to see who was blocking him. He turned his head so the two behind him could hear him, "Get this guy out of my way!"

Why Mathis never thought to wonder how he couldn't move the guy and yet his Were guards were supposed to accomplish it was beyond Stephen. He figured this Mathis must be taking something that affected his sense of smell.

"Hello Mathis." Stephen tried to look cordial, but he was starting to get irritated at having his first night out with ladies in over… well, too many years to count, ruined.

Mathis looked at Stephen, trying to figure out how this guy knew him. The Were behind and to the left of Mathis reached over to grab Stephen's shoulder and Stephen casually caught his wrist and broke it. The Were grunted in pain and pulled his arm back. Stephen looked at the other guy. "If you try that, I'll just cut it off and it will be a pain to regrow, do you understand?" The other Were looked at his buddy and nodded.

Mathis finally caught on. "Look, I don't know who you are, but I run Frankfurt. You need to get your little white ass out of my town before I take you out." Mathis gasped in pain and looked down. Stephen's nails had grown and become like small knives. Presently, he had all five fingers of his right hand embedded three inches into Mathis' abdomen.

Stephen stepped closer so no one could see Mathis bleeding. He lowered his voice so that only the vampire and Weres could hear him. "No one runs Frankfurt unless I allow it, Mathis." Stephen made the end of his name a hiss. "If you don't come to me tomorrow night at nine at the Steigenberger Frankfurter Hof, I will find you and I will take you to your maker so he can reprimand you. If he doesn't satisfy me, I'll just kill him and then kill you." Stephen spread his fingers and Mathis hissed as additional pain shot through his stomach. "This underground you are running is over. Your partner has one week to leave Europe on pain of death. Every Were that is part of the underground will re-submit to the Pack council here, or will leave Europe within that same week. Do you hear what I am telling you, Mathis?"

Mathis grunted as Stephen twisted his razor sharp nails causing new muscles to be sliced apart. He gasped out, "Who are you?"

"I am Stephen, the son of Michael, and the bondservant of the Queen, Bethany Anne. By her declaration I am lord of Europe and by my decree, your underground efforts are outlawed. Do you understand this decree, Mathis?"

Mathis just sucked in as much breath as he could. Not only because of the continuing pain Stephen was causing him, but because this was the sun-walker and he had heard rumors of the female vampire. If she had one of Michael's children answering to her, then the UnknownWorld was changing radically. This also meant their dead partner's maker presently had his hand halfway into Mathis' stomach. He nodded. "I'll be there tomorrow night."

Stephen pulled in his nails and surreptitiously wiped the blood on Mathis' clothes. "Now leave, Mathis. Take your two Were and get out of my sight. If you so much as think about failing to show up tomorrow, I'll just find you during the day and drag you into the sun. No muss, no fuss and no mess. Stay away from any humans, you have these hours to do as I command." He looked at the two Were who had finally realized how close they stood to death walking. "Take my commands back to your pack. You either submit, leave or commit suicide. If I find you I will make it a very painful death so you will be the lesson mothers tell their children about, do you two understand me?" They both nodded. "Now turn around and leave." All three turned away from Stephen and walked back down the stairs. They were significantly less boisterous leaving. Stephen looked down and noticed he had some blood on his white shirt. "Gott Verdammt!"

Ivan came up behind him. "I suppose we're done for the night?"

Stephen sighed. "Yes, we need to sleep and prepare for tomorrow night. I'm afraid there will be no taking ladies back to my room tonight, it would be too dangerous."

"I thought as much. I've paid for all of the drinks, by the way, Evangeline asked me to give you this." He handed Stephen a napkin that had a lipstick kiss and ladies handwriting on it, 'Call me, Terry' and her phone number. He had thought she had given him a fake name. He smiled and slid the napkin into his jacket. Maybe the night wasn't a total bust.

CHAPTER FOURTEEN

The Queen Bitch's Ship Ad Aeternitatem, En Route to Costa Rica

Bethany Anne was in the medical room on TOM's ship, going over the pod readings. It had been four days since Gabrielle had lain down in the device and it was time to wake her up. She could use another two days of rest, but needs must and the devil was driving. Or in this case, the Nosferatu outbreak was the driver.

She entered the code to wake Gabrielle up. TOM had explained how to make part of the pod cover transparent so she could see in, and Gabrielle would be able to see out. It wasn't a big area, maybe six inches square but she remembered her first experience feeling claustrophobic when she woke up.

She was standing over the pod looking at Gabrielle's face when she opened her eyes. She had a strong sense of deja vu, she was there when her father woke up, too.

Gabrielle's eyes went from staring into the distance to focused and quickly found Bethany Anne looking down at her.

She smiled in recognition at her friend. She heard Bethany Anne explain how to open the pod from the inside, so she felt around until she found the lever and pulled it. The pod door opened and Bethany Anne stood back, out of her way. Eric and John were out in the hallway, on the other side of the closed door.

"I feel different."

TOM?

It looks like a few deficiencies were detected and corrected. She is approximately an inch taller and her muscles have been tightened up. Her bones had some of the same work to strengthen them as yours did. She can walk in the sun without any issues and generally, her nanocytes have been upgraded. She has a small direct pull on the Etheric now.

That's kick-ass, my own six-million dollar vampire girl.

"Well, you've been modified some by the process. I can tell you that you'll need a new wardrobe. You're about an inch taller, and by just eyeballing you, I'd say the inch is in your legs. You look a little tighter all over." Bethany Anne pointed to her breasts, "Ecaterina is going to be jealous, no support necessary there. Not that a lot was needed before."

Gabrielle looked down. "Did I get enlarged a cup?"

"No, at least TOM didn't mention it, probably just a general re-shape. Good thing you don't wear black spandex, or the guys wouldn't be able to focus on their jobs." Gabrielle stuck her tongue out at Bethany Anne who was making a 'turn around' gesture. "Yup, you get to learn how to get rid of the tattoo."

"That figures."

Bethany Anne turned and grabbed the pile of clothes, "The pants will probably be a little short and it all might be just a touch larger than you're used to, but overall I think you'll like this."

Gabrielle started putting on the clothes, "I feel a little awkward at the moment."

"You're just getting accustomed to the new height and different size. Your muscle memory is confused. We'll need to spar to get you comfortable quicker. Speaking of sparring, I had to pull you out of the pod early. We have some trouble."

Gabrielle looked at Bethany Anne as she pulled her shirt on. "What trouble?"

"We are almost to Costa Rica. The power vacuum has caused all sorts of Forsaken fighting including random rampages by Nosferatu after their makers were killed. We're going in."

"What about Anton?"

"That schlong midget is shoot to kill."

Gabrielle sat down on the small bench connected to the wall and grabbed the combat boots. "I still can't believe you're looking to kill one of Michael's children."

"Believe it. Michael is either dead, in which case one of his kids probably killed him. Or he's captured, in which case see the kid comment just mentioned or he is purposefully hiding. If he's hiding, then Carl is probably with him and they are aware of what is going on. He's welcome to pick up the fucking phone and call me, but I'll just hang up on his ass. If he was going to deal with Anton before, it would have been centuries ago. That we have evidence Anton was involved in the worst of the Nazi atrocities is enough for me to condemn his sorry ass. Michael knew my background before he changed me, so it can't be a surprise I care about the rights of the deceased. Even the deceased of seventy years ago."

Gabrielle could feel the righteous fury Bethany Anne

barely held in check. There was no changing Bethany Anne's mind on this subject. Either Bethany Anne or Anton was going to die, and Gabrielle was going to do her fucking best to make sure it wasn't Bethany Anne. She stomped her feet to get them to settle in the boots and stood up. The clothes fit much better than she had a right to expect. "Then Anton had better say his final prayers, hadn't he?" She smiled at Bethany Anne who nodded.

Bethany Anne looked around the room and made sure it was clean. She turned and programmed the pod to close and to ready itself for use. Maybe she would be able to talk Stephen into it.

She walked to the door and let it open before continuing out. John and Eric had been lounging against the wall opposite the door and stood up as she exited. They looked behind her and she saw the surprise on their faces. Yeah, TOM had to have tweaked the Pod for attractive parameters. Both men took a second to get their game faces back on.

Eric stuck out his hand to Gabrielle, "Are you finished sleeping? Ready to get your lazy ass up and help us take care of some Nosferatu?"

Gabrielle noticed the change in Eric's demeanor. This wasn't a guy that was picking on her as a woman, this was a guy who was picking on his teammate when they wanted them aboard. She shook his hand, and then started squeezing while smiling. Eric grunted and then started to go down to one knee. "Eric, you sheep-loving ass herder. You can't run into the light and hide from me anymore. You ready to make sure someone isn't on your six so I don't take a bullet to the chest?"

"I will be if you don't break my trigger finger!" Eric was able to smile. Gabrielle let go and then hugged both Eric and John.

"Gabrielle, since you seem to be so happy showing off your strength, we need to go over to the Polarus and spar to get you ready again."

Gabrielle turned and looked at Bethany Anne, who was walking down the hallway towards the ship's exit. John and Eric started to smile at her. Bethany Anne called out, "By the way, we will be working swords without protection. Hope you're up to it."

Gabrielle's face went a little white. Her team was decimated when it was the five of them against Bethany Anne alone. Now she was going to spar with her by herself? With edged weapons? Oh, this was not going to be fun. She just looked at the two men whose grins were twice as large as they had been a moment before. She started walking after Bethany Anne and flipped the guys the finger over her shoulder. She called out to them, "Stop looking at my ass!"

All she heard was the laughter from her teammates. The three of them heard Bethany Anne from down the hall. "After I finish with you, I want you to work on the team. Four guards against one highly capable Nosferatu."

She turned around to see John and Eric's faces look like they had eaten lemons. She smiled and pointed to herself. "Payback's this bitch, you two!"

Eric looked over at John. "We can hope Bethany Anne puts her back in the medical pod, right?"

John retorted, "You're the one who had to make the lazy ass comment."

Eric mumbled, "Seemed funny at the time."

Bethany Anne waited until her team was with her. She hit the open sequence and when the door opened, John stepped off first.

Washington D.C., USA

Frank Kurns came out of his room at the Mandarin Oriental Hotel, set his laptop bag down and turned to lock the door. A second later, Lance Reynolds opened his door a few feet over to the right. "Good morning, Lance." Frank grabbed his bag again and shouldered it. He never liked the look of the backpack bags for men his age. Hell, even his new age. Ok, he just had to admit he hated the backpack look on anyone not in school.

"Morning, Frank." Lance turned to shut his door and put up the sign to let housekeeping know to stay out. Lance dealt with his own room needs as he had ever since his wife Meredith had passed away.

Frank looked a little closer at Lance who noticed Frank's scrutiny and looked back at him, "Yes?"

"You seem a little, just a little, better rested this morning than normal."

"Bethany Anne."

"Ah." The two of them started for the elevators. "I thought you were going to wait a while."

"She pulled a dirty trick."

Frank laughed a little. "Stuck the blood in your drink?"

"No, emotional terrorism. She told me she didn't want to watch her father age in front of her eyes, it hurt her too much and then hugged me like I was going to die that night."

"She cried on your shoulder, huh?"

"Yup."

"Effective."

Lance grunted his agreement. They hit the button to go

down to the ground floor. "It worked."

The two stepped onto the elevator. Both had on D.C. power suits. Dark blue with light colored blue shirts, Hermes ties which didn't associate them with either party and black Oxford shoes. Ecaterina had dressed them.

Now, the older man looked the younger as Lance took the lead coming out of the elevator. The valet brought their rental car around and Frank jumped in the driver's seat. This was his town, so he was the best choice to drive around.

Their task was to find out what was going on with the review into Bethany Anne's companies and who was behind the research. If it wasn't politically motivated, they might be able to set up a couple of meetings, answer some questions and leave. If it was politically motivated, they would have to find out if it was a set up by outside forces or inside movers trying to find someone to shake for political gain.

Either way, they needed to quash this interest in Bethany Anne's corporation before the information became too well known.

They stopped at a small pancake house and got a booth. Both had coffee while Lance had pancakes with eggs and bacon and Frank chose oatmeal.

After their food was served, Lance started the conversation, "Any luck last night?" Frank had spent the evening in his room after going to his office. Some of the information he needed wasn't in the core computer he accessed from his secured laptop.

"Yes and no. The original information did come from the companies that Patriarch had done the financial research on. That report sat without a priority and no notice for almost a year. Then, a minor staffer to a significant congressman out of Florida made a request about a couple of businesses, which turned up the Patriarch information. From there, more data mining was requested. Until the last few months, it had been sporadic. Since about two months before the Miami incident, it started to get significantly higher."

"So, is the staffer working for someone else, or is the congressman asking the staffer to do this for him?" Lance drank his coffee, pleasantly surprised at the quality.

"Both good questions."

"So, we don't know if the congressman is in on it or not. Based on the information you and Dan told me about the situation back in the Everglades and the terrorist attacks, it seems likely the request for information is connected. What if the attacks on the companies that you guys broke up wasn't going for fiscal gain?"

"Well, we can ask two of the hackers on that job."

"That's right, Nathan took them in, right?" Frank nodded.

"Ok. It's looking possible that the information from Patriarch Research is a tool to help find and locate other companies in our group. We need to know if it was a financial attack, data attack or a fishing expedition."

Frank pulled out his phone and hit Nathan's number. After a minute of talking with Nathan, who promised to get the two employees to call him, he hung up.

By the time the waitress refilled their coffees, Frank's phone had a call coming in from Texas. "Frank Kurns. Yes, thank you for taking the time to call, Ben. I am looking into what information you were directed to procure during your job in Miami a while back. Yes, the job before you took work with Mr. Lowell's company. I work for the lady who was in charge of the security during that job. Yes, her. Really? You want to meet her?" Frank looked at Lance, who just shrugged.

"I can't tell you if that is or isn't possible right now, Ben. The better person to ask would be Mr. Lowell. I don't know of any reason the lady wouldn't be willing to meet with you, but make it known to Mr. Lowell and let him know I asked you to do so."

Frank listened to the phone for a bit while Lance finished his eggs.

"So, you guys were looking to create back doors into the organization to extract what, exactly? Right, I understand what you're talking about. Yes, I have had some experience with that technology. Interesting, so the last item was to transfer money from bank accounts to hide the Trojan horse and the worms? Ok… No, I don't think it was a problem we didn't go into more detail before now. That's what I needed to know, thank you for your help." Frank said his good bye and hung up.

Lance pushed his plate away. "So, rob them to hide the data attack?"

"Pretty much. He said that they had some good code that should have been pretty untraceable once it was installed. But he and the female hacker have already given Nathan's company, or I guess I should say Bethany Anne's company, everything they know about the code. So, their product, Guardian, has the ability to look inside firewalls and protect the network. The company is discretely passing the word around to companies who aren't their customers. They've picked up two consultations and one client so far just by being nice people."

"Ok, but where does this get us? We know that the attacks would have been financially successful, but the real desire was to get inside the companies. What are they looking for?"

The waitress came and took their dishes and topped off their coffees. Frank voiced his first thought. "What if they don't know?"

Lance reached over for the Splenda. "Just a fishing expedition?"

"No, what if there are rumors that Michael has something, but they don't know what it is. If I was in charge of a project like that, I would first limit my scope."

"All of Michael's companies."

Frank nodded. "The second would be to get into each one and start a massive digging expedition. They're getting cash, new research they might or might not be able to use and still searching for the answer."

Lance took a sip, too sweet. "To the question they don't know how to ask. That only works if they don't fear getting caught."

Frank thought about that. "They were already operating in America. I think they either didn't fear getting caught, or considered it worth the risk. For them to push so hard while Michael was gone and have attacked his companies directly speaks to them having inside information. They believe the risk from Michael is small or nonexistent."

"Until Bethany Anne came along, that was true. Her busting up the Miami operation had to put a crimp in their plans."

Frank thought back to the fight and the aftermath. "I bet we have a bigger Miami connection than we think right now. The congressman and the staffer come from that area. I need to see if there are any phone records I can procure for that time frame from the congressmen himself."

"Who is it?"

"William Pepper. Pretty powerful in the Appropriations Committee. Been in office for six terms so far. I have some background tasks running to get more information on him. That will probably take until this evening or tomorrow before

I have a good brief."

"Do we need to be here in D.C., or go back to Miami?" Lance called the waitress over to top him off and dilute the oversweet coffee.

"Both of the suspects are here in D.C., plus some of my own support is back in my office and I need to be there to use those old computers."

"Do we need to move them?" Taking a sip, Lance seemed pleased with his coffee.

"Eventually. But I don't know where I would feel safe if we moved them. So best to leave them here in D.C. until we get our own location with better security." Frank pushed his coffee away and grabbed his water, the caffeine was starting to make him jittery.

Frank's phone rang again, another Texas number. "Hello, Frank Kurns. Hello Tabitha, I appreciate the call back." Frank went through the same discussion with Tabitha that he had with Ben. He politely said good bye and hung up. "Same information that Ben gave me earlier. She had the same instructions as the other two."

"Bethany Anne hit one too hard when trying to incapacitate them, right?"

"Yes. I asked her about it and she mentioned the last time she had done that was to a Wechselbalg, so she hadn't adjusted for the 'human eggshell,' her words not mine."

Lance snorted. "That sounds like her. I don't know any other person who can get so righteously angry for a person who has been in the grave for years and then turn around and be the one who puts a person into the grave just seconds later."

Frank raised his water to Lance. "Strangely enough, that's why I follow her, Lance. By the way, did I ever tell you the first time I listened in on her operation and heard her call someone ass-munch on the team radios? God, I thought I was going to die of laughter that night." Frank was on the cusp of laughing right there in the pancake house. "I think that night was when I started to think I could live a little while longer."

"Really? Here, let me tell you a story about when she was in high school and we were at a martial arts tournament…"

Frank put his water down. "Wait, wait. Let me get my journal out of my bag. I'm collecting stories, hold on."

The two men sat another hour while Lance thought of three different stories about his young daughter and told them to Frank. By the time the men finished, both had been laughing for the last thirty minutes. Frank had to fight to contain himself enough to jot down any notes. They left a large tip for the waitress and left the restaurant.

CHAPTER FIFTEEN

The Queen Bitch's Ship Polarus, near Costa Rica

The clanging of swords had the staccato sound of a string of fireworks going off. There would be a fast set of sounds with moments of silence and then an occasional clang and then the fury would start again.

Gabrielle was dripping with sweat while Bethany Anne walked calmly around her, seeking weakness. Gabrielle had endured almost thirty minutes of hard sparring to get comfortable with her new body. She failed to enjoy the moment as Bethany Anne had been soundly defeating all of her attacks and then Gabrielle's bell had been rung hard when Bethany Anne hit it with flat of her blade. When Gabrielle looked up from the floor, she saw Bethany Anne's red eyes and heard her simple 'Get up' command.

She struggled to push off of the floor and fight through her exhaustion. She wanted to at least mark the younger woman. This was getting embarrassing. At first, the guys who were watching which included John, Eric, Scott, Darryl, Pete and Todd Jenkins supported both women. After about five minutes it became obvious that Bethany Anne didn't need a cheering section and they all were yelling for Gabrielle to 'get back up' and to 'stop laying around.' Actually, that last one came from Darryl and Scott. She never heard John or Eric support that comment. She would enjoy that more if she wasn't getting her ass kicked so soundly at the moment.

They started another pass.

Bethany Anne started talking.

Clang—Clang—Clang. "You." Clang—Clang. "Have." Clang. "To." Clang-Clang-Clang. "Reach." Clang—Clang—Clang. "Deeper!" Clang—Clang.

Gabrielle stepped back. "What are you talking about?" She tried to catch her breath as quickly as possible.

Bethany Anne started walking in a circle around her in the other direction, forcing Gabrielle to pivot.

"You aren't using your Etheric power. Haven't you ever felt strength beyond what you have now? Speed that exceeds your present abilities?"

Gabrielle almost dropped her guard as she thought about that question, but quickly put her swords back up. It would be just like Bethany Anne to slap the side of her head again as an object lesson. "I don't remember. Maybe? But it happened so fast I could never be sure what happened."

"This is what can happen, Gabrielle." Bethany Anne's eyes went even redder and her fangs grew. It was the only warning Gabrielle had before Bethany Anne attacked. Gabrielle was able to stop two blows before her left hand went numb from a block to Bethany Anne's strike and her hand dropped the sword. She tried to pull her right sword up in time while Bethany Anne was already spinning around and Gabrielle's feet were swept out from underneath her. She hit the floor hard enough to make her ancestors flinch in their graves.

Bethany Anne's fangs were on her throat. She froze, not wanting to do anything to push the woman over any edge. Bethany Anne spoke into her ear, "You will learn to pull from the Etheric, you will learn to walk the roads with me between the dimensions, Gabrielle. You are your own challenge. You are stopping yourself from your destiny, Gabrielle. Are you ready to embrace it, or do you want to be my bitch, always lying on the ground after I kick your ass? Hmmm little girl? What is it going to be? Speak!"

Gabrielle didn't move, but anger was in her whisper. "I… Will… Kick… Your… Skinny… Ass…Bitch!"

Gabrielle could feel Bethany Anne's lips curve into a smile. "Yes, there is the fire. I can feel your blood right now, Gabrielle. Calling to me, telling me I should take it. Should I give in, hmmm? Should I just take a little, to see what you taste like? Maybe not this time, but the next time you call me 'Bitch,' it better have the title 'Queen' in the front, or I will teach you what being my bitch really means. Do you understand me?"

Gabrielle nodded slowly, trying not to cause Bethany Anne's fangs to cut into her skin. She wasn't sure if her blood would cause a reaction, but she didn't want to find out.

Bethany Anne was breathing over her neck one second, and the next she was standing beside her, with her hand outstretched to help Gabrielle to stand up.

When she was standing, Bethany Anne waved Pete to come over and hand her the sword she had dropped. Pete just looked at Gabrielle with sympathy and stepped back out of the sparring area.

"Now, I want you to stand there and feel your body, feel your core. Inside that core is an opening, as if you are a mountain and it is a small cave with the air blowing through. That is your connection to the Etheric. It fills you up, slowly. It's the same energy that blood provides you. You can use this energy to increase your power, your speed, your abilities. In the beginning it is limited, you run out quickly. In time you become more proficient in the use." Bethany Anne thought about what she needed Gabrielle to learn. "We need to try something else, hold on."

She called over to John, "Can you bring me the fifteen sticks?" John jogged over with fifteen six-inch long by half-inch in diameter dowel rods that Chief Engineer Rodriquez had cut for Bethany Anne. She took them. "Thank you. Now give John one of your swords." Gabrielle handed John the sword that she had in her left hand. That rat bastard had skipped out and left her in previous fight, so he was in the doghouse as far as she was concerned. John took the sword and went back to watching from the sidelines.

"How many of these do you think you can hit if I toss them all up in the air?"

Gabrielle thought about that. "Probably most of them."

"And if I have you close your eyes until they are already falling back down?"

She pursed her lips. "Maybe half?"

"Let's see," Bethany Anne split the dowels between her hands. "Turn around."

Gabrielle knew Bethany Anne wasn't going to make this too easy on her, but turning around? What a way to make the challenge a real pain in the ass.

"Close your eyes. You may open them when I say 'go.'"

Gabrielle turned to face away from Bethany Anne and put her sword up. She heard Bethany Anne step back a few steps away from her. "Go!"

Gabrielle opened her eyes and turned around. The damn dowels were coming right at her! She started to react, striking the dowels as quickly as possible. She missed two and clipped four. One dropped from above and hit her in the head. "Gott Verdammt!" She rubbed the top of her head.

They both went around and picked up the dowels. They now had sixteen because Gabrielle had sliced one into two pieces.

"Here. Hold this one up as high as you can." Gabrielle did as instructed. Bethan Anne turned around. "Now, I'm going to react as fast as I can without pulling from the Etheric."

Gabrielle dropped the dowel and yelled 'Go!' Bethany Anne had it in her hand before it dropped four inches. Blazing fast, but certainly not enough to explain her abilities.

Bethany Anne handed the dowel back to her. "Now I will turn around again, but this time don't say a word, just let go of the dowel, ok?"

Gabrielle nodded and Bethany Anne turned around. She thought of dropping more than one of the dowels, but she considered that Bethany Anne was trying to help her, regardless of how inadequate it was making her feel at the moment. She raised her hand and immediately let go. This time, Bethany Anne had it in her fingers before it had dropped even an eighth of an inch.

"That, Gabrielle, is the difference between enhanced speed and Etheric speed." Bethany Anne stared at her, eyes glowing. "Are you ready to embrace your heritage?"

Gabrielle started to understand how her father felt. This wasn't just some woman who was powerful. No, this was someone you followed because she embodied your beliefs. She led you through the times that were tough. Both pulling you along, and pushing you over the edge. You became more as a member of her team than you might ever become on your own. In the future, when she was asked, Gabrielle would point to that moment in time when Bethany Anne became more than her boss, she became her Queen.

A Queen whose ass she was still going to kick.

"Yes, Queen Bitch, I'm ready." Bethany Anne smiled at her and raised the dowel up in the air. "This is what you need to do…"

It took almost ten more minutes before Gabrielle was able to switch over to what Bethany Anne called her 'Vamp speed.' She was able to make it happen on purpose after another ten minutes. Then, she had to stop and drink a bag of blood as the guys came over and congratulated her. She enjoyed their enthusiasm. In her centuries of life, she had never belonged as she did here with her friends, her teammates and now her Queen. She looked around and didn't see Bethany Anne.

She finished her blood pack and looked at the guys. "Guess it's your turn, boys." She smiled as everyone looked around for Bethany Anne and realized she meant they were about to be schooled by the latest new super-vamp. Eric looked resigned to an ass kicking.

———

Frankfurt, Germany

Ivan and Stephen had gone back to the hotel from the club. While Stephen had been alert for any issues, nothing untoward happened.

Stephen nodded to the doorman who was very congenial and the two of them took the 'secret' door to their rooms. By now, everyone in the hotel had heard the stories surrounding

Stephen and Ivan and it was an exciting event when the two came and went. That Stephen seemed to have a little blood on his shirt as he came in caused a big buzz in the rumors after he passed through. One of the ladies in the restaurant asked the gossipers if they were sure it wasn't just chocolate?

As they came into the room, Stephen put a hand back to stop Ivan from entering with him. Stephen started sniffing the air, moving his head first one way, and then the other noticing a human scent having been in their room recently. He followed the scent to his bedroom and then saw that he had mints on his pillow. He smiled to himself and grabbed the mints and went back outside to where Ivan had stayed at the front door. He held up the two mints. "We have unexpected contraband."

Ivan snorted and then laughed at the situation. "I take it you haven't been to a hotel in a few years?" He came into the suite and closed the door.

"Few years? I've been asleep for nearly decades, only occasionally getting up to handle something minor and sleeping again. You should have seen me when Bethany Anne woke me up. I was old enough to act the part of a skeleton in a play, without the need for makeup." Stephen gave one of the mints to Ivan and popped the other into his mouth. "Mmm, this is good. I think I missed a few treats along the way."

"Like Evangeline?"

Stephen smiled. "You mean Terry? Exactly so." He reached into his coat pocket and pulled out her note. "She has nice lips." He pulled out his phone and entered her number into the address book.

"You're going to call her?"

"You never know, how am I going to grow my little black…" He looked down at his phone and turned it front to back and then to the front again. "Whatever. How am I supposed to grow my list of ladies again? All of the names in my last book have certainly moved on. Actually, considering the year, they've probably moved on to the afterlife, sad to say."

Ivan had to laugh at that as he walked into his room, leaving the door open. He called out, "So your first name is from a lady who failed to tell you her real name up front? I thought Paula was going to be your first. Well, your first this century."

Ivan heard Stephen from his own room. "Who says she would be my first this century?"

Ivan thought about the old rickety looking Stephen. "Stephen, that's just… ick, Stephen." He heard laughing from Stephen's room.

Ivan changed into casual clothes and walked back into the central part of the suite. "Hey, what did you do to Mathis? I couldn't see too well from the table, but it certainly got his attention."

Stephen came out of his room in a pair of jeans and his dress socks. He was getting a white t-shirt ready to put on. Even Ivan had to admire the man's six-pack. "Damn, Stephen. Do you even need to work out?"

Stephen looked at Ivan and then looked down to his stomach where Ivan was looking. "No, compliments of the nanocytes as I understand it." He finished pulling the t-shirt on over his head.

"Now I know why Ecaterina is jealous of Bethany Anne."

"Why is that?"

"Because Bethany Anne has gravity defying breasts that make men loose their senses anytime they get near her. Ecaterina is bitching about how Bethany Anne never has to wear a bra and is usually clueless on how it makes the men react."

Stephen sat down on the sofa. "I doubt she is clueless, I imagine she is probably ignoring it."

Ivan grabbed a water from the cooler the hotel had left in their room. They had never upgraded the suite to have a kitchen. He sat down on the chair, facing Stephen. "I can believe that. She has a way of picking and choosing what she notices. So, back to my question about what you did with Mathis?"

"Oh that. The young fool never noticed me before he tried to stomp right on top of me. I'm guessing he was hopped up on some sort of drug. He must have taken them pretty soon before he went into the club, otherwise our nanocytes get rid of them effectively. We suck as drug users."

"No pun intended."

"True. So when he stopped I stabbed him with all five of my fingers. I could have reached in and pulled his stomach out if he gave me too much grief. As a younger vampire, his healing ability could have handled the crises, but it would have hurt for a long time. There are muscles that are a bitch to heal."

"Sounds like experience."

"It was, a sword cut in the 1800s in… well, somewhere in France."

"Over a woman?"

"Of course."

"How in the world did you get a sword cut from a human?"

"If I remember, I was having a fling with the unwed daughter of a count. Her brother had tracked me down to an inn and I was doing my best to not kill him for her sake. After he sliced open my stomach, I punched him in the head to disorient him and left with a horse. I made it just fine, unfortunately I had to walk since the horse was drained pretty good to heal me up quickly."

"Damn, hard on your horses?"

"No, I'm very good with my own horses. It wasn't my horse I grabbed."

Ivan started chuckling and eventually Stephen had to see the humor and chuckled as well.

"So, you expect this Mathis here tomorrow night?"

"Yes. He will either come by himself, which would surprise me greatly. Or, he will come with muscle to support his ego, or he will send a group to kill me. Unfortunately, he didn't seem very smart so I am thinking option number three."

"Not going to need me for this, are you?"

"No. In fact we need to find a nice place for you to hole up for the night. I told Bethany Anne I would keep you safe. I didn't even think about you having any guns until it was too late. We will rectify that in the morning."

"How am I going to go about with guns in Germany? In case you didn't know, being asleep and all, Germany has some of the strictest gun laws. You can't really have a gun, unless it is on your personal property and then you need separate licenses to even buy the ammunition. You are not allowed to carry in public. This isn't the wild west, like in America."

"I'll do it the same way I did it the last time I was here."

"Really, how was that?"

"Diplomatic immunity."

"Ok, When was that?"

"I think the twenties."

"Which century?"

"Ah, 1920s. Between the two wars. The Allies had placed hard restrictions on what the government of Germany could arm themselves with. Or in this case, not arm themselves with. So, the government introduced civilian gun control laws so the government couldn't be overthrown."

"Is not having personal weapons here in Germany why Mathis had bodyguards?"

"No. He is a third or fourth generation vampire. He's still

stronger than a few Were, but if enough were to jump him, they could take him out. I imagine John Grimes could do it by himself. My personal belief is he has the Were with him to support his ego."

"You don't seem too concerned with him showing back up here tonight."

Stephen sighed, "I'm not. When you have lived life long enough, the same record gets played with different instruments. Maybe it's just Frankfurt, but this same situation occurred the last time I was here."

"Is that why the door is in the wall?"

"Not exactly. Every vampire who stays alive has a bolthole or two. I had this built because I'm cautious. But I did need it right away that time."

Stephen looked at his watch, "If you want to go to sleep, I'll stay up until dawn to confirm no vampire problems."

Ivan looked around. "Ok. I don't know if I'll sleep, but I will at least rest."

Stephen got his phone charger. It was a good thing that he was wealthy, because his data usage here in Germany was going to cost through the roof. He sat back down in the front room. Tomorrow would be an interesting day.

CHAPTER SIXTEEN

San Jose, Costa Rica

Giannini Oviedo was working the streets trying to find out more about the rumored attacks that had happened in the last couple of weeks in downtown San Jose. Normally, San Jose was a safe place, at least in the daytime. Now, even the small gangs that dealt in drugs, small robberies and vandalism seemed to stay off of the streets at night and she couldn't get any of her contacts in the police department to admit anything.

At 5' 2" tall, Giannini wasn't going to scare away anyone who might decide she was easy pickings, that's why she had the mace and the Taser she had borrowed from the editor of her paper. At twenty-two years of age, she wanted to make a name for herself and she would have to take a few risks to accomplish it.

She wore blue jeans and a black t-shirt with her sneakers. She wasn't a bimbo that would wear high heels at night when she might need to run. The lack of people on the street was a little weird. The night was occasionally broken up by a car or two passing by. One time, she had a guy make a U-turn behind her so she turned around and watched as this American pulled up beside her and rolled down his rental car window and asked her in broken Spanish how much for a hook-up.

She almost maced the asshole for thinking she was a prostitute. She cussed him out in Spanish and he took off.

It wasn't until she got her anger in check that she realized she was offering her body for a story, potentially. It wasn't the same as providing sex for money. Then again, it was a very backhanded compliment that she decided she didn't want or need. Asshole.

She stayed two hours on the streets before she got back to where she left her vehicle. The last five minutes, she kept looking over her shoulder feeling eyes watching her. Maybe next time she would bring someone along.

She took off in her car, screeching the tires as she turned on the main road back to her house.

————

The Queen Bitch's Ship Polarus, near Costa Rica

Bethany Anne was walking down the hall back to her suite when she heard a commotion coming from the main conference room.

She walked in, hearing Ecaterina saying, "Oh my god, I love this," in her sexy Romanian accent. Hoping she wasn't about to interrupt a make out session between Ecaterina and Nathan, she was surprised to see what Ecaterina was stroking so lovingly in her hands.

It was a new sniper rifle.

Nathan had opened up another large box and was working to pull a gun case out.

"I'm sorry, do you need a moment between you and the… rifle?" Bethany Anne smiled at the surprise on Ecaterina's face. Nathan didn't stop taking the rifle case out of the packing box. Undoubtedly he hadn't been surprised at all by her sudden appearance.

"You have to feel this, Bethany Anne. It is sex to hold, yes?" Ecaterina's smile was mischievous. Bethany Anne was the foil to her conversation with Nathan.

Bethany Anne played along. "You mean it's hard, strong, long and makes a bang when you pull the trigger?"

"Yes, all of that. Plus I get a total of ten bangs before it has to reload, I'll be spent before the rifle will."

Nathan stood up, set the carrying case on the table and opened it up. "I'm going to need a cold shower."

Ecaterina put the rifle in the case. "I'll warm up the water for you."

"You'll just steam up the place and I won't be able to see anything."

"Who needs to see? Can't you use your hands to feel around in the dark?"

Bethany Anne started walking out of the room before she saw something she wouldn't be able to un-see. She yelled back, "Get a room. Wait, you have one. Go to your room!" She heard them laughing as she continued walking to her suite. She cleaned her swords and returned them to their case. Her swords were top quality, but they weren't special from an historical standpoint.

Seeing Ecaterina with the sniper rifle caused her to

consider how to take Anton out.

She grabbed a Coke from the fridge and called Frank. It went to voicemail so she left him a message to call her when he could.

She sat at the conference table in the meeting room outside of her private quarters and pulled out a pen and pad from one of the small drawers built into the table. There was a knock on her door. She got back up and went to the door. "Who is it?"

Todd Jenkins answered from the other side, "Your security."

She opened the door and smiled at the large Marine.

He looked down at her. "Are you trying to play hooky from your security team, ma'am?"

Bethany Anne turned around and left the door open for Todd to enter the meeting room. He could stay out in the area that was set up for security before you got into the rooms that eventually led to her suite, but here was good enough and truth be told, Bethany Anne was feeling a little lonely. "Of course not, Mr. Jenkins. However, the team needs to practice and they can't possibly do that while being with me here, right?"

"Nice way to use logic to try and obfuscate the question. If I had used that a couple of years ago, I might not have gotten in trouble with the congressman as much as I did."

She lifted her bottle of Coke, "Drink?"

In moments like this, Todd was almost able to see the woman behind the mask the fickle bitch of fate had placed on Bethany Anne. "Don't mind if I do, leaded is much better than unleaded." He walked to the fridge and grabbed a Pepsi from deep behind the Cokes.

"What the hell is that?" Bethany Anne was pointing at

the plastic Pepsi bottle in his hand.

Todd Jenkins looked down at his Pepsi and decided to play along. "A Coke?"

"Hell no that isn't a Coke! That is the vile filth from a disgusting dimension. How did that shit end up in my fridge?" Bethany Anne got up, went back to her fridge and then bent over to look inside. The view she gave Todd was pretty damn hard on his blood pressure, but Bethany Anne was thinking about the other two Pepsis somebody had tried to hide in her fridge and didn't hear Todd's heart rate increase or his breathing get a fraction heavier. She reached into the fridge and pulled the Pepsis out from behind her Cokes. She considered what to do about this heresy. This had to be Ecaterina since she was the one who made sure her suite was stocked.

Somehow, she would get that little Romanian back. She opened both Pepsis and poured a couple of ounces out of each one. She then tightened the lids back and stuck them in the freezer part of her refrigerator. If it didn't take forever to freeze, she would sneak them into her bed later that night.

Satisfied that justice might be done, she turned back and sat down at the table.

Todd watched from his location near the door. "What are you doing?"

"I'm trying to figure out how to take Anton out. So far, we only know he's in South America, is rarely seen and is a crafty bastard."

"How did you get Clarita?"

"She worked by some Forsaken rules of who determines the top dog. We took out some of her businesses, which made her send the protection around her to go and try to stop the team, thinking that Gabrielle was me. She didn't realize our team had two female vampires. We spent that load."

Todd was a little surprised hearing Bethany Anne's casual use of what many would consider vulgar language. He had been told she did it, but he thought it was mostly on operations. "So, what's your first thought?"

"Shoot him from afar, then go in close to finish him off. Unless we get real lucky, he could probably come back from a round to the head."

Todd couldn't help but feel a little awe for the vampire, he had seen the results of sniper rounds. "He can shrug off a sniper shot?"

Bethany Anne looked over at him. "Not easily, no. If it was a non-killing blow, he wouldn't be able to move himself for a while. But if he's in a car then all we've done is make him aware he's a target. After he heals, he'll be practically impossible to track down."

"He doesn't already know he's a target?"

She thought about that. "He should, but the rules he's lived by for hundreds of years have preconditioned him to think the most that might happen is a slap on the hand. Unless Michael himself shows up, he won't believe there is anyone stronger than he is. I'm sure his siblings are probably close in strength, but they can't overpower him. Since Michael has never killed one of his kids, that leaves humans. His defense against humanity at large is a strong ability to implant suggestions in human minds."

"Like hypnosis?"

"Not sure. We took out a grandchild of his by the name of Adrian. Adrian talked to me as if he expected me to simply obey him and he expected immediate results. Very traditional ability attributed to vampires in popular fiction. Since it didn't work on me, I can't tell you how accurate that guess is."

"What happened to this guy when his coercion didn't affect you?"

"Incredible pain when I impaled him and threw him down on the concrete. He was very surprised, I assure you. In fact, we used a sniper on that job to get me close enough to Adrian. That reminds me, I wonder where Killian is. Have you seen him around the ship?"

"Yes, he was up top in his hide a couple of hours ago."

"That's right, I forgot he's always on duty up there. Or it seems like he's up there all of the time."

"Well, there are a lot of boat bunnies out on the smaller yachts that float around a yacht this big. I imagine he needs to confirm that none of them are hiding an AK-47 in their bikinis."

"Yes, I see where that might be a benefit to an otherwise incredibly boring job." Bethany Anne started doodling on her paper.

Todd thought about that statement. "I don't think you understand the makeup of a sniper. They have patience that is beyond understanding. I've known a few to go out and get in position for a hot LZ days in advance."

"Hmmm, I've never held a long conversation with Killian to understand what makes him tick. I might have to locate him sometime to have a discussion. But this isn't getting me closer to my goal of figuring out how to take Anton out."

"Well, anything that talks, even tangentially, to the subject has the chance of providing an idea. You mentioned that you don't know how to find him. Does he have any attributes we can look for?"

"You mean, like a missing arm?"

"No. For example, we know he has to get around at night, or I guess be very covered up…"

Bethany Anne interrupted, "Holy crap, that could be a point." She put a hand to forestall anything from Todd for a second. "If I was Anton, I would move around covered up during the day from one location to another. Easy enough to do, jump in a covered van in one garage and get out in another garage."

"They don't sleep during the day?" Todd asked.

"It isn't necessary. It's practical, if you can't walk in the sun you'll probably start staying up later at night when you can move around more freely. Hmmm, a lot of Anton's power comes from his persuasion or mind ju-ju, whatever he has. I need to see if Gabrielle knows more about it. Hell, I should just ask TOM."

"The alien?"

"Hmm? Yes, sorry. TOM is an acronym for his full name. He has insights into the way vampires have changed and how their different powers might conceivably work. We have a specific injection that we could use on Anton. If we shot him with this stuff, he would die within a couple of weeks. It's a slow death, but an assured death."

TOM, did we make sure that Gabrielle is protected against the same serum used on Adrian?

No, everything was corrected, but I did not think about protecting her from what we did to Adrian.

Ok, it's something we need to deal with for those who are on our side. If we thought about changing the nanocytes in Forsaken, the idea can be used against us as well.

Wouldn't they first have to figure out how to work with the nanocytes?

Yes, but this technology is something that scientists are working on right now. I'm pretty confident that the earth doesn't have something as advanced as what you have implemented, but that doesn't mean they can't figure out enough to turn it against us.

You humans are a challenging species.

That we are, that we are.

As far as Todd could tell, Bethany Anne was still in his conversation. "How else could we inject him?"

Bethany Anne got her head back into her conversation with Todd, "So long as we injected him with enough nanocytes, they would eventually saturate his body. If he drinks blood, he would…"

Todd recognized the 'eureka' moment. "What are you thinking?"

Bethany Anne turned back to face him. "If we could figure out how to get his blood supply contaminated with the nanocytes it would work, but that has to be, like, plan 'F' or something. Why can't this motherfucker be an arrogant ass that just has to show himself all of the time? He sure is messing up my life right now."

"You could always skip killing him, but make it so that he is impotent."

"Sounds like a great plan, but then he would just make more kids. Since he's first generation vamp, they would be powerful. No, we have to neutralize him, we just don't have enough information to make a plan. This sucks." She sat back in her chair, feeling defeated before she began.

Todd thought to some of the team's operations. "Seems like you need to grab some of his inner circle and ask them."

Bethany Anne sat back up. "That might be possible." The next thing Todd knew, he was in an empty room and the door behind him going out to the hallway was open.

He turned around and started walking and mumbling to no one in particular, "How the hell are you supposed to guard someone that can run so fast you don't have a fucking clue where they went? I need to GPS tag her ass…"

You could hear him asking people every few seconds as he passed them walking down the hallway, "Have you seen Bethany Anne? No? Thank you." It took him a few minutes to find her back in the conference room with Ecaterina, getting contact information for Clarita's kids.

She was talking as Todd came into the room. "Yes, I know I have to wait based on the time. But they should be up in a couple of hours, right? Good." She turned around. "Oh, Hi Todd. Sorry, I should have told you where I was going. Good job on the idea, by the way." She started walking past Todd again. "Heading to the suite, see you there in a minute!" She blitzed away again leaving Todd staring at Ecaterina and Nathan.

Ecaterina shook her head. "You might get used to it, but I doubt it. She is usually better about not leaving her security behind if that is any consolation. What is she so worked up about?"

"Trying to figure out how to take Anton down." Todd replied.

Ecaterina said, "You should ask her what the bait is."

"I'll see if I can work it into any conversation." Todd nodded thanks, waved to the two of them and started his walk back to her suite.

———

Frankfurt, Germany

Ivan got up and went into the bathroom, the incredibly small bathroom, and splashed a little water on his eyes. It had taken him the better part of an hour to get to sleep after saying goodnight to Stephen.

He walked out of his room to find Stephen sleeping on the couch. He had his phone in his hands and it looked like he just laid his head back and fell asleep.

"Stephen?"

Stephen's eyes flew open and his head came upright and immediately surveyed the room. He finally focused on Ivan. "Sorry, I must have fallen asleep." He looked down at his phone. "Ah, it is almost 11:00 AM. The morning is already gone." He looked at Ivan. "So, shall we get dressed and go get something to eat?"

Ivan shrugged. "Sure, what's the plan for today?"

Stephen stood up. "I'm thinking that we will deposit you in a safe hotel, one not connected to this one, for tonight. If, for some reason, I do not make it through the night you have enough money to make it out of Frankfurt, correct?"

"Sure."

"Well, I doubt anyone would be looking for you directly if they have taken me out. Unfortunately, individual humans do not normally rank very high on a vampire's danger scale."

"Yes, I remember how Petre didn't give Ecaterina a second's thought even though he was running from Bethany Anne." Ivan remembered a bit late that Petre was Stephen's child. "Sorry."

Stephen waved at him. "It is no worry. After speaking with Josef yesterday, I am getting to a point I am regretting not taking care of Petre myself. I only have more appreciation for my Queen the more I learn about this underground Petre was a part of. That comment about Ecaterina. What is it she says about catching her prey?"

Ivan smiled. "If you want to catch something, you need the right bait."

Stephen smiled and played with his phone. "I think I

know what the right bait is, or rather who the right bait is."

Ivan's voice turned incredulous. "You would use Terry as bait to get Mathis to come to you?"

Stephen shook his head. "No, but I would use Terry's voice to get Mathis to come to her. Or, at least where he thinks she is. He is the type that won't expect a double-cross, because at the end of the day what woman can contain herself around him? That she has been pushing him off is what makes him need her so badly. She is causing a disconnect with his ego. If he could get her to bed him because she wants to, it will set the world back in the right orbit. One that revolves around Mathis."

"How are you going to get her to play along?"

"Well, I can use my vampiric powers of mental control and command her to say what I want her to say."

"Shit! You can do that?" Ivan's face was the picture of surprise.

Stephen paused, then answered Ivan's question. "No. but you should have seen the look on your face when I said it." Stephen put his fingers to his lips and kissed them, "Priceless!"

"You vampiric ass-munch."

Stephen laughed at the embarrassed Ivan. "No, I cannot command her to do this, and Bethany Anne might find the idea repulsive as well. Terry has a personal stake in making sure Mathis is unable to harass her anymore. Plus, I told Mathis to meet me at nine tonight and sunset is a little after four fifteen. He will have plenty of time to meet with Terry, get his ego stroked and plan on meeting me." Stephen paused as he thought about what he just said. "Maybe that was a poor choice of words."

Ivan just snorted. "How are we going to get Mathis' phone number?"

"Well, Josef should have it. If he doesn't, I'm sure he

knows someone who does. I haven't informed him that we met Mathis last night, so hopefully I won't raise any concerns asking for his phone number. It would be a bit annoying if he turned my ambush against me."

Both men got ready and Stephen called Terry. He got her voice mail so he left a message where he said he would provide another drink if she would answer one question for him and left his phone number.

CHAPTER SEVENTEEN

Las Vegas, Nevada

Jeffrey Diamantz and Tom Billings were closed up in the conference room at Patriarch Research. They had cold pizza and beer bottles on the table while Chinese food detritus awaited its eventual retrieval from the trash by the late night janitors.

Nathan Lowell had called them and outlined the technology infrastructure he wanted to have built to bring on the software code that had caused them so many sleepless nights for the last two years. They changed the name of the project to Adam and all hoped they didn't need to change it to Cain in the future.

Both had the frenzied look of people working on too much caffeine and not enough rest. If you had asked either one, they would admit it was the most important project of their life. They had asked for a project budget of two million to test the next stage. Nathan informed them that they had a thirty million dollar budget, to be paid in increments of five million to get the building rented and the infrastructure done.

The CEO expected many assurances they would not bring about the end of civilization by doing this project. But the CEO needed to know if they truly had the beginning of a strong AI in mere weeks. They had expected a couple of years to work on the project.

Cost, they were told, was not a concern.

Both felt like they had been handpicked to help usher in the next stage of human civilization. Now if they could just design a system that would protect the rest of humanity if the new entity was malevolent they were golden.

They called it quits at two in the morning. They needed a few hours of sleep before they met the real estate agent at ten to view possible buildings.

Nathan had explained that the unnamed CEO had asked how they would move the new AI if they were successful? Both had been at a loss for words. Their assumption was wherever they built the infrastructure would be where it was housed.

Nathan told them not a chance. Once it was proven, they should expect a new location to be named and that wherever it was, they would be asked to move to the new location to stay with the project. He had other, even more exciting information to discuss with them soon.

Neither could figure out how you could top the possible existence of a new sentience.

After the call was over and they had both whooped for joy at the challenge and the opportunity to see their project through, they talked about what could possibly be more exciting than a new AI?

Tom mentioned the Tsoukalos meme from Ancient Aliens. "I'm not saying it was aliens, but ALIENS!" Both busted out laughing at that idea then quickly forgot Nathan's statement as they got wrapped up in the effort to make his challenge a reality.

Jeffrey was notified late that afternoon the company's account had a wire transfer for five million dollars pending which would clear the account by midnight.

If he had any doubts on how fast Nathan wanted them moving, a wire hitting the same day was a clear indication that they had better push the gas pedal to the floorboard and never hit the brakes.

The Queen Bitch's Ship Polarus, near Costa Rica

Bethany Anne had spoken with Claudia and her brothers Juan and Scott. They had provided a good group of vampire names she could try to track down and ended up texting the names to Frank. Eventually, she would talk to him.

Ecaterina had spoken with him, however. They had received permission to fly Shelly into San Jose. Since Costa Rica abolished their military in 1948, there wasn't a base in the capital they could land at. The Juan Santamaria International Airport was too far away from downtown San Jose, and Bethany Anne refused the request from the police for them to land at that location. They finally found a landing spot close to a small hospital that was next to a metro train station near downtown. They would tell reporters it was a mercy mission to get someone to the hospital.

If things didn't work out well, they might have need of the place.

That evening, Bethany Anne and Gabrielle both suited up in black with their swords and pistols. Bethany Anne had her leather pants on. Killian was on the bird with them, with Ecaterina taking on his responsibilities back on the Polarus. Nathan, Dan, Pete and Todd had stayed behind to help cover any security concerns.

Bobcat had flight duties and John, Eric, Darryl and Scott were suited up in their team suits. Everyone had one pistol loaded with darts that put humans to sleep.

Unlike Michael's interventions in the past, Bethany Anne's group wasn't here to just take care of Nosferatu whose makers had been killed, but also any Forsaken they could find.

The San Jose Police had narrowed the search pattern for the Nosferatu to a twelve block area. There had been three missing persons reported a week before. Then another two had been horribly murdered two nights ago. The corpses looked like something had ripped their throats out.

Those who were naturally skeptical blamed it on a wild animal. That was ludicrous, but for some it was a blanket to cover their worries before they became outright fears.

They broke into two teams of three. Bethany Anne, John and Darryl went up the first street, while Gabrielle, Eric and Scott took the next block over. At ten o'clock at night, the stillness in a major city was disturbing. Everyone was scared to be out at night. The rumors had become outrageous enough that some had come close to the truth. The zombie stories were the most frightening to the populace. Bethany Anne's teams were described to the citizens as a small American special operations force brought in to handle the drug addled citizens who had been taking cocaine mixed with a new drug which had calamitous side effects.

Those that knew the missing argued that they were never into drugs. Between the police telling their story and the neighbors who wanted to believe the police, they got the 'truth tellers' to keep quiet.

They were about ten minutes into their patrol when Bethany Anne paused. They were in the middle of a street, trying to make sure nothing could surprise them when she spotted a human female approaching them, five blocks away.

She was rapidly walking towards them but was looking over her shoulder.

She couldn't be more than twenty-five, but looked closer to twenty and pretty short. The guys were able to see her as she passed under a streetlight. That's when they heard the screech.

CHAPTER EIGHTEEN

Downtown San Jose, Costa Rica

Giannini Oviedo was scared. This evening wasn't like the previous night. She drove to a different part of town, where the murders had happened. She parked ten blocks away and carefully made her way towards the area where the bodies had been found, their throats ripped out.

She hadn't made it two blocks when she felt her skin crawl. She looked behind her and swore when she saw two eyes, glowing in the dark and staring at her. The eyes were between her and her car.

She panicked and started walking faster without thinking that each step she took, she was a step farther away from transportation.

After five blocks, she could see a second pair of eyes when she glanced behind her. Unlike the previous night, no cars had been driving on the road. It was like the whole city had shut down and was hiding behind their doors.

Now she understood why. The mace and Taser in her hands were little comfort compared to the fear she felt. One of the stories was that the people were killed by wild animals. She had been told before that you never ran from a wild animal as it would immediately chase you down. She didn't have long enough legs to even consider trying to outrun an animal.

When she saw the pair of eyes behind her, she calculated the animal was either very tall, or walked on two legs.

Her heart was beating loud enough that someone standing next to her could hear it. If anyone had been willing to come with her that night. Even her best friend Enrique had told her she was crazy and she shouldn't go. Nothing she said would persuade him to go with her. But she needed the story to move up at the paper, so she grabbed the mace and the Taser and left him to go downtown.

Now, she was sure she was going to die for her desire to get ahead. She started praying the prayers she learned at church as a kid. Hopefully, the ten years between this evening and the last time she darkened the church doors wouldn't be held against her.

There was a bone-chilling screech behind her, her mind lost it and she started running. When she looked behind her, she saw two figures loping towards her. Both had eyes that seemed to glow a dull red and bloodstains on their jaws and down their necks to shirts that had seen better days. They were easily catching up.

She put everything she had into running and stopped looking behind her, it wasn't helping and she didn't want to slam into anything.

That was when she saw the three people a block ahead of her. Two had military weapons and the closest, a female, had pistols in holsters on each side of her chest and sword handles over her shoulders. She angled to run towards them.

She heard the footfalls of the things behind her. They were getting closer. She heard the woman in front of her yell as she turned to look behind her again. Breaking the rule she had just given herself not to look.

Bethany Anne yelled, "Get…"

Giannini Oviedo tripped when she stepped into a small pothole in the road, falling to the ground trying desperately to protect her head.

"Down." Bethany Anne fired both pistols, three bullets at each of the Nosferatu's heads. Both stumbled, falling as their ability to think left out the back of their skulls when .45 rounds blew chunks out of their heads. The most they could do as Bethany Anne walked up to them was twitch their limbs. Bethany Anne took out a sword and cut off their heads. Their twitching stopped. John and Darryl kept watch beside and behind them.

She pulled out a small radio device. "BA here, two down." She put the small radio back on the clip by her waist. She hated the short name, but it was agreed no real names on the radios tonight. Ecaterina had voted to have the guys use the 'P' names from the Washington D.C. operation, but John told her it was only good for one op. Bethany Anne replaced her spent ammunition. Her gun with the darts was in a holster on her hip. She was used to drawing the guns from the shoulder holsters so didn't want to change anything with them.

Darryl knelt down next to the woman who was shaking uncontrollably, the aftereffects of the adrenaline rush her body had subjected her to. He set aside the mace and Taser to make sure she didn't spray or Tase them as they tried to help her.

Darryl made sure she was ok, talking in a soothing tone. He pulled out a small packet of antibiotic cream and a sterile pad that he used to gently clean her wounds. After a minute, he was able to get her name.

Bethany Anne cocked her head; she heard footfalls. Lots and lots of footfalls coming in their direction. She pulled her radio back out. "Hey G. Get your team over to our location, I think we have company. You read?" She got back an affirmative. They were three blocks over. While Gabrielle could make it easily, she could only go as fast as their slowest runner, which was Scott as Eric was taller and had a longer stride.

She clipped the radio back on. "Guys, we need to get her to safety, fast. Ideas?"

John spied a metal dumpster and pointed, "There?"

She followed his finger. "Works, let's go." Darryl picked up the woman in a fireman's carry over his shoulder and they jogged together the half block. The dumpster had three bags of trash in it. John easily reached down and pulled them out.

"It's disgusting," he said, "But it will be better than being with us and the smell might protect her if she doesn't make a sound."

Bethany Anne thought about that for a second. "Good point." She grabbed the pistol at her hip and calmly shot the woman in the ass. The lady over Darryl's shoulder started to say something, then she was completely out. John reached over and pulled the dart out. He tossed it to Bethany Anne who put it into a small pocket that protected her from the needles. John helped Darryl put the woman into the garbage dumpster and shut the lid.

The guys could hear the Nosferatu at that point. Now, Bethany Anne could see the Nosferatu all racing in their direction, there were eight in this pack. She could hear

Gabrielle and her team coming up the side street.

Bethany Anne quipped, "I'm not sure this is going to be reason to even break a sweat."

John saw the eight Nosferatu and considered what she said. "Yeah, you might be right." If John had seen eight Nosferatu running down the street late at night just a few months back, he would have soiled his pants.

Gabrielle and the guys joined them and the Nosferatu slowed a bit when the reinforcements came into sight.

Scott whistled. "Well, what the hell are we going to do? That's only eight. Are you going to leave any of the sticky fuck-balls for us Bethany Anne?" Bethany Anne snorted.

Gabrielle looked back at Scott. Even with her new moves and better body, she didn't want to try and attack all eight by herself and Scott didn't seem at all worried.

"Tell you what. If Gabrielle can't handle them, I'll let you finish them off, how does that sound?"

Gabrielle turned back to Bethany Anne. "What?" She was looking right at Bethany Anne when the beautiful woman's face lost her humanity and took on the visage of the destroyer.

Bethany Anne turned back to the Nosferatu and spoke in a deeper, bone chilling voice, "Watch and learn, little vampire girl." Gabrielle didn't have a good reply for that before the destruction came.

Bethany Anne's hands blurred into action, pulling her pistols and shooting four of the Nosferatu twice in the head and two of them once in the head before jamming both pistols back in their holsters and reaching for her blades. The two front Nosferatu didn't notice that their six compatriots behind them were sprawled on the ground. Bethany Anne started racing ahead to meet them as the two front ones continued running to get to the fresh meat. The left Nosferatu was five feet closer than the other one. That just meant it was the first one to have its head cut off. The second lasted a full half second longer. The two Nosferatu who had suffered just one bullet to their heads had made it as far as standing up before they lost their heads. The final four were twitching and screeching on the ground as Bethany Anne calmly walked over and dispatched each one.

She looked up, eyes still glowing red and fangs extended. She smiled at Gabrielle, "Did you learn anything?"

Gabrielle nodded. She learned how to cut a group of Nosferatu down to size before slicing off their heads and this woman was even more scary fucking dangerous than she had originally thought.

They were able to draw out two more small groups of Nosferatu in the next fifteen blocks. Bethany Anne made Gabrielle work both small groups with two guys backing her up. The closest the Nosferatu got was a small rip in Gabrielle's protective vest before Scott shot it in the head and Gabrielle quickly dispatched it.

Occasionally, they would see a person trying to peek out at the gunshots. After each fight, she radioed Bobcat who would give the street address to the police to take care of the bodies. After their first fight, she made sure to relay where they had dropped off the drugged woman for safety.

They had cleaned out fifteen Nosferatu by the time they got back to the helicopter. It was a good trip back, everyone happy to have been in a fight that went so well.

The second night provided more practice and the third a chance to capture a Forsaken leader.

———

Giannini slowly woke up in a small hospital room. Both hands were bandaged and there was a lady in a suit reading some clipped together papers sitting in the corner.

"Hello?"

The lady had dark black hair, glasses and was probably in her forties.

"Hello, Señorita Oviedo. How are you feeling?"

"Drowsy, disoriented. Where am I?"

"You are at the clinic near the police headquarters. I am Superintendent Rodriguez of the Costa Rica Police. I am one of the officers in charge of the task force for investigating missing persons and murder cases. Do you feel up to giving me an interview? I apologize for interrupting your rest, but we need to acquire as much information as we can right now. Time is important and don't be embarrassed, let me know all of your impressions from last night."

"Sure, sure." Giannini hit the button to make her bed sit up. She wasn't feeling bad, and the drowsiness was slowly receding. "Where do you want me to start?"

"How about what time you went downtown and why you were on the road?"

Giannini blew out her breath. "Well, the why is easy enough. I am a reporter for the Tico Times and I want to crack open a story to get my work seen. Being a reporter is a dog eat dog job, and if I can't break my own story I will be stuck fact checking other people's work and that is boring me to death. So, I heard about the people disappearing and the murders." She looked over at Rodriguez. "You will be happy to hear that none of my contacts in the police force would tell me anything." Rodriguez smiled. "So, two nights ago I went out and while it was creepy, nothing happened. I heard about the murders and decided I would try to find something out last night."

"You went by yourself?"

"Yes, but not because I didn't try to get some people to go with me. Even my best friend told me I was crazy in the head but I wanted a story."

As Giannini warmed up to telling what happened the previous night, she realized she had a story if the Superintendent would let her write it.

She continued, "So, I parked the car and was walking to the area where the murders were supposed to have happened. I probably had only made it two blocks before I heard something behind me. I panicked and started running away from the sound, which was away from my car as well. After a couple of blocks I could see eyes glowing behind me."

"Glowing?" The Superintendent had been writing down Giannini's story, but stopped to question her.

"Yes, I could first see one, then two pairs of dark red eyes behind me as I was running. They were humans."

"Not animals?"

"Certainly not animals." Giannini noticed the Superintendent didn't seem surprised to hear this, but rather was making sure that Giannini was certain of what she saw. "I was able to see them in the light. It was two people, and they had bloodstains on their face and their shirts.

"What happened then?"

"As they got closer to me, I saw three people standing out in the middle of the street, two men and a woman. All had guns and were dressed in black. The men had military guns, rifles and the woman had pistols and I think swords."

"The woman had swords?"

"Oh, certainly. The woman was the closest to me. She started to tell me something but I looked behind me and got my foot caught in a pothole or something and stumbled.

There were lots of gunshots and then nothing. I was so terrified. One of the men, a black man, came over and helped me." She looked down at her hands. "He cleaned up my scraped hands and then the lady said something about more coming. I was freaking out. The black gentleman threw me over his shoulder and then I felt something hit my butt, like they pinched me, and then I woke up here."

"They shot you with a dart to knock you out. We believe they stuck you in a dumpster to keep you safe."

"I was in a dumpster?"

"Yes. It makes sense in a way. They told us where to find you and we brought you here."

"Am I going to be free to leave?"

The Superintendent closed her notebook. "I'm told there is nothing wrong with you. However, I have to ask you to not write the story you paid a high price to get." Rodriguez held up her hand. "I'm not saying that we can't work something out. Your information is the first we have on what is happening. The team you saw last night are foreigners, they cleaned out a total of fifteen of these drug crazed murderers."

"Who are you trying to lie to? I'm not the public that is willing to accept whatever you say instead of what I saw. Normal drugs do not result in people whose eyes glow red."

Rodriguez had to give this young lady credit, she wasn't going to be pushed around with the official line. "It is how I must talk about the situation. As I was saying, they killed fifteen of these things. We had a group of five of our police officers get attacked by one of them. We lost two of the men, another might not live and the other two are seriously hurt, but will survive. Our team is presently canvassing the neighborhoods to see if anyone will talk to us. So far no one is. They believe that if they talk to us, this group of foreigners might either come for them, or worse, not help them any more."

"Why are you working to find out more about them, don't you already know who they are?"

"No. But you might be able to help me. While I can't authorize you to write your story, I will give you greater access to what I know and you will be able to write some of what is going on. Enough that it will help your career. Are you interested?"

"Why do you need me? Don't you have people in the force willing to do whatever you need done?"

"Yes, but they are part of the agency. If I use them, and this other group finds out, they might leave and we cannot risk that happening. But if they are followed by a reporter, what could we do about it? We have freedom of the press."

Giannini made a face that called that statement into question.

"Ok, when we have a chance of our city going up in flames from everyone feeling they are not safe, we will not allow inflammatory newspaper articles."

"I haven't even written the story yet."

"Yes, but you would. The problem is that you have your own experiences backing up your story and people might start to believe you. We would be fighting in the streets at night, and fighting the people during the day."

"Actually, I understand. I'm not going to incite anarchy, but if I help you will you promise to help me? Not the police force, but you personally. Will you help me with this story and stories in the future?"

Superintendent Rodriguez sighed. Why were reporters always the hardest to work with? "Yes, I personally will help you when and as I can. This isn't an agreement that I will tell you whatever you want, but I will help as my responsibilities permit."

That was all that Giannini was going to receive from the Superintendent. It was more than she had yesterday and the best she could salvage from her brush with death.

CHAPTER NINETEEN

Frankfurt, Germany

Ivan had been surprised at how quickly Stephen had gotten Terry's agreement to help. It seemed she had been terribly afraid for her life and had been surprised how easily Mathis had been rebuffed by Stephen in the club the previous evening.

She was concerned when Stephen explained that she would have to invite him to her apartment, but he gave her his assurances that Mathis would not be allowed to bother her again. Ever. She decided to not ask any questions for answers she didn't want to know. She knew that without Stephen's help, Mathis would never stop stalking her and was afraid that she wouldn't survive. If Stephen didn't make this happen, she would leave town the next day.

Stephen told her that Ivan would stay with her in a suite at the Hotel Hessischer Hof. They would be provided two suites next to each other under assumed names.

Stephen and Ivan took a taxi to her apartment complex, which had three floors. The taxi waited outside as the two men went upstairs. She let them in and gave them a quick tour before Ivan took her downstairs to the taxi that delivered them to their hotel for the evening.

When Ivan checked them in, he was happy that Stephen was picking up the bill. Even with his monthly salary for working and helping Stephen, this was beyond his means.

Stephen looked around the apartment. It was small, having one bedroom and a kitchen. Instead of a separate area for dining and living room it had a larger living room with a bar. Stephen needed her apartment for two reasons, the first was if Mathis was smart enough to confirm her name and address. The second was for her scent.

Mathis would be controlled by his urge to take the woman. When he opened this door, her scent would overwhelm him and he would lose a lot of his ability to think clearly. It was the same experience for human men, but pushed harder by his vampiric abilities and temperament.

Stephen found an Apple iPod on a speaker in her bedroom. He looked for and easily found some romantic music. It seemed the lady who was so bossy at the club was a romantic at heart. He liked her taste in music. He picked her 'Romantic Interludes Vol 1 - English' selection which started off with The Righteous Brothers Unchained Melody. He set it loud enough that Mathis would believe she wouldn't hear him come in, and Mathis would certainly hear it out in the hallway. He left the door unlocked and then went across the hall from her bedroom and stepped into her small bathroom to wait.

Set the right bait, indeed.

He got a text from Ivan that he and Terry were in their

rooms at the hotel. It was half past three o'clock, so Stephen went online. He found Terry's Facebook page. Facebook had taken over the previously most popular social media website StudiVZ. He made a request to friend her. She hid most of her posts from the general public, so he would have to see if she noticed the request anytime soon.

He opened up Tinder and started looking through the app. He had yet to swipe on any of the women so far, but he loved just browsing. Since he was in Germany, he filtered to those around him.

He got a ping on his phone from Facebook. He quickly turned off the sound on his phone and chided himself for missing the audio switch earlier. The last thing he needed was his phone to give him away. He noticed the time, it was fifteen minutes to five o'clock. Terry had accepted his request to friend him on Facebook. He felt giddy, the thrill of the hunt hadn't waned for him in all the centuries he had been alive. He wasn't sure he was capable of being with only one woman in his life. He had no problems giving his allegiance to Bethany Anne, but that was not the same as settling down for decades with the same woman.

If he made no promises, either way, it worked for him. It wasn't only the modern women who would have dalliances. Women in the far past had informed him before that he was a casual fling. Even the count's daughter knew she would be a political prize and was happy with who she was going to eventually marry. He was a casual roll in the hay, so to speak. He took their love and gave in return for a night and expected nothing else the next morning. Except, perhaps, angry brothers. Fortunately, it didn't look like that would be a problem in the present day.

He turned his phone off and waited in the darkened

bathroom. Almost ten minutes later, while Percy Sledge sang, 'When a Man Loves a Woman' on the iPod, Stephen heard her front door open and Mathis speak her name out loud, just not too loud. The door closed and the footsteps came closer.

Stephen's face broke into a smile. As he heard the footsteps enter the open door to her room, he flushed the commode. If he were Mathis, he would jump into the room and quickly strip and get into her bed. Hopefully the idiot had at least one small romantic bone in his body and brought roses. Stephen peeked out of the bathroom. Yes, her door was closed.

Stephen stepped out, went over to the bedroom door and opened it. Mathis was under the covers. Stephen enjoyed the shocked expression on Mathis' face. "What Mathis, no flowers? Didn't I tell you to stay away from humans, Mathis? If I can't trust you with this one simple command, then I simply can't trust you."

Stephen closed the door behind him. There was one short shriek and then silence.

Twenty-five minutes later, a white Mercedes Benz van rolled up to the front of the apartment complex and put on its hazard lights. Three of the four men in the van went into the building and came out less than ten minutes later carrying something heavy wrapped in bed linens. One came down behind them and threw in two garbage bags. Two went back up and brought down a mattress that seemed stained. They got in their van and pulled back into traffic.

The next day, they would open the linen per the instructions and Mathis's body would receive the full sun. Within the next few hours, his body would disintegrate. The Weres then dug a grave and unceremoniously dumped Mathis's remains inside. Until the previous day, they had been a part of his underground. They had been made to do this as an object lesson as to what they should expect if they chose to ignore the vampire Stephen's command.

For these three, they re-committed themselves to the pack. They had become believers that any other choice would be death.

Stephen had called over to the hotel and was able to find a taxi in time to get to the hotel and go out shopping for a new mattress and a new set of linens with Terry. She didn't want to know why her mattress and linen needed to be replaced. She had a good enough idea what had happened. The shopping was done in time for a late dinner with Stephen, which she enjoyed.

He was mysterious, which attracted her. But he was obviously very dangerous and right then, Terry needed to feel a little less danger in her life. She wished him well from her hotel room. Stephen knocked on Ivan's door and let him know that he would go back to his own hotel room for the night. He would catch up in the morning. Ivan was enjoying his room and agreed to take a taxi back to their hotel by eleven the next morning.

Stephen turned around and went downstairs. It wasn't the first time that he had to take care of business and have it mess up a good thing. It wouldn't be his last, he was sure.

He had the name of the vampire in Paris. He would deal with that problem after he went to talk with Clarita's children.

He spoke with Bethany Anne and gave her a quick update. She was very pleased with the results and commiserated over his loss of the woman. "Don't give up hope, Stephen, she might just need to get over her reaction to everything. She knows someone was killed in her apartment."

He agreed and decided he would see if Terry needed to move in the morning. It was the least he could do for her helping him as his bait. They hung up and he went back to his room. His somber mood was noticed by everyone on the floor, and also that his friend wasn't with him. The gossip speculated that his friend must have gotten lucky and he was shot down. Three of the women were quick to say they were willing to make sure he was feeling ok, but they all knew Stephen had requested to be left alone unless he or Ivan called.

The manager had caught one of the ladies, Felicity, when she seemed to be heading to the door that Stephen always used. He quietly told her to either go to the other side of the hotel, or go home and stay home.

———

Washington D.C., USA

Lance and Frank met in the restaurant at the Mandarin Oriental. Frank's research programs had finished the morning before and together they went through the results.

It seemed the esteemed Congressman William Pepper was up to his eyeballs in communications to South America. They had their guilty party, and they had the beginnings of a plan to have Congressman Pepper work for them.

Frank had spoken with Bethany Anne and she explained they needed someone on the inside, and a congressman who was already dirty just voted himself 'to become my sock puppet bitch; I want to move my hand and he speaks my words.' Frank made sure to write down that phrase for his book. While there were certainly good men and women on both sides of the floor in Congress and the Senate, it was also true that some were as dirty as coal.

That one was about to change his allegiance to become

her dirty politician didn't bother Bethany Anne at all. At least she would allow him to support his constituency as he should, and if he became involved with anyone else she would kill him. She was a jealous blackmailer who wouldn't allow any freelancing for her congressman.

She explained she was looking for ways to get to Anton and Frank shared all of the telephone calls they had traced back to South America. "Out-fucking-standing, Can you figure out where they go?" He could, he allowed, but it would take a few days.

She told him that wasn't a problem, they were stuck in San Jose with the Nosferatu issue. So long as no one fucked with them, they might be out of San Jose in a few days.

Lance drank the coffee the waitress had poured for him. It was good, but the two-bit pancake house they went to the other morning had better. "How do we persuade Pepper to fight the good fight?"

Frank smiled as he used real sugar in his coffee for the first time in ages. With his body recuperating, he doubted a few calories of the good stuff was going to do too much damage. "By giving him a package delivered by hand courier with all of his bank accounts and the tracing info. He's over a barrel and it isn't good. If I were to give this info to the press, his goose is cooked."

"What?" Lance asked with a faked look of shock on his face, "We aren't going to bring in my daughter to talk with him? What the hell, we're going old school?"

Frank raised his mug to Lance. "Who are you calling old, you geezer?" Lance had to laugh, with Frank's hair coming back dark, he certainly looked younger than Lance. After his haircut, which got rid of his grey hair, and with his almost ever-present grin Frank looked less than half his real age.

"I'd tell you to respect your elders, but you're older on the inside than this new coat of paint, jackass."

"Ass-munch."

"My daughter would have you doing push-ups for the consistent use of the same cuss word."

"What, are you going to tell on me?"

"Hell no, you cock stain on a two-bit whore's Thursday panties. I'd hate to see your heart burst. I'm warning you, fuckhead."

They burst out laughing and the others in the small restaurant looked over at them. They got their outburst back in check.

Lance took a sip of the coffee. He was wishing they had gone back to the other place. "So, we ship a copy of the papers without it getting traced back to us. What then?"

"We leave Washington and go back to Miami is my suggestion. Hole up in the house while we let the bastard sweat like the little greasy pig he is. We can't possibly do more to upset his sense of well being than him knowing someone has that information and waiting for them to get in touch with him."

"You're a real son-of-a-bitch, aren't you?"

"Maybe. Did I tell you the time that I had one ass… hole spouting off shit and I wanted him to focus on something else? No? Well, it turns out he was diddling three women at the same time. I got all three of them…"

"Oh hell no, you didn't!"

"Yes I did."

"How did it end up?"

"One of the women stabbed his ass with a butter knife if I remember correctly. Worked out better than I could have hoped."

Lance slapped the table laughing and people looked over at them again. He wiped a tear away and called for the check. "God, that's great. Oh, shit. This has to be one of the funniest meetings I've been a part of… since breakfast at the pancake house."

Lance's phone started ringing, he looked down at it. "Frank, one second, it's Patricia." Frank just nodded and sipped on his coffee. "Good morning, Patricia. No, I'm in Washington D.C., so I've been up a while already. No, I'm not playing ten toes up and ten toes down with anyone you hussy, how could you think something like that? Ok, you got me there, it is probably one of the only reasons I might come to D.C.. No, it's on business. Yes, I was serious when I mentioned a job for you if you ever decided to quit the military. Why, what's changed your mind? Oh, rumors the base is being closed down?"

Lance looked at Frank and raised an eyebrow. Frank signed the check and pulled out his laptop. He should be able to get into some different databases to find out more about this development.

"Certainly, but you might have to move. I travel a lot. Well, I'm based in Miami right now, but that could change to England or it might change back to near there. I can't tell right now, you would probably have to consider living out of a suitcase for the foreseeable future. Salary? How about twenty percent higher than what you make right now, plus another thirty percent for travel. If we stop traveling so much, you will lose that added amount. God, what are you now, your own agent? What kind of bonus are you talking about?"

Lance winked at Frank who had looked at him over his laptop. Frank realized Lance was as happy as he had seen him lately.

"Fine, but not all at once. I'll approve a 10k bonus when

you sign on, and an additional 10k at ninety days and another at one year. Damn, what now? You want cost of living assurances? When did you leave the military and become a mercenary? Uh huh, you know the pain in the ass you will be working for? Just for that I should hang up. That's what I thought, kidding me my ass. Yes, that's fine. Call me back when you've put in for your transfer to TQB Enterprises. Yeah, I'll have my present secretary send you tickets. No, she might not have been with me as long as you, but she has a very sexy accent. Hell, I just call her to hear her read me the paper."

Everyone turned when Lance couldn't keep his laughter in a third time due to Patricia's scathing retort. He finally put the phone back to his ear. Frank could hear her cussing Lance out from across the booth. "I didn't know you still had that kind of language in you, I thought you were a refined woman, imagine my surprise to be learning all of this now. I can tell you aren't prepared to go on interviews in the private sector, Patricia. You had better hope you get the first job or I don't think much of your chances otherwise." He pulled the phone a couple of inches away from his ear for ten seconds. "Ok, look, joking aside I want you on my team. So, figure out how soon you can get to Miami. Sorry, pets aren't an option. I didn't know you had any pets. No, sorry you can't get that cat you've always wanted. Get a stuffed one from Toys R Us. Yeah, I'm a coldhearted bastard, trust me, you'll thank me later. Yeah, give me a call within forty-eight hours to update me. Bye."

Lance hung up the phone. Frank didn't look up from his laptop, "First glance suggests that without you being back at the base, a couple of higher-ups decided it might be the best to close your base down for budgetary reasons. Almost everyone would get moved to other locations. The group that is puttering in the lower levels is trying to keep it open for research, but they don't have the budget."

"Hell, I'd shut it down just to get rid of those bastards. They were always a pain in my ass."

Frank shut his laptop. "The research will continue on my main computer, but the behind the scenes maneuvering is going hot and heavy. Since your base isn't close to any major cities, there aren't too many politicians concerned with it."

"It was always a pain to get the best personnel stationed at the base due to decent entertainment being so far away, but it would work like a charm for what we want to do."

"Think we could buy it?" Frank asked.

Lance considered the question. "Probably not soon enough. We can't move in next week or anything, but probably within a year, maybe two. We can possibly do a partial, I'll have to call some old friends and see what's happening."

"We won't have the same infrastructure as one of the bases in Great Britain." Frank pointed out.

"Yes, but we have all of the buildings and we can afford to move people on base. We have a chance to really handle who gets on and who doesn't. I'll take it up with Bethany Anne. It would be a good place to run the company from. We would have our own airport and if we start letting men on the base know a company is going to be buying the place and would need security, some would be willing to stay. They have family and houses in Denver."

Frank put his laptop back in his bag and stood up. "Well, let's get busy with operation sock-puppet bitch and go back to Miami."

Lance grunted in laughter. "Let me guess, my daughter?"

Frank just smiled. "Who else?"

CHAPTER TWENTY

San Jose, Costa Rica

The same team was back on Shelly for the third time. They had handled another two smaller groups of Nosferatu the previous night. Now, they finally had some good intel on the location of a couple of Forsaken with Nosferatu on the north side. Bethany Anne had hopes that they could capture one of the vampires.

The police had been asking more questions than she liked, so she told them that they would be welcome to handle the rest of their problems without her team if they insisted on answers. They quickly backed down.

It wasn't that she didn't understand the police's desire to know. They had a tough job dealing with the UnknownWorld without a good background. More than likely, there would be some in their government who knew what was happening, but they hadn't contacted Frank to open any communications so Bethany Anne assumed they worked for the other side.

Their helicopter had gotten noticed. Costa Rica has a multicultural respect for languages and while Spanish is the official language, many languages are spoken, including English. So that made it easier to get information from some of their news sites.

There wasn't much she could do about others seeing her helicopter. They were going to ride Shelly to their landing site, and they took the Black Hawk down fully loaded. After the first night, it was decided to add Pete to the group that stayed with the helicopter in case someone got the idea that it would be a nice addition to their personal collection. Bethany Anne never left the area before marking off a quick return zone. If things went to shit, they could call her back if the zone was clear.

She had seen the report on the police officers that had run into the Nosferatu and had died. Until you fought one, and lived, no one would realize how hard it would be for humans to kill the bastards.

Gabrielle was coming along well with her fighting and her leadership. After a couple of other snide remarks, Gabrielle came out swinging every time a Nosferatu group was found. The guys protected her very well. Bethany Anne would stand back with the other two and observe the melee. After the fight was over, she would give pointers and Gabrielle had stepped her already impressive abilities up a few notches.

Shelly could almost make the trip from the Polarus to San Jose and back twice before refueling. So Bethany Anne instructed Bobcat to stay up in the air until they either saw something themselves, or she called them down. Pete was up front with Bobcat. She gave the hand signal for everyone to get ready. She was anxious to get stuck in. Tonight was going to be a slaughter, and she was the Angel of Death. Her eyes started to glow against her will and she felt her fangs starting to protrude. She was having trouble keeping her emotions in check. She made sure Darryl and Eric by the door were safe and then opened the side door, she needed air.

Eric looked over at Darryl who shrugged his shoulders. If the boss wanted to check out the view, who were they to tell her she couldn't do it? It was her helicopter for fuck's sake.

She strapped her arm into a hold and hung out the door. She had no skid to step on, as Shelly had three wheels. Some of the armament was in her way as she searched the streets below with her superior vision. It took fifteen minutes before she spotted a disturbance over in a major park to the west of a cemetery. She called to Bobcat over the headphones to head in that direction. She was itching to get into the fight and it was driving her mad. She wasn't sure what was going on, as she hadn't felt this kind of influence before.

TOM, why am I feeling on edge?
One moment, I don't know.

"Bobcat, get me over in that area soon before I decide I need to start kicking something and Shelly is the best choice at the moment!" He didn't respond, but Shelly dropped suddenly and Bethany Anne's face lit up in a feral grin. "Fuck YEAAAAAAHHHH!"

Her attitude was infectious; the team prepped their weapons. Everyone knew, loved and respected Gabrielle and believed she was a kickass leader for their group. But going into a battle behind Bethany Anne was an addiction for these men. "Pete!" He turned to look at her as best he could, "When everyone is off, I want you, Killian and Bobcat up top giving us cover. If it gets too much for us on the ground, then use those door guns and fuck everything that isn't us up. Got it?"

"Yes ma'am!" He started unbuckling.

Bobcat had them coming in at only a hundred feet above the buildings, no one that night would be able to mistake what was flying through their neighborhoods. Many windows were opened as the 'protector of the night' came screaming right past them with a woman hanging out, eyes unmistakably glowing.

She saw two Forsaken teams coming together, probably over forty bodies down in that mess. "GET ME THERE NOW, BOBCAT!" She was straining, trying to hold in her desire to rip, to tear, to destroy. She hadn't felt this out of control since she'd destroyed the wall in TOM's spacecraft.

Bobcat came over the teams' radios, "I'll land in that spot three blocks to the north, I'll have you down in thirty seconds."

"FUCK THAT!" Bethany Anne swung over the edge and disappeared.

"BETHANY ANNE!" John screamed her name as she disappeared. "GOD DAMMIT! Get us down Bobcat." The team all popped their safety harnesses and prepared to jump, Killian prepped his rifle.

"What the fuck happened?" Bobcat pitched Shelly in a tight ass turn and Pete jumped into the back to man the guns.

"She jumped already, I swear to God if she makes it out of this I'm going to put her over my knee and spank the fuck out of her. I can't believe this shit." John was heated, worried about his boss.

Gabrielle yelled into the group, "C'mon Bitches, let's go get our fucking Queen or we won't have shit to do ourselves!"

Gabrielle jumped from twenty feet up. The men, as prepared as they were, waited until Bobcat was hovering a few feet in the air before jumping off themselves. Bobcat quickly pulled Shelly back up, Killian giving cover.

Bethany Anne had slipped through the Etheric to come out fifty feet behind the Forsaken group coming in from the cemetery side of the park. Her night vision had a red haze.

Bethany Anne. TOM got no response.

BETHANY ANNE.

WHAT?

I've got that answer, what's going on with you.

What the fuck is it? She took off after the stragglers in the group in front of her. She could hear Shelly screaming in a tight turn behind her.

You're having your period. You can get pregnant.

WHAT? How the hell was that possible? TOM had told her that wasn't going to happen. She had figured it was better for her to never have children, so it had only been a relief when she had first learned of her lost cycle. Her anger was making better sense now. She had always been easy to piss off, but during her cycle she was a perpetual anger machine.

Now, she was infinitely stronger, vastly more dangerous and utterly and totally enraged.

Well, it would just suck to be a Forsaken tonight.

She pulled her pistols and started firing, one shot per head. She didn't want them dead right away, she needed to get her anger out and so fuck 'em if you have 'em and she was going to fuck them up tonight.

She shot ten right away, and two more turned at the noise. That left eleven continuing on to attack the other team. Those two groups had just started their own attacks against each other in the park.

She heard Gabrielle catching up with her. "Fucking hell, Bethany Anne. Wait for your backup!"

"I AM MY OWN FUCKING BACKUP!"

The first group of five Forsaken running at her broke against the indomitable rock that was Bethany Anne. Gabrielle, who had been training to spar against Bethany Anne when she was in Vamp mode, was momentarily shocked at the blurring speed and the destruction in front of her.

Gabrielle just caught out of the corner of her eye a German Shepherd tearing through the park. The dog tore into a Forsaken that was coming at Bethany Anne from her right side. The dog dragged it down and ripped its throat out.

Gabrielle heard her team rapidly catching up while she watched the dog attack. "Gott Verdammt. She even has dogs following her into this crazy fucking mess."

She turned to her team. "Don't get in her way, this is a contain campaign. There's no talking to her right now." The men just nodded and chased after Bethany Anne and the dog; both were covered in blood.

Shelly flew over and the heavy thump-thump-thump of the door guns ripped through the bodies fighting in front of them before it flew across. They heard the occasional shot from Killian. That would be the last safe pass for Shelly before Bethany Anne would be right in the middle of the carnage ahead.

It was later said that the dead rose from the cemetery to fight that night and the screams would infest the dreams of those who lived near the park forever.

The fight was swords, scattered gunshots, ripping and tearing of flesh, shrieks, screams and cussing. Lots and lots of cussing. Most of the cussing aimed at the Forsaken. Some of it aimed at their own boss.

But there wasn't one face in the Queen Bitch's Guard that wasn't smiling during the thrill of the battle. The team fought like a single entity, where everyone knew what would happen next. Scott would duck as Darryl shot over him and then Scott would turn around and shoot a Forsaken in the head. The same head would then be sliced off of its neck by Gabrielle almost instantly afterwards. The team killed, they fought, they protected and they contained the Forsaken.

What they couldn't do was contain Bethany Anne and the damn devil incarnate dog that had joined her. Eric had been aiming at a Forsaken that had stepped far enough away to be a safe shot when he saw Bethany Anne rip an arm off of one Nosferatu and then use the arm to beat another Nosferatu before turning in a half circle and kicking in the ribs of the Nosferatu missing its arm, knocking it back. Completing the turn she sliced off the second Nosferatu's head. He noticed she suddenly turned her head to look over at a grove of trees and just disappeared.

Eric screamed to the group, "She's fucking disappeared again!" Gabrielle had just taken the head of a Nosferatu John had impaled with his knife. John ripped his knife back out of the dead chest and looked around, "Where?"

Gabrielle pointed to a grove of trees. "Look, the dog is running that way." All of the remaining Nosferatu turned in the dog's direction. Gabrielle wanted to go after the crazy woman, but her job was to make sure that every one of the Queen's Guard made it through this fight. Gabrielle wasn't sure where or why Bethany Anne left but she doubted anything was going to be able to harm her.

Gabrielle pulled her pistols and started firing at the Nosferatu as she had been taught. "Target practice for hell, boys!" One bullet, one head. She missed her shot on the fourteenth Nosferatu. She was disgusted with herself, "Fuck me! Bethany Anne's going to laugh her ass off."

The guys grinned as Darryl and Scott plugged the last two. Gabrielle holstered her pistols as she ran towards the farthest Nosferatu. The guys ran and shot each one of the Nosferatu as they healed until Gabrielle came around and removed their heads. It took a vampire's strength to slice through their necks.

They heard a yelp of pain from the dog and a fierce sword fight going on inside the trees. Finishing up the remaining Nosferatu, Gabrielle led the team into the grove. Twenty yards in, they found the dog mortally wounded.

Gabrielle didn't think, she just reacted. She pulled her sword across her wrist and forced the dog's mouth open. John came up to her, "Put the blood into the wounds as well, Bethany Anne helped my chest that way."

She held her other wrist and John didn't hesitate to slice it with his Bowie. She forced as much of her blood into the wound as she could. The dog was having trouble breathing. It was all she could do at the moment.

She looked at John. "Detail protection."

John pointed to Darryl and Scott and then to the dog and got two nods.

Gabrielle's wrists were bloody, but they had stopped bleeding. "Let's go."

Gabrielle, John and Eric made up a quick triangle with Gabrielle in the front and ran into the brush. As they came out into a small glade, Gabrielle was surprised by an object the size of a soccer ball sailing through the air at her. She stabbed it and quickly found out it was a severed head. The face had a look of shock. "That's just gross!" She put the head on the ground and used a foot to help her pull the sword out.

She looked up to see Bethany Anne fighting with a taller vampire.

Both John and Eric had put their weapons down in the ready position. It was obvious to the three of them that Bethany Anne was toying with this guy.

The team heard her talking throughout the battle, "Is that," clang-clang, "the fucking," clang-clang-clang-clang, "best you got you," clang-clang-clang-clang-clang-clang, "cunt lipped bum fucker?"

The other vampire screamed in frustration and attacked with all he had. Bethany Anne just tightened her concentration up a notch as she started laughing.

"You will not laugh at me, you fucking bitch!"

The team started yelling into the fight, "Bad form on that over swing. If you're going to try and hit her, you need to pull your… Nope, not that way fucktard!"

The vampire was not pleased with the help the newcomers were offering, "I will kill this bitch first, then you are next!"

"Uh oh," said Eric.

"Yup," John agreed.

"Geez, you would think he would use a different curse word." Gabrielle opined.

John and Eric both said at the same time, "Sucks to be him… JINX!"

The team heard movement behind them and turned around. It was Darryl carrying the dog and Scott coming up behind him. Scott asked, "What the hell, are you guys having a party?"

The sword fight continued behind them. "No beer near here," said John. "We're waiting for Bethany Anne to …"

They heard a sudden thud and turned around to see Bethany Anne crush the vampire's ribs and then they heard his skull crack from a punch. He was lying on the ground holding his ribs moaning in pain each time he tried to breathe.

Bethany Anne pulled out a pistol and shot him in both kneecaps. "Stay the fuck down or I'll do worse." She holstered her pistol, "You're just lucky it was the other galactic jizz midget that hurt my dog."

She turned to the team. "Gabrielle, detail this asswipe to bring with us. Call Bobcat and make the update to the police." She walked over to the team, covered in blood and guts. Her eyes were back to normal and her fangs had retracted. She went to Darryl and checked on the German Shepherd. She noticed the slow healing. She looked up at Darryl who used his head to indicate Gabrielle.

She gently took the German Shepherd from Darryl. When she was holding him, he started licking her face. She gently laid him on the ground and lifted an arm in the air. Darryl pulled his Bowie and sliced her wrist. Bethany Anne was able to get more of her blood into his mouth. The dog licked her wrist clean, so she had Darryl slice it once again.

They heard Bobcat landing Shelly and the police sirens in the distance. She picked up the dog and heard another gunshot behind her, so she turned around. Gabrielle looked up, "The twit-lip mouthed off, so I gave him something to complain about. If he does it again, I'll shoot his dick off." Bethany Anne just shook her head and started back through the bushes to get the fuck out of there before they had people to talk to.

Listening to the approaching police, she muttered to herself, "Am I ever going to be able to tell San Jose to kiss my ass and be able to make it stick?"

Pete watched as Bethany Anne approached the helicopter carrying a dog. He looked around and Bobcat told him where the blankets were stored. He grabbed two and laid them on the floor. Bethany Anne jumped into the helicopter and sat on the blankets, cradling the dog.

The rest of the team climbed into the helicopter with the vampire in tow, Killian closed the door and Shelly rose into the night. The people who lived in the area and had seen the group named them the Protectores del Infierno.

Giannini had been driving down a street heading north after Superintendent Rodriguez informed her what area of town was expected to be a hot spot that night.

She had been driving normally until a Black Hawk helicopter screamed above her, heading north like they were heading to battle. Giannini broke the law, driving like a wild woman after that happened. She was able to see half of the fight from a nearby roof. She watched as they came out of the trees and headed over to the helicopter. She thought of them as Ángeles Oscuros and that was the name that was printed.

Twenty minutes later, Bethany Anne called ahead to the Ad Aeternitatem and had them confirm no one was in TOM's ship. She had Bobcat hover over the boat. She held on to the dog and slipped through the Etheric from the helicopter directly into TOM's cabin. She made her way into the medical room and awkwardly punched in the sequence to open the pod while holding the dog. She gently placed the dog, who was unconscious, into the pod and hit the sequence to close the pod.

TOM directed her to enter a new sequence to work up a genetic report on the canine. She sat down, tired, on the little ledge bench. Twenty minutes later, she heard a banging on the outside of the craft. It sounded like metal hitting the door. She got up and went to the door and hit the button to open it. Gabrielle and Ecaterina stood there. Ecaterina had a bag with her. She waved them in. She hit the switch to close the door, she didn't feel like talking right now, but she appreciated the women coming over.

She walked back to the medical room and checked the readout. Which is to say she looked at the readout and TOM told her it was working appropriately.

She sat back down, a bloody streak going down the wall where she rested.

Gabrielle reached into the back of her bag and pulled out a pouch of blood. Bethany Anne's face scrunched up in distaste, but she did need to drink a pouch.

"Thanks." She took it from Gabrielle. She opened the pouch and drank the contents. Ecaterina handed her baby wipes.

She raised an eyebrow at Ecaterina. "Bobcat suggested you might want to clean up a bit before you get a chance to take a shower."

That Bobcat was a keeper.

She cleaned off her face, neck and hands. She stripped out of the over shirt and took off her protective vest. Ecaterina had pulled out a heavy duty plastic bag and held it open to take the bloody clothes.

Bethany Anne looked Ecaterina in the eye. "You know, I found Pepsis in my fridge." Ecaterina hesitated, just a second, before acting as if she didn't know what Bethany Anne was talking about.

"Really? Imagine that. I'm sure they infected the Cokes through all of that protective plastic."

Bethany Anne dropped her stuff into the bag and grabbed a couple of baby wipes to wipe down her arms better. "I imagine they did. They'll probably turn into mutant Pepsis that can move in the Etheric, right out of my fridge."

Ecaterina was noncommittal.

Gabrielle spoke, "So, you want to share what went on back there?"

Bethany Anne didn't try to be smart, or cute, or dodge the question. What she had done in the fight wasn't the tactically correct thing to do, but it had been the right thing for her to do.

"Yeah, the Bitch is Back."

"So? You were angry, that wasn't a good reason to jump without the rest of us."

Bethany Anne looked up confused, then remembered that neither of these women were from the States.

"Ok, let's try this again. It's shark week?"

Both women looked puzzled.

"The storm has made landfall?"

Gabrielle just shrugged. "No?"

"The uterus ninjas are here?"

"Nope, nothing."

"My bloody buddy is here?"

Ecaterina caught on, since she was the only one presently normal. "You're having a period?"

Bethany Anne nodded, Gabrielle put her hand to her mouth, "How is this possible?"

"Fuck all if I know."

Ecaterina asked her, "So, your emotions went nuclear?"

Bethany Anne nodded again. "Pretty much, if I didn't get off that helicopter I was going to start punching Shelly in frustration. I, literally, wanted to kill something. As it turned out, a lot of somethings."

TOM, have you figured out what went on?

Yes, I've made the adjustments. Your rising use of the Etheric overcame the original settings and I've had to adjust. This means that eventually, Gabrielle will also run into this. I can adjust once I see what is going on otherwise I'm just guessing.

Bethany Anne looked over at Gabrielle, "Guess what?"

"What?" Gabrielle looked confused.

"You're next. Well, eventually."

Gabrielle's mouth opened and she slid down next to the pod dock and sat on the floor. "I'm going to have a period again?"

"Yeah, if you want it. TOM says that he can adjust you after it happens, but until then he doesn't want to mess with anything. So, you know, practice safe sex with Ivan."

"Oh god, I've not dealt with this for centuries."

"I thought I had already made this choice for my life and had been ok with the decision not to have kids. Now I have a choice again and I don't know what the hell I'm going to do. Hell, I can't keep a dog safe. I almost got him killed."

Ecaterina asked, "Dog?"

Bethany Anne pointed to the pod. "Yeah. Right at the start of my ape-shit maneuvers, this German Shepherd comes in like terror on four legs and rips the neck right out of a Nosferatu. He stayed with me through the whole fight and even found me when I translocated to where the two vampires were fighting. They tried to gang up on me and when the dog joined us, one of the pricks sliced up his side and kicked him hard. It probably broke some of his ribs. It pissed me off so I cut off his head and kicked it."

Gabrielle snorted. "I was wondering why a flying head attacked me."

Bethany Anne smiled at that. "I've got him in the medical pod and TOM is running some genetic testing right now. Between Gabrielle helping him right away, and my blood later, he will survive. We're seeing what we can do for him."

Ecaterina looked back at the pod. "Oh."

Bethany Anne stood up. "So, nothing to be done right

now and he won't age in the pod. Want to see the spaceship, Ecaterina?" She smiled and Ecaterina grinned.

"Of course!"

Bethany Anne took her around and gave her the fifteen minute tour. When they ended back up in the medical pod she checked it. TOM gave her instructions to program into the pod, when she finished she looked up.

"Ok, the little warrior will be good for a few days. Time to go back out to the real world."

While Bethany Anne was paying attention to the dog and the medical pod, Gabrielle had used the baby wipes on the wall.

The ladies left the ship. It was time to face the music with the Guards.

CHAPTER TWENTY-ONE

The Queen Bitch's Ship Polarus near Costa Rica

Chris piloted the Sikorsky from the Ad Aeternitatem over to the Polarus. Dan had Bobcat flying Shelly as an overwatch for the next couple of hours. There had been a large amount of chatter on the military and police bands due to the significant battle in Costa Rica's capital.

No keeping that fight under wraps.

She got off the helicopter and the rest of the guards were waiting for her. They tried to be stern, but soon their grins won out. Together, they had accomplished kicking some serious Forsaken ass and not one of her team had a serious wound. Many had cuts and scrapes and Darryl would have a black eye, but that was it. John was the last to crack trying to give her a stern look, but he finally just shook his head. "You know, you're going to give me a heart attack."

She reached up, way up, and ruffled his hair. "Well, seeing how you guys kicked ass tonight, that might be the only way you die early, Mr. Grimes." She gave him a ten thousand watt smile. "Where's our new visitor?"

John turned around. "Pete and Dan have him down in the hold. He's making a horrible racket."

Together, they walked off the helipad.

Bethany Anne asked, "He's healed up?"

John snorted. "Well, he was. Dan told him to quiet down until you got there and he mouthed off. So, Dan shot him with a silver frangible. He isn't healing so quick from that."

"Yeah, I'm surprised he isn't bellyaching about the poor treatment."

"He yelled, and I quote, 'Is shooting someone the only way you people know how to negotiate?'"

"Well, he should be happy to know I also rip off limbs and negotiate whether I give them back or not."

Eric laughed and then commented from behind her, "I saw you rip an arm off one of the Nosferatu and beat another one with it."

"Which time?" she asked.

"Right before you disappeared."

"Ok, right, that time." Honestly, Bethany Anne had lost track.

"How many times did you do that?"

"More than once, less than fifteen. The whole fight was a little blurry."

They could hear the bitching and bellyaching coming from the prisoner from way down the corridor. Dan and Pete were talking as they arrived.

Bethany Anne looked at Dan. "How's our guest?"

She heard him from inside the cell. "In fucking pain, you cunt!"

Bethany Anne's head tracked over to the door, her eyes

quickly glowing red and her fangs started protruding. "One second, Dan." The voice Dan first heard in a crappy tent down in the Florida Everglades was speaking again. Dan just stepped back and smiled.

Dan had enjoyed shooting the prick earlier, but he suspected he was about to enjoy Bethany Anne's discussion with him a bit more.

A look came over Dan's face as he started patting down his pants.

Pete watched him for a second. "Watcha looking for?"

"Phone! I want to record this." Dan was getting a little frantic, he didn't want to miss recording this episode.

Pete lifted up his phone, with the audio recorder already set up. "Got you covered."

Dan was relieved, and they both smiled. Bethany Anne wouldn't allow video recordings, but some of the most fun the team had was listening to older audio recordings and Dan said this beat down looked like it was going to become an instant classic.

Bethany Anne looked into the room from the small slit. She suddenly stepped back when a hand and wrist appeared between the bars. The ass had tried to punch her in her skull! She grabbed his hand and yanked it down, breaking his wrist. The scream was immediate. He pulled his hand back in and backpedaled until he hit the wall, screaming obscenities the whole time.

She calmly talked to the vampire as she pulled her weapons and handed them to Pete and Dan. She cracked her knuckles. "Really? Fucking cunt, fucking bitch, slit-faced whore? That's the best you got? You douchy-scrotum-licking-shit-eating-nut-sack-cellist. Bite This." She disappeared and reappeared in his cell and immediately beat the living shit out of him. By the time Pete turned off his phone, the vampire was on the floor begging Bethany Anne to forgive him for his disrespect. He got it right the third time. The other two times she merely said, 'not good enough' and tore into him again.

Gabrielle asked the guys at one point if anyone had a nail file, because it seemed this idiot was too stupid to get the message and she wanted something constructive to do.

That was when Bethany Anne started breaking bones. He got the message after she broke the first leg.

John looked over at Dan. "You're right, that is an instant classic. I counted at least forty-seven cusswords and not one duplication in the bunch. Frank is going to love this."

Dan nodded agreement.

Bethany Anne had Dan join her inside the cell and stayed next to him for protection as he asked questions. Dan started with his name, which was Muerto. Bethany Anne busted out laughing at this and the vampire looked like he was going to say something and then stopped himself.

Dan was able to get two more high-level vampire names that would be closer to Anton. Unfortunately, this guy knew nothing directly about Anton himself. There was a rumor Anton was in Argentina, but that was all. It looked like that bastard was still too hard to fucking find.

Bethany Anne was impatient and she was getting worse. She hoped Frank would be able to track down something based on the phone information he had found.

Maybe she had killed Clarita a little too soon.

———

BITE THIS

Jeffrey and Tom had met and been driven around Las Vegas and the nearby desert towns for the last two days. They finally found three well-insulated, very thick concrete buildings that fit the specifications for what they needed.

These buildings had been used by Nellis Air Force Base in the past. Now, they sat on the outside of the base's security fence and were in an area that could be wired for a gob-smacking large amount of internet throughput for less than a hundred grand.

They called Nathan and went through the details. Nathan confirmed they had figured out a way to protect everything outside of the buildings in case they had to detonate a small EMP inside the main AI building. He agreed with their assessment on the purchase and closed the call.

Jeffrey was able to purchase the buildings for a quarter million dollars. They didn't argue, they didn't try to negotiate at all. They were on a deadline and the price was half what they had guessed they might have to spend. It was a good thing, because the additional cooling buildout to keep the computers cold enough was going to eat into the leftover budget pretty significantly.

They needed the 3 Ps of computer server complexes. These are power, ping and pipe. There was plenty of power as the last use of the buildings for the Air Force had been as a machine shop whose large industrial lathes and drilling machines took a huge amount of power. The ping and pipe was going to cost a hundred grand and then they just needed to have an electrician make sure the power lines were still good to go to pull the power without a meltdown.

Tom thought about it. They weren't going to provide ping

outside of these buildings, so the 3P statement was a little off, but he didn't correct Jeffrey.

The guys had a large argument over max CPU Cores vs. max memory needs. They agreed to go Intel CPUs over AMD and while they liked IBM, they didn't want to chance Lenovo and had concerns over possible spying software and other shenanigans Lenovo had been accused of in the last couple of years. After a while, they realized most of the brands had a constraint on network connectivity input, so they chose to go with Cisco blade servers for Adam Ver 1.0.

Their call to the Cisco corporate office started pretty slow until Jeffrey mentioned they had a P.O. that would exceed a million dollars and the computers needed to be available fast. There would be a premium payment if the computers could be at their location within eight days.

The two boxes of one terabyte SSD hard drives were going to cost more than a Tesla, but they agreed the speed the SSDs provided more than made up for the high cost. For long-term storage they would use the larger and cheaper platter hard drives. The two men acted like little boys in a candy store as they spent the budget on their computer setups.

Once they had spec'd out the primary server setup and the secondary internet download system for the second building they called Nathan. After a two hour discussion going through every possible angle of CPU, short and long term storage, maximum memory and type of memory and bus speed Nathan approved the expenditures.

During the second hour, Tom mentioned they might be wasting their time. When Nathan asked why, Tom said that if ADAM came online, it would probably design the next computer for itself.

That cooled the excitement of all of the men a little when

they realized they would have a computer designing itself.

"Good point," said Nathan. "So, go with the picks we've agreed to so far. We're just nitpicking and I'm doing it because I'm a geek at heart. So, we'll let ADAM 1.0 figure out ADAM 2.0. I'm going to put the second five million in the company's account by tomorrow at noon. I don't want you waiting on anything. Make it happen, guys!" They agreed they would and signed off.

They called CISCO and ordered ADAM's brains.

They called it an early day in order to rest and let Jeffrey spend a little time with his family. Nothing was going to happen that evening and getting a good night's sleep would help as they got started on the next phase of their project in the morning.

They raised a toast with their soft drinks, shook hands and left for their homes. Both suffered niggling concerns about whether they had thought of everything as they went through the day's events in their heads.

————

Miami Florida, USA

Lance and Frank decided to eat at a favorite steak house on the way to Key Biscayne from the airport. While flying first class was nice, the food is still a pale imitation of a real restaurant meal.

As they sat down, Frank pulled out his laptop. He had been running some programs to try and capture phone conversations and on his third recording, he hit pay dirt. He listened for a minute on headphones and Lance could tell something was going well by Frank's smile.

He pulled the headphones off and set them aside. "I think I can confirm that Anton is in Argentina."

Lance smiled at the news. "Why is that?"

"Because I just heard someone I think is Anton on a short call with Congressman Pepper. Anton uses throwaway cell phones, so that makes my tracking him extremely difficult unless I know one side of the conversation. I was able to capture a comment about the SNAFU in Costa Rica and that he had another one to deal with in Argentina. The Argentinian government just changed hands and he was going to have to meet with a few politicians he hadn't had conversations with so far. Apparently, he had expected the female incumbent to win."

Lance took a roll the waiter delivered and bit into it. He loved steakhouses, they all seemed to know how to bake a good roll to go with the food. After finishing his bite he said, "Argentina has been politically messed up since World War II. If he's been a part of the influential elites, it makes sense why they've made so many bad decisions and focused on the elite and not the people over the years."

Frank thought about that for a second. "I imagine he is the 'influential' in influential elite."

"Good point." Lance reached for the butter.

"So, we can tell Bethany Anne that we have him narrowed down to one country. It will take surveillance to find him now. He has to come out to work with the people."

"Not if he has them come to him." Lance looked up in surprise after that comment came out, unbidden.

"That, my good sir, deserves a toast." Frank reached over to get the wine menu.

Lance waved to a nearby waiter. "I agree. I know a few good wines that would work very well."

"Really? Would this have anything to do with that last goodbye night on the town before Bethany Anne left with Michael?"

Lance grinned. "God, that was a hell of a night! Yes, it would have to do with that night."

"Care to tell me more of that story?" Frank raised an eyebrow.

Lance reviewed the wine list. "I don't mind telling you more of that story at all. You need a second to…"

"Get out my notebook, yes I do." Frank dug into his notebook bag for his notepad and pen.

The next hour, Frank and Lance enjoyed two wonderful steaks as Lance regaled him with the night he and Bethany Anne went out tasting the best wines they could afford on credit cards she wouldn't be around to pay off.

CHAPTER TWENTY-TWO

Frankfurt, Germany

Stephen closed out his stay at the hotel. He talked with the day manager and gave him instructions on changes he desired to his suite. He wanted a new fridge and microwave to be added and large flat screen TVs to be added to each room.

He needed the suite updated since he would be in Frankfurt to engage with the Wechselbalg council more often.

Stephen went and picked Terry up, in order to both take her to the apartment and be with her when the new mattress and linens were delivered.

It didn't take long for her to get the room set up how she wanted it. She never asked exactly what happened, and Stephen didn't offer any explanations.

He asked if she had any issues staying in the apartment considering the events. She was happy to keep her apartment, it was home. Stephen made sure she had the contact information for both he and Ivan.

Stephen said his goodbyes and caught up with Ivan who had stayed at Hotel Hessischer Hof. Ivan jumped into the taxi with Stephen and the two of them went to the airport. Stephen was going back to Romania to meet Clarita's kids. The situation in Paris could wait until after his discussion with them.

Europe wasn't finished as far as he was concerned, but it was on its way to being a better place for his Queen.

———

Buenos Aries, Argentina

Anton grabbed the throwaway phone he had used earlier to talk with Pepper. His face was a moue of disgust. What a pompous American ass that congressman had become. Pepper had visited Argentina years ago and had been invited to one of the parties held at his house. While Pepper was there, he took the opportunity to enthrall him. He couldn't make the man do everything he asked, that would require him to meet with him more often. But he had been able to make him highly suggestible to Anton's requests.

He dialed a number that didn't exist on any piece of paper or was saved on any digital piece of equipment: Anton was a security freak. After the fall of the Third Reich and his own close call with death leaving Germany, he had been very particular about his own protection.

Now, he had all sorts of problems occurring in his area.

The phone was ringing. A cultured voice spoke on the other line, "Hello."

"David, it's Anton. I'm losing top-level people here. Are

you positive you have him under control?"

"Yes Anton, I am sure. The human computer support person with him gave me enough information to figure out what he does to disappear."

"Can you confirm with the human once more?"

"Sadly, no. It seems the instruments I used were not calibrated as effectively as I had hoped. What did you expect? I haven't used them since the war."

"Ok, if he is in your glass prison, then the rumors of another powerful vampire—this Bethany Anne—are true."

"Then you need to take care of her, Anton. We've been working on this solution for over seven decades. I would be very annoyed if we had to start all over. I've got Michael— who was supposed to be the hardest part of our plan— under control. This female is a wild card and I really don't like to hear whining about it."

"You're preaching to the choir, David. You keep dear old Dad out of this, or kill him if you can and I will deal with this Bethany Anne."

"I can't kill him if he won't become corporeal. I don't know how long he can stay in this gaseous form his servant was guessing he used. He can't get out of the glass cage, it is airtight. He is only safe if he isn't in his body. If he shows himself, we will be able to destroy his body. That would be a satisfying end to the problem."

"Good enough. Have a good night, brother."

"Same to you, good night."

Anton hung up and crushed the phone. Making sure the sim card was destroyed, he took the pieces to a special furnace he used to destroy any technology he got rid of. He watched the pieces melt.

Thousands of miles away, on a computer under an old

building in Washington D.C., a computer software program closed out the recording and sent a message to notify the programmer that new information was available.

MICHAEL'S NOTES

Bite This - The Kurtherian Gambit 04:
Written Dec 11th, 2015

PLEASE NOTE, this is a MUCH longer note as I go into a rant at the end. Please ignore that part if the thoughts of an Indie Author aren't interesting :-)

———

Thank you, I cannot express my appreciation enough that not only did you pick up the fourth book, but you read it all the way to the end and NOW, you're reading this as well. Since this book is part of a series, I am presuming you have blessed me by reading them all and what a fantastic feeling that is for me!

So, in my notes in Love Lost, I mentioned the third book took 13 days. I am on a more reasonable writing timeline and this book (I am writing this note on the Dec 11th, for putting it online on the 15th) took 11 days to get through the core writing, leaving myself and my advance read team 4 days to review, make changes and get it online. (Mind you, at this time my 'advance read team' is one awesome fan in Australia.) I took a week off from writing after Love Lost before I started this book (editing effort etcetera).

I mention on my website that I have engaged an editor who is presently working on the first book. From there, Queen Bitch and so on through the series. Death Becomes Her was edited and the new version placed online. Only problem? You have to DELETE your existing file to get the new download.

A personal preference of mine, as a reader, is that I would rather read through the small (hopefully) editorial glitches rather than wait the extra month for the editing. I completely understand how it can drag you back out of a story for some readers who would prefer to wait for the professional editor. So, I am going to add a conversation thread on my Author Page (http://www.amazon.com/Michael-Anderle/e/B017J2WANQ) to get your input.

I have had one stalwart fan from down under (hint hint) that has already helped immeasurably with insights into military (Navy) life. I am hoping he will permit me to put the information he has shared up on my website. I think all of us who enjoy this type of military fiction would find his insights fascinating and appreciate the significant amount of time he has already spent providing me with a better grasp of the realities of working on a submarine.

I mentioned on my blog post (http://kurtherianbooks.com) that an author's success usually entails LOTS of pre-work before you release your book. However, I just put Death Becomes Her and Queen Bitch out in the wild with no notice and no advertising. I really hope that if you enjoy reading these stories, you will share with your friends the link and encourage them to read them as well.

Purchased vs. Kindle Unlimited update. As we go into book four, the purchased side is ahead in gross sales vs. The Kindle Unlimited group. Even after we pull the 30% that Amazon takes for purchased sales, the total is still 10% higher. So, my best guess being so new to this author business might have to do with the reviews making the difference. I am assuming that Amazon is going to pay the same amount per page (.0048) as they did to authors in November, if they drop it again for December then full copy sales vs. Kindle

Unlimited will only be that much more ahead.

Feel free to jump on the Facebook page to ask me any questions about being an author on Amazon. I'm happy to share what experiences I can.

Here is my regularly scheduled comment related to my type of writing: I've mentioned before, my writing is more escapist. I love a good action story, but more than that I want to engage with the characters. I want to feel what they are going through if possible. I want situations that make me get excited, worried, laugh and say 'take that, sucka!' out loud. The challenges faced by the protagonists don't have to be life threatening, it could be a challenge to ask that special someone out for a date that keeps the story flowing. I'm not really into books that keep you constantly afraid for the characters. If I care about a character, I'll turn the page, and buy the next book, just to see them reach a personal milestone that is challenging to that character. Having said all of that, action is still what drives the story forward.

In this story, we find the team working to locate Anton, and cleaning up some of the Forsaken crap that is lying around Europe and South America. We finally get insights into Michael's situation leading us to Never Forsaken— TKG05 (Ok, so I'm not exactly hiding whether Bethany Anne will ignore Michael's plight.)

Then, as always, there is the emotional side to the story. I'm not sure WHAT the thoughts of my readers will be to Bethany Anne's cycle coming back and her reactions. Will the guys who read the story be too uncomfortable with the subject? Personally, I have always believed that great accomplishments meant huge challenges and often the heroes have lost significantly in other areas of their lives. One of the biggest areas of loss for Bethany Anne had been related to her not having children. When she was dying, she was happy to know she wasn't going to leave a child behind who would go through life like she had. Now what will her decision be? I think I know, but until I write that part of the story I can't be sure. I think as an author I can't have that large of an issue be brought up without a significant introduction. Hopefully, I didn't offend anyone in the interim.

What would you do if you needed to save the universe, but wouldn't leave any children of your own to appreciate your sacrifice? I've got the utmost respect for what Bethany Anne has to go through. It isn't easy, I understand, but that just makes me want to support her even more. One piece I had not considered was the relationship with Gabrielle and Ivan, and Gabrielle's expected change to be able to conceive again after hundreds of years. What will Ivan think? What will Gabrielle think?

Wouldn't it be hilarious if Ivan & Ecaterina's mom (who I am NOT fond of) had to burp a little vampire child? (Edit scene: little cute baby is being held with such loving care by Grandma, Grandma is cooing about how cute the baby is, snuggling down and kissing Grandma's neck, Grandma's eyes fly open in alarm… the little vampire baby is KISSING HER NECK!!!)

Ok, that makes me smile. Would Ivan's mom still be the raging… something… that we left behind in Queen Bitch? I'm not sure.

Personal favorite scenes in this book include Stephen and Ivan in Frankfurt, and the scene at the end where Bethany Anne goes postal on the Forsaken. Is postal a U.S. term only? The term had to do with U.S. Post Office workers getting so stressed out they would go home, get a gun and come back and shoot their co-workers. Since the whole beginning of the term started with a U.S. POSTAL WORKER, it makes the term rather localized. I'm curious if the phrase has caught on around the world?

There are presently 13 titles sketched out and I expect

more after that. Bite This is the fourth in the series.

Please, if you enjoyed this book give it a good rating on Amazon? Your kind words and encouragement help any author. I will continue to the next story whether you provide an OUTSTANDING review or not. But it might get done a wee bit faster with the encouragement (smile).

As of today (12/11/2015), 39 days since I released the first book I have three 5-Star ratings and two 4-Star rating on Death Becomes Her, four 5-Star and one 4-Star Rating on Queen Bitch, and the same four 5-Star and one 4-Star Ratings on Love Lost. Some of the reviews make ME stand up and cheer. Your insights and comments on what makes you laugh, grin, cheer, and feel about the story edify me as I continue to write the next in the series. I read every one of your reviews (often multiple times) and take your comments to heart. I appreciate anyone who takes the time to both praise the story and describe the issues.

A quick note about authors responding to reviews. I responded to an early reviewer that I would be going back to edit a book. Not an hour later, I read on the Amazon Authors forum where the suggestion was NOT to get involved in reviews in any way, shape or form as an author. It is the reader's area and shouldn't be touched. So, I'm not doing this however much I WANT to talk with you regarding your amazing input. However, I would LOVE to have a conversation with you and suggest the Author's Page as a great place if you want to converse in public, or hit me up on Facebook or email. Your choice!

Unless I go back and fix something huge, then all bets are off.

All of the links to the different areas (email, Facebook, website etc.) are below the rant ;-)

———

\<STEP ON SOAPBOX\>

So, finally my soapbox comment related to Indie Authors. This discussion has to do with something I read last night on the Amazon Author forums that the original poster claimed, with absolute assurance, that a black and white way to tell if an author was professional was whether they paid to have a professional cover done.

I don't pay to have my covers done. Will I in the future? Probably. Possibly not for this series, but another one wouldn't make me cringe. Why didn't I, and the tangential, why didn't I have a professional editor work on Death Becomes Her before I released it?

It has to do with a lot of different reasons, but one of them is the MVP concept. MVP is 'Minimally Viable Product.' The idea started, (I believe) with the software profession where programmers and small software companies would build just enough of a solution to test the waters. As it can be expensive and take a long time to accomplish a full and robust software program you don't want to invest a significant amount to find out the whole thing is a bust.

Similarly, as a brand new, wet behind the ears author who had dreamt of putting something out since he was in high school, I didn't want to invest the expense and effort of a professional cover and professional editing if no one was going to buy the book in the first place.

Most of the author biz stuff I was reading before I released my first book or listening to on podcasts said most authors might be lucky to sell a book a day. That meant they would be bringing in $60 a month. It would take me almost a year to recoup the income for testing the waters if this happened. The MVP strategy would put the book out and find out if any interest and sales in my books occurred and fix anything else if it became successful. Basically, try to fix fast.

This is the industry I came out of after twenty years.

Now, I've learned a lot. You can buy a cover for somewhere between $35 to $100 and up. An editing job usually starts at $400 for simple spelling and grammatical effort for 70k words to $1,000s for help fixing your story. Only recently have I found an editor in England who will go through a manuscript and charge you by the pass (making it 1/3 as expensive).

So, the MVP strategy is what I followed. Guess what? There was a much bigger desire for Bethany Anne's stories than I thought. It will still take me a little while to recoup the investment, but I don't feel like it will take a freaking YEAR to accomplish. Now, I'm behind the eight ball getting caught up. I'm ok with that, and the greatest fans in the world (you!) are helping me deal with it.

As for the cover image, I know enough to be ok with Photoshop. Would a professional do better? I'm sure they could. But now, my cover brand is stuck so I guess I'll just be an unprofessional Indie Author doing something I love.

Personally, I always thought a professional was someone who got paid to do something. I get paid to write these stories, ergo, I was a professional.

So, I checked out the definitions of professional. Seems that the closest definition states a professional is someone 'engaged in a specified activity, especially a sport or branch of the performing arts, as a main paid occupation rather than as a pastime.'

I certainly spend way more time writing than I should to call it a pastime, but it isn't my main source of income right now. So, even if I paid to have a cover done by a professional, that wouldn't qualify me as a professional.

I guess it's good my hobby is generating income and I can write off the expenses. (Hear that, IRS?)

So, at the end of the day I realize this author who was

stating their opinion was probably bemoaning the state of indie authors (such as myself) who released their story into Kindle Unlimited before triple checking the editing. I'm certainly guilty of doing this and I apologize to my readers who slogged through the stories before the cleanup efforts. You deserve something amazing. I don't have amazing yet, but I can try for cool.

So, let's try this. I'll start the price for Never Forsaken - TKG05 at $0.99 for the first 24 hours when it comes out in January. If you sign up for my email list before then, I will make sure to email you at least twice to remind you of the reduced price coming up. I'll email a couple of days before the release, and when it goes live. (Email list link below).

Unfortunately, I can't make it 'free' without pulling down my Amazon book ranking.

<\ STEP OFF SOAP BOX>

————

If you want to help make the books better and receive an advanced copy, please consider the Advance Team project and email me: mike@kurtherianbooks.com or on Facebook and let me know your interested. I am thinking five positions at the beginning to keep it small enough to be manageable for me to handle.

You can find book links on my Amazon Author Page here: http://www.amazon.com/Michael-Anderle/e/B017J2WANQ/

Want to comment on the best (scene, comment, event, shoes or gun for Bethany Anne, weapon Nathan would prefer…you name it) join me on Facebook: https://www.facebook.com/TheKurtherianGambitBooks/

Want to know when the next book or major update is ready? Join the email list - http://kurtherianbooks.com/email-list/

Software used to write this book is Scrivener (Windows and Mac): https://www.literatureandlatte.com/scrivener.php

Book Cover Images purchased at PhotoDune.net: http://photodune.net

Image software to make the cover (Mac): http://www.pixelmator.com/mac/ (1.6 ratio @ 300dpi)

Thank you,

Michael Anderle, Dec 2015

*All credit for me having ANY shoe knowledge goes to my wife, who still works to provide me with even a finger's amount of fashion sense. Why she asks me to comment on her outfits in the morning still confuses me to this day. Second note, the suggestion to include special canines also came from my wife.

P.S. - The dog's name will be Ashur

P.S.S. - "Protectores del infierno" - Protectors from Hell

P.S.S.S. - "Ángeles Oscuros" - Dark Angels

P.S.S.S.S. - David Down Under has permitted me to release his work, so I'll be putting up his comments regarding military life on my website soon.

WANT MORE?

Join the email list here:

http://kurtherianbooks.com/email-list/

Join the Facebook group here:

https://www.facebook.com/TheKurtherianGambitBooks/

The email list will be sporadic with more 'major' updates, the Facebook group will be for updates and the 'behind the curtains' information on writing the next stories. Basically conversing!

Since I can't confirm that something I put up on Facebook will absolutely be updated for you, I need the email list to update all fans for any major release or updates that you might want to read on the website.

I hope you enjoy the book!

Michael Anderle Nov 2015.

SERIES TITLES INCLUDE:

KURTHERIAN GAMBIT SERIES TITLES INCLUDE:

First Arc

Death Becomes Her (01) - Queen Bitch (02) - Love Lost (03) - Bite This (04)
Never Forsaken (05) - Under My Heel (06) Kneel Or Die (07)

Second Arc

We Will Build (08) - It's Hell To Choose (09) - Release The Dogs of War (10)
Sued For Peace (11) - We Have Contact (12) - My Ride is a Bitch (13)
Don't Cross This Line (14)

Third Arc (Due 2017)

Never Submit (15) - Never Surrender (16) - Forever Defend (17)
Might Makes Right (18) - Ahead Full (19) - Capture Death (20)
Life Goes On (21)

New Series

THE SECOND DARK AGES

The Dark Messiah (01)
(Michael's Return)
12.25.2016

THE BORIS CHRONICLES
* With Paul C. Middleton *

Evacuation
Retaliation
Revelation
Restitution 2017

RECLAIMING HONOR
* With JUSTIN SLOAN *

Justice Is Calling (01)
Claimed By Honor (02)
Judgement Has Fallen (03) Feb 2017

THE ETHERIC ACADEMY
* With TS PAUL *

ALPHA CLASS (01) Dec 2016
ALPHA CLASS (02) Mar 2017
ALPHA CLASS (03) May 2017

TERRY HENRY "TH" WALTON CHRONICLES
* With CRAIG MARTELLE *

Nomad Found (01)
Nomad Redeemed (02)
Nomad Unleashed (03)
Nomad Supreme (04) (Mar 17)

TRIALS AND TRIBULATIONS
* With Natalie Grey *

Risk Be Damned (01)
Damned to Hell (02) coming soon
Hell's Worst Nightmare (03) coming soon

SHORT STORIES

Frank Kurns Stories of the Unknownworld 01 (7.5)
You Don't Mess with John's Cousin

Frank Kurns Stories of the Unknownworld 02 (9.5)
Bitch's Night Out

Frank Kurns Stories of the Unknownworld 02 (13.25)
With Natalie Grey
Bellatrix

AUDIOBOOKS
Available at Audible.com and iTunes

THE KURTHERIAN GAMBIT

Death Becomes Her - Available Now
Queen Bitch – Available Now
Love Lost – Coming Soon

RECLAIMING HONOR SERIES

Justice Is Calling – Available Now
Claimed By Honor – Coming Soon

TERRY HENRY "TH" WALTON CHRONI-CLES

Nomad Found - Coming Soon

ANTHOLOGIES

Glimpse
Honor in Death
(Michael's First Few Days)

Beyond the Stars: At Galaxy's Edge
Tabitha's Vacation

Manufactured by Amazon.ca
Bolton, ON